Would the doomsday numbers roll against him?

If they did, it wouldn't bother Bolan. Years ago he had made peace with the fact that he would die in battle, even before he began his crusade against the Mafia.

Now, here he was, fighting an enemy so close to that original pack of demons he had stocked the halls of hell with, cruel scum who stole youth and innocence through sexual slavery.

Ruiners of human life, who broke almost everyone with whom they came in contact.

They had earned their judgment.

MACK BOLAN ®
The Executioner

DON PENDLETON'S
EXECUTIONER®
THE
BLOOD TRADE

A GOLD EAGLE BOOK FROM
WORLDWIDE.

TORONTO • NEW YORK • LONDON
AMSTERDAM • PARIS • SYDNEY • HAMBURG
STOCKHOLM • ATHENS • TOKYO • MILAN
MADRID • WARSAW • BUDAPEST • AUCKLAND

First edition February 2003
ISBN 0-373-64291-1

Special thanks and acknowledgment to
Douglas P. Wojtowicz for his contribution to this work.

BLOOD TRADE

If you strike a child, take care that you strike it in anger, even at the risk of maiming it for life. A blow in cold blood neither can nor should be forgiven.

—George Bernard Shaw
Man and Superman

In my War Everlasting, I have found that there are crueler things that can, and have, been done to children than striking them in anger or cold blood. These things neither can, nor should be forgiven. They can only be avenged.

—Mack Bolan

To adoptive parents.

True love is worth more than mere accident of birth.

Prologue

Yakov Katzenelenbogen looked around the banquet hall of the Willard Inter-Continental Hotel, his steely gray eyes searching for his friend. With his wineglass precisely balanced in his artificial right hand he kept his left hand free. Decades of having the artificial limb meant he could drink from a wineglass in the stiff prosthetic fingers without a problem, leaving his good hand free in case he needed to do something important.

Such as draw the Beretta 84 tucked under his right armpit, in case of trouble.

Katz shook off the thought. He wasn't expecting the world to explode into violence.

But violence had been a way of life for the gruff Israeli. During World War II, as a mere boy, Katz was a member of the French Resistance, killing Nazis at an age when American boys had been baseball players. Later, as a young man, Katz was part of Israel's struggle for independence, and the battles to keep it free in the decades that followed. For the Jewish homeland, Katz had sacrificed a son and his right arm below the elbow. But he didn't sacrifice his fighting spirit. Instead, he struggled harder, trained harder, until he was deadlier with one hand and a prosthesis than most two-handed men had ever been. It was for this no-quit attitude that, when Mack Bolan finished his war with the Mafia, Katz was selected to head the Executioner's foreign legion—Phoenix Force, five men assembled from around the globe to combat terrorism. After a long tenure as the field commander of the team, finally Katz decided he had seen enough combat. He shifted to a desk job, using his brain more than his body to combat the specters that haunted the shadows of humanity.

Where is he? he thought, looking around the room. He shrugged and took another sip of ginger ale. Two glasses of wine had been his limit. The big man was either off to one side, observing the festivities, or he was simply partaking in some light conversation with an attractive woman.

Katz hoped deep in his heart that it was the latter.

Mack Bolan rarely had enough time in his life to actually socialize. Finding a little slice of heaven, even for only an evening, before cementing yet another mission, would be a nice change of pace for the man known as the Executioner. Katz stifled a grin. If Bolan didn't want Katz to find him, he wouldn't.

As he strolled to the banquet table, Katz's steely gaze kept flickering over the crowd with practiced timing. Each face was noted or recognized, including the hired help. Nobody tripped his instincts or showed up on his mental lists of known Stony Man or Mossad enemies, old, new or neutral. There were plenty of Caucasians about, but this banquet was being held in honor of Thai Prime minister Xiang Di Hua in particular, and in total for ECPAT—End Child Prostitution in Asian Tourism.

Though Phoenix Force had spent some time in Thailand, it wasn't because of the 1.5-billion-dollar child-prostitution trade. Rather, it was the murders of American DEA agents who had stumbled onto a plot by a coalition of rebel factions in Thailand to use heroin to finance even more political power for themselves. The coalition had been crushed, actually incinerated by a well-placed thermite grenade, but there were still some missing pieces from that particular battle.

The San United Army had been one of them, a particularly vicious cabal of murderous thugs who had been led by Chang Chi Fu. The SUA still existed, and according to Thai news reports, their brutal leader was never announced as killed. As such,

Katz had Aaron Kurtzman put the San United Army, Thailand and Chang Chi Fu into a search program. Any references to these three would be brought to the wily old Israeli's attention.

As an afterthought, however, Katz had gone into the computer and added another set of parameters. The first was the Thai heroin trade. A strong heroin trade financed almost every serious threat force in the region of Myanmar and Thailand. The second bit of information was about something that Katz had glimpsed only slightly while Phoenix force was preparing to leave Thailand for home: child prostitution.

Katz set his jaw firmly. There were people here who were only present to pay lip service to the cause of ending child prostitution. Some of these people were even so ill educated as to think that the Asian children willingly took part in it. But as he'd seen, and as had been explained to him by Narong Poolsri, these were children, sometimes bought, other times simply kidnapped, but most likely taken at gunpoint by an armed force.

Back then Katzenelenbogen had felt his insides churning, and he had considered requesting Hal Brognola leave Phoenix Force in Thailand to clean out the foul trade. Narong, however, explained that five men couldn't obliterate a 1.5-billion-dollar industry. Even though the men from Stony Man had just given the heroin trade in Thailand a bloody nose, the peddlers of innocence were too deeply rooted, their tentacles too deep and wrapped too tightly around the heart of the government.

So Phoenix Force walked away from that conflict reluctantly. Other battles were awaiting them.

But Yakov Katzenelenbogen vowed that one day, Stony Man would give these animals a taste of the cleansing fire...if not the burning flames of Phoenix Force, then it would be the attention of one man to whom justice was his life, and battling impossible enemies was on his daily plate.

"Good evening," a voice said, drawing Katz out of his reverie. "I don't believe I know you."

Katz was smoothly assessing the man when he recognized him. It was Prime minister Xiang. He held out his left hand to shake. "Yakov Rosenberg. I'm a law-enforcement consultant."

The prime minister smiled. "Ah, yes. We could always use someone with actual enforcement experience in ECPAT."

"Alas, I have current responsibilities right now, Mr. Prime Minister. Otherwise I would throw all of my efforts into this cause," Katz said.

A glimpse out of the corner of his eye, and there was Bolan, finally. Something tingled at the base of the Israeli's skull, an impression of danger that was almost supernatural.

"And what brought the existence of this meager little cause to your attention?" the prime minister asked.

Katz moved to one side, facing away from Bolan, his feet pointed at right angles to each other. Just a natural stance, but one that would provide him a perfect base to spin, move or brace himself. "I had been a part of an investigation in Thailand a while back. I was working for the DEA at the time."

It wasn't a lie. Back then, when Katz was still an active field agent, instead of serving as a tactical adviser, he was leading Phoenix Force on behalf of the DEA to avenge the deaths of four agents. The clever old fighter had since lost some of his physical edge, but not his mental prowess. He was still positioned well to be conversing with Xiang, but his eyes were flashing in an arc to spot what had set off his instincts.

Whatever had set them off had also spurred the Executioner into combat mode. At that moment, Katz had already had the plan that was formulated in the big warrior's mind. He'd tackle and cover the prime minister, and give cover fire as Bolan went into action.

Not exactly the best plan, and Katz was already searching for Xiang's bodyguards, seeing them distracted by beautiful young Thai women. On closer examination, Katz's gaze grew grim and more intense. Too squared in the shoulders to be women.

"Something wrong?" the prime minister asked.

"Only if you're not disturbed by your bodyguards being distracted by *kra-toeys.*"

The prime minister glanced over his shoulder at one of his men, then his lips parted. "That can't..."

Katz hoped that Bolan caught the reference. An after-action report by Rafael Encizo and David McCarter had revealed this dangerous little bit of information about the Thais. *Kra-toeys* were transvestite prostitutes, and while most were as harmless as any regular female prostitute, the very fact that they were men could make them ideal muscle, especially if it was hidden behind an evening gown and makeup.

A glance back over his own shoulder, and Katz noted that the Executioner had disappeared once more.

This time, it reassured the former Phoenix Force commander.

Mack Bolan was no Superman. He couldn't see through jackets and detect guns. He had no paranormal sense of hostility and intent to kill. No tingling danger sense.

But an observant and alert soldier didn't need X-ray eyes to know the predatory type as soon as he saw it. And when the quartet of Asian men stepped through the kitchen entrance, their faces grim, eyes dark and soulless, looking intently upon the Thai prime minister, Bolan swiftly broke off his halfhearted attempt at conversation. The vapid New England rich girl had been stricken by the tall soldier and began talking to him without any bidding on his own part, but as soon as the four young predators entered, she was a distant memory.

There was a word of protest, but Bolan wasn't paying attention to her anymore. Someone was planning a hit, and from the way objects beneath the quartet's loose tuxedo jackets jutted oddly, it was going to be some serious mayhem. The four killers, however, weren't going to be the only ones on the scene. Nobody who supplied concealable weapons to hitters was going to have only four killers on the scene.

Luckily Bolan had one of the world's most experienced warriors for backup, even if he was no longer a field operative. Just a glimpse of trouble in Katz's peripheral vision had sent the Israeli into combat mode. In only a matter of seconds, Katz's announcement of the Thai transvestites had doubled the opposing force on scene, if not the firepower. The Executioner wasn't certain of their plans, or how well the transvestites were armed, but he was betting on at least two more men perhaps covering the four killers' retreats, and maybe a driver or two, with a shotgun rider.

Long odds.

It also meant a lot of money and organization behind the hit. As he glided out of the peripheral vision of the newcomers, Bolan also realized that these eight had managed to slip past the State Department's diplomatic security team, no small feat, and the prime minister's own protection force. This wasn't just a hit. It was a full-blown coup, and someone, possibly a lot of people, from either the U.S. or Thai contingents, had somehow been flipped, giving aid to an enemy intent on bloodshed.

Plain and simple betrayal, fueled by greed, blackmail or blind ambition.

Nothing that Mack Bolan hadn't seen before, and the numbers willing, he'd most likely see again after tonight.

A quick mental assessment of his arsenal made the odds grim. Not expecting the need for either the force of the .44 Magnum Desert Eagle or the autofire and silent killing power of his Beretta 93-R, he had left them at Stony Man Farm, instead relying on a conventional 14-shot Beretta 92-F Compact for his off-duty weapon of the evening. The Centurion was nothing more than a standard Beretta 92, or a U.S. Military Spec M-9 autoloader with its barrel shortened by three-quarters of an inch and its handle shortened by the height of two staggered 9 mm cartridges. Compared to his usual side arms, it was a dainty gun, but then, he was six foot three and powerfully built. The "little" Compact would provide plenty of killing power...just not at the rate of mayhem that a machine pistol would afford. Bolan was hardly without a few other backup tools; he also had a garrote in one pocket of his tuxedo, and in his pants pocket was an Applegate-Fairbairn Combat Folding knife.

The gunmen were angling along the buffet table, and Bolan was moving along the other side, his ice-blue eyes scanning for a further advantage when he saw a Sterno-heated server. He paused. It was stainless steel, and weighted down with a platter full of steaming hot noodles. He gave the server a touch. Hot enough to make his lip flicker, but not too hot to pick up and use as a weapon.

It would prove to be the first time he used a hot-noodle grenade.

The gunmen looked to one another, giving themselves nods of encouragement, then started to open their jackets, going for weapons. None of them had thought to look over their shoulders, to note that they were being stalked. They'd counted entirely on the prime minister's bodyguards to be distracted by their cross-dressing friends and the diplomatic security team to be outside, having to get through heavy doors. By the time they got inside the banquet hall, the deed would have been done.

The moment the first one reached to open his jacket, the Executioner was moving into action. Grabbing up the hot server, he launched it like a Frisbee, his arm protesting at the sudden weight forced onto it unnaturally. All told, the server had to have weighed close to twenty pounds, and it caromed off the shoulder of one of the Asian hit men, sending him tumbling forward in middraw, then came apart. Heavy stainless steel slammed into the shoulder of the second gunman and vomited hot noodles all across his face.

With a scream, the second gunman recoiled and backpedaled into the third of the killers as the fourth whirled, ripping an Uzi from under his coat, looking to see that three of his partners had been momentarily taken by surprise.

Screams filled the air as Katz, on the other side of the table, elbowed the prime minister out of the way with his right arm, his left hand snaking free his Beretta .380 even as the Executioner was grabbing his own Beretta out of shoulder leather. The Uzi gunner, unsure of which suddenly armed Westerner to chop to pieces first, was hit by a wave of 9 mm and .380 rounds, sporting five new holes in his torso and a single bloody wound in his forehead before he went tumbling back to the floor.

"Get the Uzi!" Bolan commanded, leaping onto the buffet

table, Beretta leading the way as he took three quick steps across it. The gunman who'd been first hit was rolling and tracking Katz. The Executioner came off the table, his foot landing in the small of the killer's back, making an ugly cracking sound.

Never one to leave an enemy to suffer, or shoot an ally in the back, Bolan sent the Asian murderer to his just reward with a pair of 9 mm taps to the back of his head, spraying the pristine white marble floor with chunks of bone and gore. Bolan checked the other two as they were still working to get up, the noodle-splattered man still growling and complaining of his burns when Katz's voice cut through the air.

"The *kra-toeys!*"

Bolan dropped from the table and into a crouch as a server full of chicken just over his head was smashed off the table by the impact of a .357 Magnum round. A transvestite was holding the smoking revolver, straddling a bodyguard who was trying to hold in his intestines and the knife that freed them. The revolver-armed killer lowered his aim, but Bolan beat the cross-dresser to the punch, pumping a single hot 9 mm round through the cleavage of the evening gown, shattering his breastbone and severing his aorta.

Katz's little Beretta crackled as he cut down the two struggling machine gunners, then tossed Bolan an Uzi. "Always nice when they give us presents we like."

Bolan spared a moment to grin as he spun the Uzi into firing position and aimed at a second *kra-toey* who was running for cover behind a pillar, holding up his skirt with one hand and a 9 mm Browning with the other, muzzle-flashes slicing from the hitter's handgun. The Uzi cut loose at 600 rounds per minute, slow for a modern submachine gun, but more than quick enough to shatter the spine of the Thai assassin and send him tumbling lifelessly to the floor.

Katz rolled to one knee as another Browning spit flame at him, hitting where he'd been moments ago, and held down the trigger on his own Uzi, the weapon an extension of the Israeli's left hand as it ripped his would-be killer from testicles to throat. The *kra-toey* took three stumbling steps backward, his eyes rolling up into his head, then slumped to the floor, his white silk evening gown splashed with blood.

The last of the killers on the scene kicked his way through a door, and the Executioner was in hot pursuit. Letting these assassins run free in Washington, D.C., wasn't Bolan's idea of public safety, and if it meant that he was exposed to gunfire from friend and foe alike, then so be it.

Still, he went through the doorway low, catching sight of the blue-gowned transvestite racing down a hallway. People were on the floor, more than one was bleeding, and the doorjamb and wall on either side of his head exploded into splinters as 9 mm autofire blasted into it. Going prone, Bolan brought up the Uzi and fired a short burst toward the spot where one muzzle-flash had flickered.

No go, but the devil in the blue dress had stopped and was aiming at the grounded Executioner.

Bolan sent him to hell with a chattering burst that tore off his wig and turned his rouge to gore.

The two gunners rose from their cover, cutting loose wildly with their machine pistols, shards and splinters pelting Bolan through his tuxedo. With the stone-cold patience of a sniper, and countless battles under his belt, the soldier breathed deeply, aimed and sliced the remainder of the Uzi's clip through the two gunmen right at belt level. Both hitters fell, one onto his face, coughing and vomiting his lifeblood, the other onto his back, his eyes turned glassy black with death.

The Executioner dumped the empty Uzi magazine and bolted down the hallway, Beretta in hand. As he reached the end of the hall, he paused only long enough to grab a couple of spare magazines from the dead, then raced down the spiral staircase and out into the lobby. People were still cowering on the floor, and the sight of the big man with his machine pistol wasn't doing anything to calm their nerves as two cars raced off down the road in front of the hotel.

Gunfire was chattering outside, and the Executioner knew instinctively that the DST had found the escape car. From the sounds of the M-16s going off outside, he also knew that they were outgunned, Bolan looked up and saw the getaway vehicle, two heavily armed Asians sweeping their weapons left and right.

One State Department gunner was lying on the ground, coughing up blood all over his torn shirt and body armor.

Bolan's blood boiled, but he knew he could do nothing for the man, not while two men were opening fire on the streets of Washington, D.C. The sound of .357 SIG-Sauer pistols barked in the air, but the pumped-up 9 mm rounds were no match for the flesh-shredding power of the M-16. The soldier dived to the floor, sliding over slick marble tiles, coming to a halt and feeling broken glass from the hotel lobby doors dig into his forearms and elbows.

One of the diplomatic-security shooters, crouched and holding one ruined arm, struggled to reload his SIG-Sauer. "Buddy! You decided to come down at the wrong time!"

"It's never a good time to join a firefight," Bolan said.

He pulled the stock of his Uzi to his shoulder and took careful aim. The two Asian gunners were heavily armed, but nothing took the place of tactics. Instead of trying to retreat or taking effective cover, they were simply laying down a hail of lead, hoping to drive everyone to the ground or kill them, and then make their fast getaway.

Unfortunately for them, they forgot that the world existed in a sphere around them, 360 degrees any direction. Looking at eye level meant a person missed things above and below him—such as how vulnerable his feet and legs were to enemy gunfire. Bolan loosed a burst toward the legs of one rifleman, pounding Parabellum shockers into flesh and bone. The guy dropped like a rock, screaming as he dropped his rifle.

Bolan ignored the fallen man, rolling to the side, knowing the other gunner would try to make a break for it. Over the sound of gunfire directed at the downed murderer who'd shot, wounded and killed innocent bystanders and at least three of their own, Bolan heard the engine on the Lincoln roar to life.

The Executioner lurched to his feet, Uzi in one fist, his hand grabbing for the Lincoln's handle with the other. There was an angry curse in Thai, and Bolan ducked his head, digging in his fingers as the passenger window exploded in a hail of glass and bullets. Shouts arose from behind him, but the Executioner plunged his Uzi through the window, feeling the impact of steel on steel as weapons clanged. Nine pounds of steel met the lighter-built M-16 and both weapons were jarred from hands, but by then, the Lincoln was accelerating in time with the curses of the irate getaway driver.

A fist hammered at Bolan's already bloody forearm, knuckles driving glass into already injured skin, but the Executioner hauled his 230 pounds up to door level, his free hand trying to yank out his Beretta as his feet bounced along the asphalt, his pants being torn and skinned, one dress shoe having been yanked off.

The driver hit the brakes, and Bolan felt himself whirl, his hips slamming against the fender of the Lincoln. The Beretta chopped loose from numbed fingers, clattering on asphalt. The driver cackled, saying something too fast for Bolan to recognize, and the Lincoln's rear tires squealed, trying to catch.

In a heartbeat, the soldier dived through the window, his left hand clutching the collar of the driver and yanking him off balance, pulling the guy's face hard into the Executioner's forehead. The driver sagged, but one hand clawed at Bolan's injured arm, the other plunging under his jacket for a side arm.

Using his own weight, Bolan slid hard back out the window, interrupting the hit man's draw, slamming his head into the roof of the car with another sickening thud. The driver tried twisting free, but Bolan slammed his fist hard behind the guy's jaw, hitting the major junction of nerves and blood vessels there. The solid punch left the Asian glassy-eyed and without any more fight. The Executioner hauled him through the car window and began making sure he was clean of weapons when the clatter of shoes on asphalt sounded behind him. He spun, drawing the Thai's pistol, but saw it was only Katz and the diplomatic security team.

Katz, winded, raced up to his side, steely eyes softening as he realized that the rest of the hit squad hadn't escaped, and they had been left with one living prisoner.

"I'm getting too old for this shit," he panted, gulping air. He held up Bolan's discarded shoe for the big guy to retrieve.

"Katz," Bolan said, accepting the shoe and pulling out his Justice Department badge.

"Yes?" Katz asked, still a bit out of breath as he slung his weapon over his shoulder and watched the D.C. Metro Police pull up.

"You needed to convince me to help ECPAT take down the flesh peddlers?"

Katz nodded.

The Executioner locked his icy gaze with his old friend's. "Consider their judgment sealed."

2

By the time Hal Brognola arrived at the Willard Inter-Continental Hotel, strobe lights were flashing all over the place, and federal agents of every alphabet agency swarmed the area. Chewing on his cigar, he realized that a gunfight a mere two blocks from the White House itself didn't bode well, especially on an evening when Mack Bolan and Yakov Katzenelenbogen were on the scene scoping out a possible mission.

As it was, nearly twenty body bags were being loaded out of the grand old landmark hotel, and ambulances were dealing with more people who suffered glancing gunshots, splinters or just anxiety attacks during the fever-pitched battle. Chewing even harder, he managed to cut his way through a crowd of men in suits who were surrounding the Executioner and his comrade in arms. Neither Bolan nor Katz looked as if he was getting any comfort from the constant after-action grilling by each dark-spectacled officer of the government, but short of whisking them away in a helicopter, one Mike Belasko and one Yakov Rosenberg were going to be thoroughly grilled.

"Excuse me, gentlemen," Brognola boomed. "I'll take their

accounts from here. Unless one of you wants to send me whatever you gleaned from them."

"And just who are you?" one suited drone asked.

"Brognola, Justice Department," he answered, showing his badge. "They're with me."

The drone, an FBI man according to the ID on his lapel, bristled. "Those two are responsible for twelve dead foreign nationals at a State Department-sponsored function. And now you're going to rush them off somewhere?"

"If you have a problem with that, don't forget that the FBI is a mere functionary arm of the Justice Department," Brognola said, tightly holding in his annoyance.

The FBI man kept pushing on. His name tag read Johnson. "So these men work for you? And we're supposed to just hand them over? After a huge international incident?"

Brognola glared at the man. "Only two questions per idiot. Anyone else have a problem?"

The rest of the assembled men knew, or at least had heard of, Hal Brognola, one of the top men at the Justice Department. They wisely backed off, and a black man whispered in Johnson's ear.

When the FBI man's eyes went wide, he stepped back with a hastily muttered, "Sorry, sir."

Brognola let his frustration pass. He had other ulcers still brewing as he turned to Bolan and Katz, their tuxedoes torn and grimy from their few minutes of combat earlier. Bolan was still holding a shoe in one hand, and Brognola was confused until he saw the bandages swathed around a foot. A wince of sympathy filled the big man.

"End Child Prostitution in Asian Tourism, eh?" Brognola asked.

Katz shrugged. "You must remember, I'm semiretired. I can look into things that interest me."

Bolan remained deadpan. "All work and no play makes Johnny a dull boy."

Brognola chuckled and removed the unlit cigar from his mouth. "Yeah, but you're Johnny's brother. And you—dull?"

The soldier shrugged.

"Striker and I feel that there's at least two insiders working this hit. Whoever's after Xiang isn't going to stop. Even after losing twelve people," Katz spoke up. "If we can get the driver to talk..."

"He won't," Bolan said. He pointed out the lobby doors at another body bag, the familiar face of the driver disappearing behind the zipper.

"You didn't hit him that hard, did you?" Katz asked. A look from Bolan, neither stern nor disbelieving, just a look of resignation, told him everything.

Brognola grimaced, looking at the multitude of faces. "There are too many people at this crime scene. FBI. Diplomatic security. Secret Service. The Thais."

"We can get information even off dead men," Bolan pointed out. "Especially since we know that somewhere, the San United Army is behind this. They've used *Kru-toey* prostitutes as hidden-in-plain-sight backup before. And we just have to figure out how they got their passes to the banquet."

"Let's at least get back to my office before..." Brognola began, when a pair of Thai men wearing official Thai Royal Guard badges showed up.

"The prime minister would like to see the men who saved his life this evening," one spoke in stilted English.

"Of course. Lead the way," Bolan said.

ON THE TWELFTH FLOOR of the hotel, the prime minister's head-of-state luxury suite was a madhouse. The Willard had long been a place where foreign dignitaries would stay, just for the convenience of being only two blocks from meetings with the President of the United States, and of course, this evening, the prime minister of Thailand was making good use of its services.

The luxury suites not only provided posh accommodations to the dignitaries, but the suites also allowed for entire staffs of secretaries, translators, bureaucrats, bodyguards and hangers-on of assorted ilk to show up and not crowd the dignitaries.

The suite also provided a nice quiet room where Bolan, Brognola and Katz could meet with the prime minister, flanked by four bodyguards and looking more tired than usual, his features wrinkled by stress. He was standing at the window, his face tense with worry as he looked down at the green park below his window, 1600 Pennsylvania Avenue shining in the distance.

For a man who'd come within inches of dying, he seemed remarkably under control.

Just another annoying day at work.

Bolan respected that aspect of the man. He also respected the goal that the man reached for. Not many leaders would make it his crusade to fight a 1.5-billion-dollar sex-tourism industry. Nor would they do it in direct opposition to corrupt police and politicians in on the traders of innocent flesh. The Executioner set his jaw grimly.

"The President told you to expect us tomorrow. I'm sorry our meeting had to be rushed this way," Bolan stated.

"Now you see what we have to deal with," Xiang said, his voice grim. He turned from the window and looked at Bolan. "The money that's commonly mentioned, 1.5 billion dollars, that's a conservative estimate. We're not even talking local Thai men or Burmese."

"It's not the money that bothers you," Bolan noted.

The Thai leader nodded. "It costs ten thousand dollars U.S. to make one of these tourist trips to my country. Think of that— 150,000 children a year, turned into—"

"It happened to my own sister," Bolan said quietly. He felt Katz and Brognola's instantaneous reactions to his statement. It was something that the Executioner always kept quiet, but not this time, to this particular man. He felt the need to let him know that this mission wouldn't fail. This time, someone would act in a way that couldn't be ignored.

"As a younger man, I used to watch as the mercenaries—I always called them mercenaries—would come down the roads with trucks full of young people, the oldest of them at best fifteen, the youngest barely old enough to stand, all being rolled down the road," the prime minister said. "It was something we were forbidden to talk about. After all, good money was being paid to them for the girls, and if we spoke up or acted, it was a bullet for us."

"It wasn't your fault," Bolan said.

"No, but when good men do nothing, it is evil that succeeds."

"You're doing something now."

The prime minister locked gazes with the Executioner. "I'm fighting a war where I do not have the ability to shoot back. Do you know that the United States government gives funds to prevent the poaching of rhinoceroses and tigers, but to stop the destruction of innocent young lives, it takes private citizens sending a few dollars here and there to assist the victims?"

Bolan nodded. Katzenelenbogen had been entirely thorough with his research and data. If there had ever been a cause long overdue in his holy crusade against Animal Man, this was one battle long past postponing.

"So tell me, Mr. Brognola, Mr. Belasko, Mr. Rosenberg. What do you intend to do about it?" the prime minister asked.

Bolan looked to Brognola and imperceptibly nodded.

"Mr. Prime Minister, you've already seen Mr. Belasko at work," Brognola started. "He's one of my most trusted allies. He may not be a miracle worker, but I'm certain he can give aid to you in these troubled times."

The prime minister, who had been watching Bolan throughout this tale, went from stern to sullen. His lips parted, and the bodyguards around him noted their leader's sudden but subtle distress.

"One man..." the prime minister began.

Bolan nodded. "One man, sir."

Xiang lowered his head, his eyes heavily lidded. He searched Mack Bolan's eyes long and hard, finding no flinch, no doubt. He rose and walked to the window. "I'll take what help I can get, then, Mr. Belasko. When can you start?"

The Executioner's voice was even and emotionless. "I have a few things to clean up in town."

The prime minister nodded, then pushed forward a thin manila envelope. As the Executioner opened it, looking into the eyes of young people, their bodies racked by disease, their eyes burned soulless from emotional damage, he heard the pronouncement.

"Mr. Belasko, it looks like you've just joined another crusade."

The Executioner fought down his bile as he closed the folder.

3

Chang Chi Fu reclined in his chair behind his desk in Chang Mai, Thailand, frowning over the news of the failed attempt on Xiang Di Hua.

"Two men stopped a dozen trained killers," Chang said, keeping his voice low and calm. "And who were these men?"

Han shook his head. "No official reports, but our man with the prime minister gave us a description. One was a tall man with black hair and blue eyes. The other was an older man, a much older man, left-handed, with an abnormally stiff right hand."

Chang sat up. "Did the hand look artificial?"

Han looked at his notes. "He didn't say specifically."

Chang cursed, looking at a burn on his arm that he'd acquired years ago, when he was riding a train holding several tons of heroin. Back then, six men attacked the train which would have provided the San United Army with the funds to stage an overthrow of the Thai government. Those six men had destroyed the train and cut down dozens of his men.

He had burned the images of their faces into his mind.

"Describe the older man," Chang said, dismissing the taller man for the moment.

"As was said, his most notable feature was an abnormally stiff right hand, and an adeptness with his left. He had gray hair, more the color of steel. His nose marked him as Arab or Jewish, though his coloration was that of a white man, so it might have been Jewish," Han explained. "He had a paunch and looked to be in his sixties, yet moved with athletic grace."

Chang's face screwed up as the man described matched the one to whom the other commandos deferred to those years. The man who had led this small unit of murderers to smash his SUA operation.

"We have people ready to check all the airports?" Chang asked.

Han nodded. "Six men each airport."

"Triple that number. Heavily armed," Chang said.

"Triple?" Han asked. "Surely an old man—"

"This old man was part of a small unit that cost us millions and slew nearly a hundred of my men in a few days. And if he's sending his old friends, we'll be in for a war even worse," Chang said.

"All right...eighteen..."

"Twenty!"

"Twenty men. Heavily armed."

"Two pistols at least. Whatever can be arranged."

"You're overreacting," Han spoke up.

Chang leaned back, his lips a tight line. "It's been almost ten hours since the hit. I'm expecting them in at least two hours. These people move quickly."

"And if they don't show in two hours?"

"I have an army. We rotate our tired watchers. Four shifts of six hours. And it's an airport...they can sit, they can eat. They just have to keep their eyes open and their guns ready."

Han sighed. "I'll see to it, sir."

Chang shook his head. "You do not believe yet. But you shall."

MICHELLE LAM FROWNED and sighed deeply before looking up from her desk. Brushing a lock of long black hair from her face, she eyed her boss, Alan Singer, for a moment as he sat. Silhouetted by his reading lamp, he was slouched low, his nose seemingly pointing down at new information. She bunched her shoulders and turned her head hard and quick, listening to her neck pop, and felt a wave of relief wash over her. She smiled to Singer, who looked up at the sudden sound.

"Need something to drink?" Lam asked in her soft, slightly accented English. She sometimes felt self-conscious around other people; having grown up in an entirely Thai-speaking household had imprinted a strong accent on her. However, Singer didn't seem to notice it and, in fact, did his best to trade quips with her in his own halting attempts at Thai.

"No, I'm fine," Singer said, his deep voice resembling the low growl of an exhausted lion.

They'd been spending most of the night going over newspaper ads and assorted personals, looking for information regarding sex trips to foreign countries, especially trips to Myanmar and Thailand. Lam suppressed a smile for a moment, thinking that American women had it relatively easy in regards to prostitution. Armed mercenaries didn't harvest them out of their simple village lives and dump them into some back-alley dive in a major city.

As she walked down the hall, feeling her back unkink and her knees give a little stutter-pop with the first few steps, Lam knew that the information that they gathered would only be more grist for the mill. A few more pages of data here and there to go into the ECPAT files, more information and useless trivia that would sit and linger while the flesh peddlers continued their harvest of innocence.

Lam shook her head at the colorful phrasing of her most recent thought. "Man, I've got to stop reading those trashy novels."

Opening the fridge by the door, she got a diet soda and nearly jumped out of her skin as she saw the bulk of two men outside the door for the New York City ECPAT offices.

There was a soft rapping at the door, and she looked back. Singer was already standing, and he'd placed himself next to the filing cabinet. Swallowing, Lam knew that the filing cabinet was where Singer kept a six-inch-barreled .38-caliber revolver. With trepidation, she turned back to the door, and opened it and saw two men standing there.

They were an odd pair. One seemed like a kindly grandfather, or perhaps an older college professor, with his wrinkles softening once rugged and handsome features. While he wasn't obese, a small spare tire around his belly showed him at a balance between fitness and the lethargy of retirement. Dressed in a dark maroon shirt, a brown suede jacket and brown corduroy pants, with a pair of wire-rimmed glasses, his professorial persona was complete, except for the rakish maroon beret on his head. Something about the tiny badge on one side struck her as oddly out of place, perhaps even military.

The other was tall, well over six feet and solidly built. Under a dark denim jacket, he wore a black T-shirt and black jeans and looked as if he could fade into the shadows at any moment. His face was as rugged as that of any Hollywood hero that she'd ever seen, bringing to mind the more distinguished and dignified men of yesteryear. His eyes, ice-blue and penetrating like an arctic wind, met hers, and she felt herself shiver.

"Excuse me," the taller man said in a voice as deep, resonant and powerful as Singer's. "This is the ECPAT office in New York, right?"

Lam nodded.

"Xiang said that Mr. Singer would be working late. My name's Mike Belasko. This is Yakov Rosenberg."

The woman looked back to Singer, who was still leaning against the filing cabinet.

"Prime Minister Xiang wouldn't have sent two armed men to me without notifying me first," Singer answered.

Lam looked back, and she realized why the tall one seemed so...lumpy. Belasko simply smiled and walked into the office.

"I'm with the Justice Department, Mr. Singer," Bolan said curtly as Katz slipped into the office.

"Um...you're both armed?" Singer asked Katz.

The gruff Israeli smiled and opened his jacket to show his SIG-Sauer P-226 with a Justice Department badge clipped to the inside-the-waistband holster. "Yeah. But Mike won't let any shooting start."

Singer ran a hand through his curly hair as Bolan pulled an envelope from his hip pocket, with a familiar signature on it. Satisfied, he looked the tall stranger in the eye. "So, what's the Justice Department doing here tonight?"

"Stopping criminal activity with the assistance of a dedicated organization," Belasko answered.

"I love straightforward Feds."

"I like most lawyers. They're not quite the bottom feeders that people make them out to be."

Singer raised an eyebrow. "You know I'm a lawyer?"

"I told you, Prime Minister Xiang asked me to see you about some help. We're looking to shut down the sex-slavery ring that made an assassination attempt on him this evening," Bolan said. "If you don't want to help bring known rapists and murderers to justice, then fine."

Singer frowned. "Tough talk."

Bolan folded his arms. "All I'm looking for is a handle. Someplace to start twisting. I got some information that there are some 'exported' Thai and Myanmar women and girls in brothels in New York City."

Singer shook his head. "Unless you have some kind of floating search warrant, you're never going to be able to swoop in there and get the main bad guys. And the worst of it is, you'll just be deporting confused, malnourished and undereducated women back to Thailand and Myanmar, which is where their problems started in the first place."

"Tell you what. You get somebody there who can actually keep those women safe, and I'll arrange for them to be much better taken care of."

Singer narrowed his eyes. "Just what do you have in mind?"

Bolan grinned without any mirth. "I need a handle. Once I have it, all I have to do is twist."

4

Aaron Kurtzman picked up the phone by the time the first ring faded.

"It's Striker," Bolan stated.

"We've been running traces on the guys you bagged and tagged tonight," the computer wizard of Stony Man Farm replied, resting his phone between a beefy shoulder and his ear. He spun his wheelchair back toward the thin client that connected him to the series of Cray supercomputers in the Stony Man Annex. "The State Department has entry records on the four transvestites."

"Anything of interest?"

"They came in at LAX and spent approximately three days traveling to Las Vegas. Then they took off from McCarran Airport out to LaGuardia, arriving a week ago. And in case you're curious, they came in as men."

"Duly noted. Who paid for their tickets?"

"Cash all the way," Kurtzman answered.

"That's why you didn't mention any hotels."

"Not a single credit-card blip showing up matching the names on the passports. We've also done a search on brand-new credit cards signed to Asian names, Thai, Japanese, Korean..."

"They don't all look alike, Aaron."

"You know that. I know that. But Poppa Billy Bob Bodunk in the Possum Flats Arms on Highway 27 isn't going to know or care about the difference."

The Executioner went quiet, the sound of a rustling paper on the other end of the phone the computer expert's only clue that he was still there. "Did you try Filipino, then?"

Kurtzman did some quick typing after setting down the handset and going to speakerphone. "What made you think that? I've got about seventy previously unregistered Filipino credit-card users coming up now."

"The Philippines is one of the most active child-sex tourism hot spots in the world, right after Thailand. I remembered a few years back, the papers were full of news about American servicemen who got transferred out of the islands because they were caught using child prostitution."

Kurtzman remembered, too. He could tell from the hollowness in Bolan's voice that the man was bothered by the thought of servicemen engaging in the spoiling of young lives.

"I'm trimming things down, trying to isolate credit cards that seemed to move in groups, like four transvestites."

"There might be more than one group. I don't think it was only a few hitters being imported," Bolan answered.

Kurtzman continued tracing the newly activated credit cards, his brow furrowing as he dedicated another of the supercomputers to running reverse traces in New York using the results of the first search. His throat went tight.

"Twenty-five possibles, Striker. They've shown up in Los Angeles, Vegas, New York, and most recently, a couple of uses in Washington, D.C. The Bamboo Emporium. Want me to see about calling in Carl and the boys on this?"

"No. I'll get Jack to pull me out of New York while Yakov's running a few leads up here."

"It's been a long night, Striker, and Hal told me you're not on all cylinders."

"I'll redo my bandages on the flight down."

"Carl's already in town, and he's not going to like being left out of the game on this one," Kurtzman said.

"He won't if you don't tell him," Bolan stated.

"Too late, big guy," a voice said behind Kurtzman.

The computer whiz wheeled around to see Carl Lyons standing there. "It'll take me less time to gear up and get there. Once you show up, I'll give you a layout for when we go in."

There was a moment of silence, and then, Bolan said, "All right but no independent action."

"Yes, Daddy."

"Striker out."

The phone went silent, and Kurtzman rolled to the coffeepot as Lyons took a look at the address for the Bamboo Emporium. "Any floor plans ahead of time on this joint?" Lyons asked.

"I already started a search of city planning records for it the moment we caught a lead."

"Good, as soon as it prints up, hand it over. It'll make my night easier."

"Yeah," Kurtzman said, pouring some of his legendary black mud into his cup. "And my night longer."

JACK GRIMALDI glanced at the big guy in the cabin of the Hughes 500D as it raced along the East Coast, cutting the distance between New York and Washington, D.C., at nearly 150 miles per hour.

"How's the foot?" he asked as he returned his attention to the instruments and the scattered diamonds of light as they zoomed along the coast.

"No infection yet, but the cuts are a little puffy," Bolan answered, rubbing salve along his asphalt-abused foot. "Luckily I can put my weight on it, and I didn't crack my ankle on the ground."

"How'd you manage that?"

"I made the decision that it would be less damaging to have my foot ground off slowly than my leg broken by flopping outside a speeding automobile," Bolan said.

"You don't have to clean out this whole nest of vipers in one night."

"Yes, I do," Bolan answered, pulling on his combat boot, lacing it back up.

The Stony Man pilot sighed. Once the Executioner took up a crusade, he usually saw it through, no matter how badly hurt he was. A case of road rash wasn't going to slow down Bolan any more than a pocketknife would stop a charging rhino.

"At least let me come along on your visit to the Bamboo Emporium," Grimaldi offered.

"I already have Ironman lending a hand."

"Is Gadgets or Pol helping?" Grimaldi inquired, asking about Carl Lyons's Able Team partners.

"No. Carl was the only one at the Farm," Bolan answered.

Grimaldi's face split in a grin. "Well, then, you'll definitely need me. I know caveman-speak. Gadgets taught me."

Bolan had gone quiet in the back. The soldier was already catching a quick nap.

"No rest for the wicked, but a catnap for a savvy soldier," Grimaldi remarked, continuing the flight to Washington in the relative silence of the helicopter's cabin.

OVER THE CELL PHONE, Aaron Kurtzman's voice was as gruff as ever. But the electronics genius of Stony Man Farm had once again proved to be one of the Sensitive Operations Group's best assets. Carl Lyons listened intently to Kurtzman's rundown on Xian Mo, the owner of the Bamboo Emporium, a warehouse-store that specialized in teak furniture smuggled from Myanmar into Thailand by heavily armed forces who were using the money from the expensive wood to fund their attempts at creating their own nation. The Teak Crisis, as it had been called by a few who cared about such things, was an unfortunate crossing of a native people fighting for their lives against drug dealers from the Golden Triangle, loggers destroying their homelands, and government and rebel troops slaughtering each other and killing and recruiting locals to die for their squabbles.

All in all, to Lyons it sounded exactly like the kind of screwed-up twelve-way battles he'd experienced in the early days of Able Team. Back in the beginning, with Able Team, when Bolan was still Colonel John Phoenix and Stony Man was given free rein to hunt down the savages, the answer to such mixed-up battlegrounds was quite simple. Flick the selector switch on the Konzak assault shotgun, and continue emptying 7- and 20-round magazines of double aught and #2 buckshot until nothing moved anymore.

Now, things were different, but that didn't mean that Lyons was more restrained in the fulfillment of his duties as one of America's best pest controllers, but getting involved in a five-sided firefight in an American city was something Hal Brognola frowned upon.

"If that's the case, why didn't he make Phoenix Force domestic? They're pretty straightforward." Lyons gave voice to his thoughts as Kurtzman put him on hold to gather some fresh data from the computers.

Jack Grimaldi chuckled. He and Mack Bolan had rendezvoused with the Able Team leader. Together, listening on the cell phone, they got more information from the Farm.

"Because, Ironman," the pilot said, "your Spanish sucks, and that's the only foreign language you even know any words of."

Lyons shrugged. "As opposed to you, Jack? You know Italian and—"

"Carl. Jack."

The Stony Man pilot and the Able Team leader stopped their bantering, turning to Bolan, in the back seat, his face illuminated by the glow of the laptop screen as he studied the layout of the Bamboo Emporium. The Executioner was in deep study, checking off spots that Lyons had pointed out with the mousepad and an in-system flag marker.

Grimaldi just shrugged, waiting for Bolan to finish concentrating, using the map and his own view, thanks to a pocket scope, to determine the course of action.

Lyons grunted, and the phone clicked off hold.

"Okay, I'm back, Carl," Kurtzman said. "Xian is definitely working something kinky. The DEA records were tough to crack, but Akira finally cut through and got a glimmer that the Bamboo Emporium is also money laundering for Thai heroin."

"Money laundering...any chance of there being smuggling involved, too?" Lyons asked.

"The DEA has been trying its best to find any," Kurtzman answered. "But nothing more than circumstantial evidence pops up at best."

Bolan spoke up from the back, listening on the cell phone's

speaker. "Circumstantial is enough for me. We have a member of the prime minister's staff calling this place, and I doubt he'd call a Thai imported- furniture store for a souvenir to bring back home."

"A word of reminder for Ironman," Kurtzman said. "This is Washington, D.C., not Sri Lanka. Try not to make too big a mess."

"Any mess we make, we'll be far away from," Lyons said. "That's why we went strictly through you guys. Nothing to connect us."

Kurtzman groaned. "Barb's going to have my ass for this."

The Able Team leader hung up. "Come on. I'm going to look for something that goes with my sofa set."

5

The Executioner left Lyons and Grimaldi to cover the corners of the store. The building took up almost a quarter of a block of strip-mall space, and was two stories high, with lots of clear glass so passersby could ooh and aah at all the pretty imported Karen region teak and bamboo furniture, handsomely crafted, Bolan knew, in sweatshops around the globe by workers who were barely skin and bones thanks to a paycheck of a nickel an hour. He had once made a mental note about the conditions of slaughter in the Karen province of Myanmar with rebels, loggers and Golden Triangle drug dealers doing their damnedest to force an entire race of people into extinction. The Executioner's war book received another mental flag—sooner or later, he'd have to deal with that particular hellhole.

But first things first. Bolan positioned himself at the service entrance, away from the front. Grimaldi and Lyons, casually dressed in windbreakers and jeans against the evening chill, loitered nonchalantly. The only clues of their lethality were bulges under the windbreakers, offset by hands in pockets, and earphone-microphones that led down into their open collars to a radio that hummed softly in Bolan's right ear.

The soldier fished around in his gear bag for a small device rigged up by Hermann Schwarz, Able Team's electronics master, and John Kissinger, Stony Man's armorer. He remembered Schwarz's description of the eight-inch-long, inch-thick pipe. "Latest toy from Cowboy and me. Silenced 12-gauge lockbuster. Fires an ounce of iron filings at about fifteen feet per second at point-blank range. Kills most locks dead."

Considering that for fast action, it'd work much better than a .44 Magnum round that could bounce off a lock, the locksnuffer, as Schwarz had christened it, would be ideal for those times when a lock pick was too slow it wouldn't be discreet to deploy. Bolan drew the small pipe from his gear bag and pressed it to the security lock of the service entrance, then pulled the ring on the end of it. The pipe jumped, and the door made a loud thumping sound. When he pulled the pipe away, the lock fell away in chunks.

Bolan eased open the door, undoing the near-silent snaps on his own dark jacket to allow free access to the suppressed Beretta under his left arm. He stepped across the doorway, his eyes closed and ears wide open in the gloom, trusting his hearing more than his unadjusted night vision to warn him of any presence inside the stockroom. After he could see a little more clearly, he moved among the stored stock, keeping low and using it for cover. No other light was visible, except the spray of moonlight coming from the cracked door behind him. The maze of stacked crates led him to the far wall, and he paused, reaching under his jacket and clicking the pocket transceiver hooked to his ear once.

Slow, agonizing seconds passed, then there were two clicks.

Grimaldi.

Three clicks.

Lyons.

The three clicks repeated, and there was a count-off of clicks. Two clicks.

Bolan knew that, according to SWAT communication procedures, a building was given four sides for better nonverbal communication. Side 1 was the front. Side 2 was the right, going clockwise. Side 3 was the back. Side 4 was the left side. Since Lyons was covering side 2, Bolan knew that something had attracted the Able Team leader's attention on that side. Stepping

softly, gingerly, ignoring the occasional flare of pain from his lac-
erated foot, the Executioner edged toward Side 2, slowing as he
reached a stack of boxes from which he saw a band of whiteness.
With his feet barely leaving the floor, he cat-footed toward his
new goal.

Finally Bolan was able to rest a shoulder against the wall near
the business office. Light leaked onto the tile floor of the storeroom, occasional shadows giving the sign that someone was behind the door.

Bolan contemplated his options for a moment, then clicked
his radio again. From the sound of it, there were only three men
inside the room. With Lyons and Grimaldi outside, there wasn't
going to be much wiggle room to get them into the stockroom
before the emporium employees inside noticed what was going
on. However, his Stony Man allies would be valuable in the
mop-up.

Instead, he reached around and knocked politely on the door.

There was a sound of startled movement rising from the crack
under the door, confused voices speaking in Thai.

Bolan knocked once more.

The door creaked open and a head poked through, leaning out.

The Executioner grabbed the man's head with both hands
and heaved, picking up the lighter Thai and hurling him backward and into a man-sized crate with a resounding crash. The
man shouted in terror before the impact drove the wind from his
lungs.

In a flash of movement, Bolan was in the office, his Beretta
covering the remaining two occupants as they were caught,
stunned by the sudden launching of their buddy into the inky
blackness of the stockroom.

One was scrambling to pull a revolver out of his waistband,
his body swinging sideways behind the relative cover of a filing
cabinet, but the Beretta 93-R snarled with brutal efficiency, catching him across his thighs with a 3-round burst. Screaming in pain,
the Asian smuggler dropped to the floor, his wheelgun clattering noisily into the warehouse. Bolan stepped forward swiftly,
snapping his foot hard into the side of the Thai gunman's head,
sending him into blissful unconsciousness.

The office's other occupant remained motionless, so Bolan

turned his attention to the first Thai smuggler who had returned to the doorway, his face a bloody mask from a cut on his head. The soldier shrugged hard, whipping his elbow to strike the angry gangster right in his nose, adding more color to his scarlet mask, sending the guy tumbling back into the arms of Carl Lyons, who'd just showed up.

Bolan kept his attention on the remaining Thai, who was calmly puffing on a cigarette.

"Anyone else?" Grimaldi asked, out of breath as he raced to the office.

"What do you punks want?"

"Cocky," Lyons spoke up, tossing aside the limp, unconscious form that had catapulted into him. "Must not have seen you two guys really at work," Grimaldi answered.

The man leaned on his elbow and blew smoke at the Stony Man trio, apparently bored with them. This was definitely the man whom the DEA profiled as their untouchable Thai heroin smuggler. A cruel, cocky smirk was on his face. "I'm a busy man. Want money? A cut of my stuff?"

"I'm here for answers, Xian," Bolan said.

The businessman shrugged. "You're pretty good. I could hire you."

"Really?" Lyons asked. He leaned in and spoke in a stage whisper to Bolan. "Hold out until you find out what his dental plan looks like."

Bolan regarded Lyons for a moment, then looked back to Xian.

"My partner wants to know what your dental plan looks like."

Xian blinked in surprise. "Um, actually, it's pretty good."

Bolan turned back to his ex-LAPD partner. "He says it's pretty good."

"I'm intrigued. Do you cover broken bridges?"

Xian looked to Lyons. "What do you mean?"

The Thai caught a flutter of movement out of the corner of his eye, and in the next moment, his vision flashed to blankness.

Grimaldi looked around at the mess in the office. "You know, I'm gonna tell Gadgets on you. One mission with Striker in charge, and suddenly you're the local comedian."

Lyons winked at the Stony Man ace pilot. "Who was joking?"

"Come on, we've got work to do," Bolan said, hauling Xian over one shoulder. "Jack, call 911 for this one—" he nodded to the gunman he'd shot "—before he bleeds to death. Consider it a gift to the DEA."

Grimaldi was dialing his cell phone even as he tried to keep up with the long strides of the two warriors.

XIAN MO WOKE UP an hour later in a garage, tied to a chair. It looked like any other suburban garage. The walls looked thick, and were well insulated, Spartan and bare without signs of the usual automotive and gardening equipment that filled shelves and walls.

However, there was some sports equipment. Baseball bats. Hockey sticks. But no balls, no gloves, no pads.

The Thai didn't think that the sports equipment was intended for any other use than breaking his bones.

He looked at the grim man with dark hair and ice-blue eyes as he sat across from him, those icy orbs boring into him as if the big man were a lion, staring at wounded prey, waiting for its struggles to cease.

Ten minutes of silence and staring.

Twenty minutes of silence and staring.

An hour.

Xian thought he was going to go mad with anticipation. Hit him, torture him, anything. Do something, please!

Then the door opened. A tall black man stood in the doorway, dressed in a completely white coverall. In his hand was a small hooked knife, and he walked slowly, nonchalantly toward the prisoner.

Though he had given his vow to never tell anything about the San United Army to any Westerner, even should it cost his dying breath, this was maddening. Now sheer terror at pains imagined and unimaginable turned his blood to ice. He squirmed, but the tall black man simply pressed his head down and lifted the knife. It gleamed evilly, glinting small suns off the reflecting edge of its blade, and Xian chewed at his tongue.

His lips already felt raw from trying to pull away the duct tape, and his heart felt as if it would burst in his chest. The knife slashed down, and the Thai wanted to scream.

But there was no pain.

Only ripping.

Tearing.

Shredding fabric.

Sharp tugs and pulls finally left him cold in the middle of the garage floor, and he trembled, the garage suddenly colder than it should have been on a warm evening.

The tall man nodded to another white man, the big blonde who was curious about dental plans. The blonde went and got a pair of large hedge clippers, resembling a giant pair of wooden-handled scissors, with all the leverage and sharpness to chop through a two-inch branch.

"Cut off his right hand" were the first words that Xian heard the newcomer say. He looked at the blond man, tall and broadly built, and the moment that the Thai met the man's eyes, there was a sudden flicker of wildness and inhuman savagery before calmness crossed his features again.

Xian felt his blood turn to ice water. He wanted to say something, but his mouth was jammed shut by the duct tape. They weren't even giving him a chance to speak yet.

"No!" he finally roared, his mustache and upper lip peeling free from the tape. It fell free, and he tasted his own blood in his mouth. "No! I'll tell you anything!"

The black man looked to the blonde with the hedge clippers.

"Procedure is not to listen to them until we carve out their eyes and genitals," the cold-eyed madman said.

"I know, but throwing all those pieces into one bag, it's just easier to kill him in one piece," the wielder of the hedge clippers said.

"His name is Thaksin Sunthonwet! He's Xiang's security chief!" Xian shouted. His chest was heaving in wild sobs. Tears were streaming down his cheeks.

"Dammit, Mr. Black, I gave you a direct order! Chop this bastard's hand off!"

"Thaksin's been taking underage boys. Xiang would cut him off at the ankles and hang him out like old laundry!"

"Fuck you, Stone! I'm sick of this. 'Cut his dick off, Black.' 'Pull his eyes out, Black.' What is your fucking damage, man? You get your rocks off on seeing naked men mutilated?" the African American asked.

"We provided him help, assistance. He has money behind him, arrange for us passports and banquet tickets and everything. I can tell you where he is, where he came into the country, what name he's hiding under!"

"You leave my personal life out of this, Black. You're paid to do what I say!" Stone spit back.

"The leader of the assassin team is Khwamwang Phattana! He's set up shop in Virginia." Xian sobbed. "Please! Please just kill me!"

But the two would-be torturers continued to argue, ignoring him. The Thai kept adding details, begging to be released from this hell.

Until finally, he felt a tap on his shoulder.

"Thank you for your cooperation," Grimaldi said waving a tape recorder. "We'll leave you here for the FBI to pick up."

Calvin James and Carl Lyons turned to Xian Mo, held hands and bowed. "Thank you. This has been a production of Dysfunctional Spy Agency Theater. Be here next week when we present *Cat on a Hot Tin Roof.*"

The Thai smuggler hung his head, tears of shame cut through by giggles of relief .

He was still laughing hours later, when the FBI found him.

6

Mack Bolan flipped open his cell phone on the first ring, already knowing who'd be calling this particular line. Inside Grimaldi's Hughes 500D, they were swooping back to Stony Man Farm to get some rest and to rearm for that evening's activities. Inside the cabin, the warble of the phone was faint, but the vibrator alerted him. Plugging the earpiece cord into his headset, he could hear clearly, flipping the phone like a microphone, speaking closely to it to overwhelm the rotor slap of the chopper in flight.

"Striker, I've got a handle," Yakov Katzenelenbogen said immediately.

"We've got another one down here, too. What's yours?"

"The New York Families weren't too happy, according to Sticker, that baby rapers were slipping through their city."

Bolan shook his head at the two-facedness. The Mob had made more than enough money with its own kiddie porn movies, as well as dealing drugs to children. The alleged high ground of the Mob wasn't anything Bolan took stock in greater than he could drop-kick the island of Manhattan. However, the news from Sticker, Bolan's longest known ally, Leo Turrin, a semiretired undercover Justice operative and member of La Commissione, was intriguing.

Of course, having Katz confer with Turrin was Bolan's primary purpose for leaving him behind in New York. Criminals often had a feeling, if not actual better intelligence, of what their neighbors and competitors were up to than law enforcement itself. The most highly placed member of the Justice Department in the most highly placed position in the old Mafia was often a vital handle on information regarding smugglers, even terrorists trading arms and muscle or just mere information, semiretired or not.

"What did Sticker have to say?" Bolan asked.

"New York has a long memory, and they're not particularly thrilled to have the heat of a kiddie porn ring operating in their town. Not when it could bring some nosy types around," Katz answered.

"So..."

"So Sticker decided to give you a preview of the lunchtime news," Katz said.

Bolan turned his head, squinting his eyes at the daylight pouring into the helicopter's cabin. Except for a quick nap the previous night, he'd been running for twenty-four hours. "Let me guess. In an apparent Mob war, a bunch of Thai businessmen were found dead. When did it happen?"

"Sticker said to give it about six minutes," Katz told him.

Bolan looked at his watch—1154 hours. "Punctual."

Katz chuckled. "I never said they didn't have their positive points."

"I agree. Deep down, they're good people. Six feet deep, at least."

"I checked again with Singer. He said that he finally made contact with a friend of his in San Francisco. Has contacts in Thailand and speaks the language."

"Good. Once I finish down here, I'll go meet him."

"Singer says you need to pick up his chop first."

Bolan sighed. "All right."

"And the woman we met. She wants to come along, too. Give you some extra local language."

"You heard her, Yakov. She was born in New York. She has a Queens accent. She'll be lost in Thailand."

"I tried to convince her of that. She was insistent."

"I'll think about it."

"She does have firearms training."

Bolan went silent for a moment. "It's no guarantee for survival if things get hairy."

"She said she didn't care. She was sick of sitting on the sidelines. Even in a support role, she'd be happy. Plus, how much experience do you have with traumatized children?"

Bolan gave a thought about Johnny, his brother, back when he began his crusade as the Executioner. "Too much. But not the way you mean. All right. She comes along to help out the kids."

"Great. Sticker says to keep your head on this one, though."

Bolan paused. "Keep my head?"

"He said you'd eventually figure it out, Striker."

"I just did. Tell him not to worry, Yakov. Striker out."

Bolan closed the cell phone.

"What was that about?" Lyons asked as the two of them sat in the back of Grimaldi's chopper.

"Just some travel plans," Bolan mentioned as he settled into the seat, watching the Blue Ridge mountains blur past the window.

"Keep your head," Leo had said.

Bolan had targeted the undercover Fed early in his campaign, thinking him a willing accomplice in the degradation of his sister that led to his father's suicidal rampage. Instead, Bolan was driven off by a fusillade of gunfire before the Executioner could pass sentence on the man he had thought led his sister to ruin.

Bolan intended to keep his head.

But he knew that others were going to start losing theirs.

THE EXECUTIONER HAD his own means of getting information that didn't involve Stony Man Farm. He'd developed a storehouse of his own personal data, a war book of information for missions that didn't interest Hal Brognola and the Sensitive Operations Group.

Not that Bolan had anything against this lack of interest.

They were protecting America from terrorists foreign and domestic.

But there were times when the Executioner had his own mission, surgery to perform that would cut the cancerous tumors out of the belly of a city. Be it a corner drug dealer who just happened to hit a three-year-old girl, or the animal who sabotaged a construction site with dozens of innocent workers just for the sake of a few dollars of insurance money.

The Executioner, when he wasn't fighting terrorism in all of its guises, was still doing justice.

And now justice was coming to a little adult bookstore in Washington, a bookstore that had shown up on a phone trace of a State Department cell-phone log, and in the confession they'd gotten from Xian Mo. There was no such thing as coincidence in Mack Bolan's line of work, so he decided to pay a visit.

He entered through the front door, his bomber jacket hanging loosely over his twin handguns, his icy stare sweeping the racks of "mild" pornography, the things that involved consenting adults doing things that Bolan himself wouldn't think of consenting to. He swept past them. Even at nearly 5:00 a.m., there were people in there, browsing, looking nervously at the big man as he moved through.

Bolan was entirely unconcerned with what they thought of him. Not in a social way, either. He projected a level of menace that darkened the store in his wake, and people moved around aisles and ducked their heads into magazines. He strode to the counter where a clerk was watching him, pinned like a deer in the headlights.

The Executioner rested his hands gently on the counter, ice stabbing deep into the clerk, who couldn't have been twenty by the pathetic wisps of chin-hair and the softness of his face.

"Where's the manager?" Bolan asked.

"Um...home...asleep..."

Bolan remained impassive, just staring.

"Who's asking?"

Bolan kept glaring.

"Man, he's just in the back."

The kid kept squirming, pinned under the ice stare.

"He said he'd kill me if I said anything about—"

"Are you involved?"

"Please, mister, I have a brother their age. It's not right, but—"

"He says he'll take your brother and do to him what he's doing to the other kids," Bolan said, the ice melting, Sergeant Mercy appearing through his voice.

The clerk nodded, tears welling in his eyes.

"Call the cops."

"What for?"

"Call the cops and get everyone, including yourself, out of the store," Bolan said, pulling his Desert Eagle. The kid blanched.

The Executioner gave him his command voice. "Do it now."

The phone was off the hook, and Bolan was around the counter, heading into the darkness of two black curtains.

The sounds that Bolan heard on the other side of the darkened hall were of raised music, pumping abnormally loud, as if to drown out everything. Everything like the crying of children.

Bolan slipped around the corner, moving slowly so as not to draw attention at his sudden movement. He saw two men speaking softly, one holding his ear to block out the music. Behind them, behind a fence of chicken wire, were small shapes shuffling in the darkness, staring blankly.

One of them was a familiar face from the list of diplomatic-security officers that Kurtzman had prepared for him. The other, seated, was the manager, sneering.

"Goddamn it, Manny!" the DSO shouted. "What the hell are you getting me into?"

"Jail," Bolan said.

The DSO, a guy named Taylor, spun, reaching for the gun on his hip. The Executioner, sworn never to fire upon a soldier of the same side, wasn't as restrained in taking a lightning stride across the room and hammering a fist deep under Taylor's solar plexus, lifting him from the ground.

Taylor collapsed against the chicken wire, and Bolan turned, seeing Manny dive for an open drawer and his own gun. The soldier extended his free arm, the one with the three pounds of Desert Eagle attached to it, and slammed the muzzle of the ten-inch-long hand cannon into Manny's face. Lips shredded against splintered teeth, and blood dribbled down his chin, but Manny was still capable of sputtering.

"Behave," Bolan snarled.

Manny was frozen in his seat.

Taylor, however, wasn't as easily convinced to quit. He snapped to his feet and lunged. Bolan sidestepped the lunge, bringing up his elbow and crashing his forearm into Taylor's face with a bloody smack. Snapping his arm straight, Bolan drove his forearm across the back of Taylor's head and sent him tumbling into the hall, legs kicking wildly.

Manny bent, and Bolan fired the Desert Eagle, the muzzle inches away from doing anything more than rupturing one of the smut-master's eardrums. The squeals of children cut through the music.

"Uh-uh," Bolan said as Manny held one of his ears, tears falling down his face.

Bolan spun, this time anticipating Taylor's recovery time. He was ahead of the man by a full second and was able to greet the pervert with a snap kick that cracked Taylor's kneecap. As his adversary stumbled, Bolan moved in, a knee to the groin and the butt of the Desert Eagle into the hollow of the DSO traitor's throat, slamming him painfully into the wall.

"Lester Taylor. Tell me what a big, formerly good-looking man like yourself is doing in a porno shop," Bolan ordered.

Taylor sprayed blood from his running, shattered nose. Bolan ignored the red rain and clutched a handful of the man's short blond hair, twisting until the DSO was forced to crane his neck back or have his scalp peeled from his skull like an orange skin.

"I'm asking you nicely, Les. Do you want me to get harsh?" Bolan asked.

Taylor winced. "Go to hell, man. I'm not saying anything!"

Bolan pressed the still hot muzzle of the Desert Eagle into Taylor's cheek. Skin sizzled, but the man didn't see that the gun was on safe, and wouldn't take his head off with a twitch of the Executioner's finger. "You're saying something now."

"Ahh!" was all Taylor could vocalize.

Bolan took a moment, his eyes adjusted to the dim light now.

The forms of three children stood, wobbling, eyes blank with fear and numbed by unspeakable acts. They were barely clothed, but from the looks of them, they looked well fed. And, no surprise to the Executioner, they were Asian children.

"Got something to tell me, Lester?"

"Man, not here, not now. They're coming for the kids."

"What?"

Just then, at the other side of the tiny office, a door swung open, the gray light of dawn spilling in, along with a pair of pistol-toting Asians.

7

The Executioner was a normal man. When confronted by surprises, he was startled like any other person, but his reflexes and his mind-set allowed him to react defensively, even when taken wholly by surprise. When the Asians burst in, they spotted Bolan, gun in hand, leaning against Taylor.

They took a moment to process that, a moment longer than the Executioner was going to give them for a free shot against him. He spun, using Taylor's body as a shield on instinct, bullets suddenly exploding in the tiny office, a gun battle at the range of arm's length taking place. Taylor vomited blood, his body slamming into Bolan as bullets cored into him.

The two men went to the ground, which was where Bolan wanted to be, but not with a mortally wounded man atop him. Especially a wounded man who could help give Bolan a mouthful of information yet. Still, the soldier was on his back now, and even though the children were still behind the two young hooligans spraying the office with gunfire, the kids would have to be ten feet tall to take a bullet at the angle the Executioner was firing from.

Bolan snapped off the safety, finally free of bystanders to open fire.

Manny screamed as a bullet smashed across his face, and Bolan felt the numbers really falling. These punks weren't taking chances, and their idea of fire discipline was dousing a failure with lighter fluid and taking a match to them. The Executioner put a double-tap of .44 slugs into the chest of one Asian tough, sending him crashing across the chicken wire. Screams again filled the air, and despite the ringing and thunder in his ears, Bolan realized that the music had suddenly stopped.

A shattered boom box on a small filing cabinet was in pieces, a speaker bouncing against the side of the cabinet. Bolan switched his attention back to the remaining gunner, who was wondering where his partner had gone and what to do about a man with half a face screaming his head off.

Bolan solved the punk's dilemma with a head shot that turned the killer into a human volcano, his body dropping as if he were a marionette with its strings suddenly sliced.

Rolling to his feet, the Executioner was in motion, heading to the doorway. Two men to come pick up the kids, just as Taylor mentioned. They'd have a driver, and they'd have a getaway car.

He hit the doorway. Sure enough, there was the driver, stuck in the middle, wondering what the sudden firefight was all about and trying to decide whether to run or to go help his friends.

The appearance of the Executioner in the budding sunrise made up the thug's mind and he started for the car, a Chevy Caprice. Bolan aimed low and blew out one of the driver's legs before he reached the open car door, folding him over it with the leg-breaking impact. In the space of a few strides, the Executioner had reached the guy, but he'd pulled a knife and drove his arm back hard. Steel deflected off the Executioner's holstered Beretta, deflecting it from where it would have plunged between his ribs.

Bolan hammered the driver across his face with the barrel of the Desert Eagle, laying open skin and cracking bone, but the wiry little driver slammed the soldier between his legs. Backing up, wanting to vomit from the impact, Bolan instead forced himself to slam against the side of the Chevy as the driver swung his knife again, this time trying to slash open his throat.

On the backswing, Bolan reached up and grabbed the arm, discarding the Desert Eagle and holding the limb in both hands. The driver tried to flip the knife to his uncaptured arm, but a hard knee to his ribs ended the toss. Swinging his whole body, Bolan rammed the driver across the trunk of the car. The rear fender dented with the impact, and the soldier was certain he heard bones snap on impact.

"Just give up, all right?" Bolan asked. He wanted another prisoner, another solid link in the chain.

Instead, the punk's foot slammed down hard on the instep of Bolan's injured foot. The soldier ignored the pain and rammed his elbow into the thug's neck, slamming it down to meet the hood of the trunk.

The ugly snap that resulted sickened Bolan.

So much for interrogation.

His leads were evaporating, and somewhere in Washington remained a skilled murderer who was gunning for the Thai prime minister.

MACK BOLAN SNAPPED back to wakefulness. Visions of his most recent nightmares were still whirling in his conscious mind as he made sense of his surroundings with the same practiced ease gained from years of living hand-to-mouth, never slowing for a second.

It was the gunfight in the office. He recalled it with crystal clarity as he settled back down, noting he was in a Stony Man Farm-rented Ford Crown Victoria, parked in a clearing by the roadside.

The fight was exactly the same, except the background, the children. They weren't little Asian kids. They were Cindy and Johnny, his younger siblings, their faces gaunt, de-aged to somewhere under fifteen, their eyes filled with a horror no child should ever have to endure.

Bolan winced at the thought and drove the dream from his mind.

"Now I remember why I don't like remembering dreams," he whispered, his throat dry.

He reached over and plucked a bottle of water from its resting place in his war bag, sipping as he plucked out his cell phone. A press of the speed dial, and he noted the time was 9:00 a.m. He'd gotten two hours of sleep, enough rest for what he had to do.

With a mouthful of water washing away the dryness of sleep, he was ready when the phone picked up.

"It's Striker," he announced.

"You don't waste much time," Kurtzman answered.

"Any news on my play this morning?"

"D.C. police hit the shop seconds after you left, finding three dead, two wounded."

"Two wounded. Taylor?"

"Among the living yet. He had on body armor, not that it was effective against the ammo the Thai gangsters were using."

"What were they using?"

"ChiCom Tokarevs."

"Odd choice," Bolan noted.

Kurtzman grunted a negative. "Word's on the street. Some big scary dude's hunting down people. The Washington Asian Crimes Task Force heard that rumor this morning."

"This rumor have a name?"

"No. But the description is seven feet tall with neon blue eyes that give off steam and a black mane of hair. He carries a howitzer in one pocket."

"No mention of my clown makeup?"

"Huh?"

"Sorry, Bear."

"Oh, *The Crow*. I remember that movie. Nope. But you are dressed in all black leather."

"Never knew I dressed so well."

"The kids are okay," Kurtzman told him. "Three of them."

"Okay?"

"Physically unharmed, I mean. Hal's trying to arrange for some psychiatric counseling for them."

"Have him ask about getting Singer's help on that."

"I already anticipated that. That's who he's calling."

"Thanks, Bear."

"Need Carl, Calvin and Jack for your next visit?"

"How'd you know there'd be one?"

"It's only been four hours since you last smashed some bad guys to a pulp."

Bolan grinned. "Hooking to cellular modem. Give me the aerial shot of the address we got from Mo."

"How'd you—never mind."

"Hell, it's been four hours. You probably had a head count of who was at the ranch house Mo described an hour before I called you."

"All right. Sending."

Bolan watched the aerial views pop up on his laptop. Studying them, his face darkened, looking at the grim odds ahead of him.

Two dozen armed men.

Excellent patrol patterns.

These guys weren't just thugs and gangsters. They were full-blown military.

Ex-military raised Bolan's concern slightly, but these soldiers were going to learn the true meaning of war.

The Bolan blitz was about to come into effect.

THE EXECUTIONER WAS getting ready for war. In the Virginia countryside already, he moved his car so that it couldn't be seen from the road, and further concealed it with some camouflage netting from his war bag. He'd anticipated the need for hiding his vehicle, so asked for it from Kissinger, Stony Man Farm's armorer.

He'd also anticipated having to fight a small-scale war.

From his war bag, he pulled the rifle case of a Heckler & Koch MSG-90, the "budget" version of the honored PSG-1 rifle. It was a rifle built to less exacting specifications, which in turn made it more rugged, and more reliable for dirty field work. Based on the G-3 battle rifle, which was as accurate and powerful as any rifle that Bolan had used without feeling his arm go numb from the recoil, the HK would prove a valuable ally to him in combat. With six spare magazines and one in the gun, he had 140 rounds to work with.

In case things got hairy at close range, Bolan could swing the MSG-90 easier than a PSG-1, but even so, he still had his Beretta machine pistol and his Desert Eagle. It was going to be tight, and while he could have used the assistance of Lyons, James and Grimaldi, they were spread across Washington, assisting in the investigation into who betrayed the prime minister.

James was at Bethesda, where Taylor had been waylaid, hoping to get more information out of the wounded man before he died.

Lyons was watching the prime minister himself, ready to act at the first sign of danger.

And Grimaldi was bringing Katz and Michelle Lam back from New York.

Michelle Lam.

She was going to be a noncombatant in the field, but none of the Stony Man staff had any experience with dealing with traumatized children. And in Thailand, they'd be dealing with plenty of kids, if Bolan had his chance.

The Executioner intended not only to lay flame to the towers of Chang and the San United Army, but to rescue as many victims of these monsters as he could.

But still, Bolan knew there were going to be complications. These missions never went smoothly. Lam, though she swore she'd stay a noncombatant, would be drawn to the front lines. She'd be dragged in, and chances were that Bolan would be facing another friendly ghost by the time this mission was over.

He dismissed the worries for the future. He'd deal with problems when they arose.

He slipped on his headset and switched it over to Stony Man Farm's tac-net.

"This is Stony Base, reading you, Striker," Barbara Price announced.

"You have a bird in the air over the ranch?"

"We have live feed right now."

"How many on-site?" Bolan found his hide, a ledge that was next to a slope.

The outcropping had a view of most of the house and grounds, and the longest shot across the clearing was a good 950 yards. It was well within the range of the .308.

Heavy wooden fences bracketed the road, so Bolan figured that if he could take out a getaway vehicle at that location, he'd have the gunmen trapped on foot, the road being only one-and-one-half car widths.

A killing box designed for the Executioner's cleansing wrath.

Bolan sighted through the 4X scope and targeted a gunman at the gate, hundreds of yards away.

"Stony Base?" Bolan asked.

"We're checking," Price answered, her voice filled with tension.

Bolan swept the whole ranch. "No perimeter guards?"

"They've taken to the tree line. Heading your way!" Price snapped.

Bolan was moving when he realized that the ledge he was standing on had a barely hidden sensor in it. A mental note was made—these guys had technology and knew how to use it. They'd probably picked this ranch house and spent the first few days figuring its vulnerabilities.

The Executioner's appreciation evaporated, and he snapped up the bipod of his rifle so it wouldn't snag or unbalance it. He'd have preferred the option of full-auto in his weapon, but single shot wouldn't be too much of a handicap considering the power of the rifle. He hit the slope and skidded, sliding down, attacking rather than retreating.

"Striker," Price called, "you're heading to a hole. They'll flank you any moment."

"Can they read this transmission?" Bolan asked.

"No sign that they are," Price answered.

"Right. I'll get back to you in a second," Bolan said, diving and rolling, a controlled tumble that dropped him past a line of shadowy figures racing uphill.

Someone got smart to Bolan's left and shouted. The Executioner targeted the guy, and a double tap of .308 rounds slammed into the brush. A blood-curdling cry split the air, a body tumbling through a bush chopped apart by high-velocity slugs.

Bolan continued his downhill tumble, not even having moved two yards when autofire sprayed where his muzzle-flash had been moments before. The cross fire swept the air around the soldier, who targeted a line of enemy muzzle-flashes and fired ten rounds as fast as he could pull the trigger. The enemy gunfire stopped, and the Executioner continued to roll, sliding to the left of where he'd opened fire.

Gunfire again erupted from the group on the left, but the gunners were aiming just behind Bolan, bullets smacking foliage and tree trunks, splinters flying. The Executioner drew his Beretta 93-R. Pressing against the trunk of a thick oak tree, he sighted on two figures who were scrambling downhill, looking for signs of the big man in black. Bolan ignored the guy closer to him, targeting the man behind him. They were smart and well spread out, so Bolan tapped a single Parabellum round into the pale moon face of one of the imported hit men. The second gunner paused, wondering what was going on with his pal.

Bolan flicked the Italian machine pistol to 3-round burst and blew out the back of the pointman's skull, sending him crashing beside his partner.

Stepping hard to the right, he found cover amid the multiple trunks of a copse of elms.

"Stony Base, anyone clearing out?"

"Negative, Striker."

"Any idea of the head count?"

"Only fifteen on site when you started."

"Bear counted twenty-four."

"Bear also counted seven cars. Now there's only four."

Bolan cursed and spun, scanning the shadows of the trees, sunlight dotting the forest floor.

Something moved, and Bolan leathered the Desert Eagle, firing a trio of shots in the direction of the movement. He was answered by a cacophony of autofire that just missed him as he went prone. As the gunners opened fire, he marked their positions, sending a barrage of muffled 9 mms and .44 Magnum slugs hammering at them as they continued to sweep the forest around them with wild autofire.

Trained soldiers, Bolan noted.

But they weren't used to someone who was skilled at ambush.

"Striker, hillside's clear!" Price announced as Bolan's pistols locked back empty. Dumping both guns' magazines, he fed them fresh sticks and holstered them, bringing back the MSG-90 to his hands. He'd need the rifle to give him cover as he crossed the open grass around the ranch house. He loaded a fresh magazine into the rifle and looked out from the tree line, keeping low.

"This wasn't fifteen men," Bolan noted.

"No," Price answered.

Bolan brought the rifle to his shoulder and scanned the house. He caught a glimpse of something in a window and quickly backtracked to it.

A man stood there holding a weapon.

Bolan squeezed the trigger, sending off his .308 missile.

But not before he saw the eruption of a rocket launcher spitting its payload right down the middle of the Executioner's sniper scope.

8

With an enemy rocket barreling towards him in the tree line, Mack Bolan's options were limited. Fortunately he subscribed to a certain bit of philosophy that had carried him against the ambush on the hill, a philosophy handed to him by the indomitable Carl Lyons, the leader of Able Team.

"When everything's fucked, nut up and do it," was Lyons's philosophy.

It wasn't Bolan's choice of words, but the idea was basically sound.

Bolan charged, bursting from the tree line. Not at the missile itself, but at an angle, he continued to charge the ranch house, running as fast as his legs would carry him, muscles burning and lungs drying out from the effort to get as far away from where the launcher was targeted.

The shock wave slammed Bolan to the ground, but he was well outside the line of the blast, no shrapnel coming close to him, even though he felt as if he might have broken a rib on the frame of the rifle, and his lungs had totally emptied.

Rolling onto his back, he gasped for breath and saw that the missile would have missed where he was by fifteen feet.

The only problem was that the radius of flames and wreckage on the tree line was more than twenty-five feet. Smoke poured skyward, and flames crackled in the woods where he'd been.

Bolan paused to examine his rifle.

The scope had been bent off its railing, one of the bipod legs was snapped off and the plastic stock had shattered. The action was smooth, a cartridge flying from the chamber. He held back the bolt, then turned the rifle, looking to see sunlight down the barrel.

Bolan tore off its cheek piece, damaged in the hit, and began a long crawl to where he knew the long grass would end. Rifle fire zipped the air around him, snipers from the house trying to get his range based on the swaying of the grass as he passed through it.

"Anyone leaving?"

"No, but two cars are swinging around to the side of the house that you're approaching from."

Bolan was intrigued, and he crawled to the edge of the grass, ripping the bent scope off its base and using it as a spyglass.

Two cars were barricading in front of the ranch house, and four gunmen were crouched with their feet behind the wheels of their vehicles. He swept the area.

Sure enough, two gunmen were flanking him. Each was armed with an M-16.

Bolan pulled the MSG-90 to his shoulder, locked his iron sights on the goon to the left and punched his brains out with a single .308 round. He was up and moving an instant later, running as fast as he could toward the second man, firing from the hip, walking rounds toward the M-16 gunner who was scrambling to bring his rifle to bear as he tried to back away.

From the cars, gunfire spit all around Bolan, but finally he disemboweled the second Thai gunman with a trio of rounds from his HK. The soldier dived to the ground beside the dying hit man, scooping up his M-16 and using the dead man as a shield. Gunfire pelted into the dying gunner as Bolan swept the two crew wagons on full-auto. Two figures collapsed to the ground, unmoving.

Reloading the MSG-90, Bolan brought it up and began punching steel-cored slugs into each of the cars. He knew the location of the gas tanks in dozens of makes, and he was aiming for them. On his ninth round, the car to the left burst into flames, a roiling blossom sweeping across one rifleman just before the eruption of superheated glass and metal sent a wave of killing shrapnel across his body.

The last gunman turned and ran, and Bolan got to his feet, tracking the fleeing man.

The time for prisoners and interrogation was over.

He had a house to ransack for clues and details.

The rifle hammered into Bolan's shoulder, and the battle for the ranch house was over.

THE EXECUTIONER MOVED silently. He needed to have his ears open, checking for any survivors who might suddenly sit up and decide to continue fighting right then and there. It could be someone who decided to play possum or was wearing armor and was just waking up from trauma. Bolan wasn't going to take chances, especially with the two men who went down with his opening salvo of gunfire.

He stopped, looking over each man.

No.

Khwamwang's face wasn't among those present here. Even the charred and shredded face of the gunman caught by the exploding car, nothing.

Bolan cursed and went into the house, flicking the line open.

"Khwamwang isn't here," Bolan said. "Did the satellites pick up any vehicles leaving?"

"Not since you got there."

"That means the other nine men, Khwamwang included, are already at the hotel."

"I'll have Phoenix Four head on over to back up Able One."

"Right," Bolan said, looking through the house. Bullet holes were in the walls, obviously from his cutting loose.

He looked at the man with the rocket launcher, surprised at the make.

"These guys have at least one AT-4 antitank rocket."

"Antitank?" Price asked.

"Yeah," Bolan said.

There was some silent muttering outside the range of Price's microphone.

"Striker, we have a theft of a half dozen AT-4s and fifty M-16s from a local National Guard base."

"Explains a lot."

"Like?"

Bolan kept moving. The place was getting slovenly from being a home of a full platoon of imported hit men.

"Explains their plans. You don't use rocket launchers to guard a place."

"What are you thinking?"

"I'm thinking that the AT-4s can be disguised as pipes, taken up to the roof of the hotel, right above the presidential suite, and bundled together."

"Like a drilling rig."

"A high-explosive drilling rig."

"How precise could it be?"

"They would have the location of the prime minister's office directly. Three AT-4s triggered at once would turn that office into a charnel pit."

"We have Secret Service and DSO on the rooftop, though."

"They were there at the gala, as well," Bolan said. "Is Jack back yet?"

"He just landed."

"Send him over."

"ETA five minutes, Striker. He's in midrefuel."

Bolan turned and saw the flicker of movement behind him just before the swinging rifle slammed hard into his shoulder. He cursed himself as he went to the floor, his arm numbed, for not checking pulses. The gunner's chest was a mass of bloody red, but from the way he was holding one arm tight to his side, and using the other, it was a shoulder hit. A lot of blood, only a little pure incapacitation.

And the damnedest thing was that Bolan was also one-armed from the opening swing. Fortune favored him, however. Had the man had two hands to swing with, the rifle blow would have crushed his skull like an egg. The man screamed and pressed his attack.

Bolan snapped up a combat boot, striking the wounded Thai right between his legs, catching him at the Y. The rifle went sailing from numbed hands, and the war cry turned into a wicked screech that would have split Bolan's ears had his heartbeat not been thundering in his skull. A second kick rammed the hit man's kneecap, splitting it with an ugly snap.

The hit man fell forward, and Bolan rolled, bringing his forearm up into the imported killer's throat. The impact jarred the Executioner's other shoulder against the floor painfully, but Bolan got enough feeling in his other arm to reach up and clutch a fistful of black hair.

The hitter choked and gasped like a landed fish, and Bolan scissored the man's head against his forearm, swinging him around to the floor. Applying his full weight, the Executioner spent what felt like an agonizing eternity crushing the breath and life from the clawing hit man. Two or three times, he was certain he had blanked out, because he'd awaken to new thrashings of the mewling life-form under him.

Finally it was over, and Bolan slumped on the hardwood floor.

After two seconds of rest, Jack Grimaldi's helicopter thundered over the ranch house and landed outside.

No rest. Not for the weary, not the wicked and truly not for the Executioner.

CALVIN JAMES DID a quick press check on the slide of his Colt Commander as his beeper went off.

He looked at Taylor, lying in the hospital bed, his eyes glaring.

"You're going to shoot me?" Taylor asked. "You have no right to judge me."

"I'm not going to shoot you," James answered, holstering his gun. "I'm being called to take care of your mess, baby raper."

"It's not rape," Taylor insisted. "It's something good and pure! I give them affection denied to them by their lives on the—"

James clamped his hand over Taylor's mouth.

"Listen. You don't know shit about the hit on the prime minister except for the blank passes you slipped to 'Manny,'" James said aloud.

Taylor squirmed as James leaned hard into him, driving his head into the pillow.

"Normally I'm not the cold-blooded murdering type, but you have two strikes in your favor."

Taylor grunted under James's weight.

"One, you betrayed a crusading, honest politician, and there ain't too many of them, to a heroin dealer."

Taylor was jerking now, trying to get a breath.

"Strike two, you rape kids. Don't tell me about affection. What you give isn't affection—it's damage. These kids are prisoners and victims and addicts, who'd starve or be killed if they didn't put out for freaks like you," James whispered. "You're a part of a deep-rooted disease. You're scum, and worth killing for that."

James's hand came away from Taylor's mouth, and he gasped deeply, catching his breath. "But like I said, I'm not a cold-blooded murderer. I can't kill you for a couple reasons."

James turned and started walking to the door of the guarded ICU room, then paused.

Taylor's eyes went wide as James turned, anger turning his dark features into a mask.

"I forgot. You're diplomatic-security office, right? A cop. A cop who betrayed his badge."

He stepped closer to Taylor.

Taylor tried to get up. He was weak; it was like moving in molasses.

"A cop who betrayed his badge and got his partners killed."

Taylor froze.

Those dark eyes burned into him.

Something dark flashed at Taylor, and he jerked, trying to sit back, and he ended up lying back onto the bed. He wondered what the guy threw, then tried to take a breath.

Nothing.

He sucked air again.

No air reached his lungs.

He tried to cough. Hot, sticky fluid poured down Taylor's cheeks.

Calvin James rubbed the edge of his hand. The blow to Taylor's throat left his hand numb, but from the way he was coughing up blood, the Phoenix Force Tae Kwon Do expert knew his chop had struck true. With a crushed trachea, Taylor had only a short, panic- and pain-filled life left as he drowned in his own blood.

He checked the beeper again, satisfied that some dead lawmen could rest, knowing that justice had been done for them.

For now, the Phoenix Force pro had a rendezvous on the roof of the hospital.

CARL LYONS CHECKED his beeper. Something was up. Lyons's instincts were buzzing. He excused himself from the DSO team and headed out into the hall, flipping open his cell phone as he did so, cutting off the ring to a single pip of the first burble.

"Lyons," he said.

"Carl, Striker and Calvin are inbound. Khwamwang is going to make his move now," Kurtzman announced. "You well armed?"

Lyons knew his Python and his backup Colt .45 might be considered heavy gear in some situations. "What kind of opposition?"

"Nine men, M-16s and an improvised explosive made out of three antitank missiles."

Lyons weighed it in his mind. "Time for me to head to my hotel room?"

"Go for it. Striker and Calvin are heading in with heavy gear, too."

"Where?"

"The roof."

"I can be up there in five minutes," Lyons grunted.

"I just hope we have that much t—"

Lyons killed the phone, but he couldn't kill the sentiment.

9

The helicopter's rear seat had enough room for Mack Bolan and Calvin James to set up their weapons. On the rooftop, and if the fight got inside the hotel, the length of an M-16 would be too much, while the power of a 9 mm SMG would still be good at rooftop ranges. Plus, if a rifle bullet went astray, it wouldn't crack a window half a mile away and hurt someone.

James was busy putting together his choice of weapon from the Stony Man helicopter's weapons locker—a Colt 635 9 mm submachine gun. Based on James's favorite rifle, the M-16, the stubby little 9 mm was accurate and much more rugged than the MP-5, with a much smoother loading mechanism. Bolan himself was business as usual with his tried and trusted Uzi submachine gun. The Executioner strapped an SWA-12 shotgun across his back in case they found Carl Lyons without a close-range-style weapon, knowing the big man's disdain for 9 mm submachine guns.

The one thing Bolan was concerned about was the status of his foot. Now that the adrenaline of combat had faded, it was throbbing, and feeling as if it were swelling to the size of a watermelon inside his boot. He tested his weight on it, pushing hard against the helicopter floor.

It would bear his weight. The bones weren't fractured. But the cuts were aggravated. His stitches were probably torn free by all the recent activity.

"Need me to check that?" James asked.

Bolan shook his head at the Phoenix Force medic's offer. "We have work to do first. Once that's done, I'll have a few hours of downtime."

"Before the next riot," James muttered.

"I'll be on an airplane. Plenty of time to rest and recover," Bolan stated.

"Do you want help?" James inquired.

Bolan wasn't thinking of the question. It took him by surprise. "What?"

"In Thailand. I spent some time there when I was with the SEALs. I speak a little of the language."

Bolan brooded on it, then looked at the roof of the hotel.

"We're there," Bolan said. "Jack!"

The two men tucked down, holding on as Grimaldi swung the Hughes 500 high and wide, a couple 5.56 mm rounds pinging against the hull of the helicopter, but most arcing into the sky around them.

The LZ was hot.

And it didn't look as if the Executioner and Calvin James would have a chance of setting foot on the roof alive, not with the concentration of firepower up there.

CARL LYONS WAS moving quickly. He'd stopped at his hotel room, shouldering through the relatively flimsy lock and going for his closet where he kept his kit bag. Anticipating a possible war for the life of the Thai prime minister, he had John "Cowboy" Kissinger, ace weaponsmith of Stony Man Farm, pack for him accordingly.

He scooped out a weapon from the open duffel, box magazines hanging and swinging heavily in nylon pouches on a sling. He was back in the hall in moments, bringing up the weapon, racking the bolt with authority. The weapon was a new manshredder that had already proved its worth in the hands of the Executioner under combat conditions. Lyons himself had burned off nearly a thousand rounds at the range with this one. It was the SWA-12 shotgun, a magazine-fed cannon that was built around the old Heckler & Koch G-3 battle rifle design. The weapon was sturdy, was full-auto capable and held 7- and 9-shot magazines of whatever 12-gauge ammunition the Ironman of Able Team desired.

Hitting the stairwell, he slung the shotgun, then worked his way up the ladder.

Lyons was sure this weapon would be sufficient. It was loaded with his old standard favorite from his days with the Konzak autoshotgun—two rounds of double aught and #4 buckshot mixed with fifty pellets per flesh-shredding shell and one rifled 12-gauge slug alternating. Buck-slug-buck-buck-slug-buck-buck-slug-buck for the 9-round magazines he carried. In case he needed pure power or range, he had two magazines of slugs on the nylon assault sling.

Reaching the top of the ladder access to the roof, he slowed. He could hear the whine of air-conditioning motors on the other side. He pushed the door open slightly and saw that he was in a corridor between two rows of the bestial machines. From one direction, he saw it was clear, but behind him he couldn't see anything. He knew anyone watching would see him clearly.

"Nut up and do it," he grunted and threw the lid open, his thick legs pushing him up through the hole. Lyons hit a shoulder roll, aiming the autoshotgun toward his former blind spot, and saw the roof was clear in that direction.

He also realized that he was completely deaf. Even the com earpiece was nothing more than a murmur at top volume. Lyons's head hurt, but suddenly the landing skids of a helicopter swept past him, nearly clipping his close-cropped blond hair. For a second, he saw the surprised face of Calvin James looking at him, then the helicopter jerked upward.

Streaks of light that could only be M-16 fire filled the sky for an instant, chasing the helicopter, and muzzle-flashes flickered from the side of the Stony Man chopper.

Lyons turned and saw that there were gunmen on the roof, all heavily armed with M-16s, two of them trying to set up a tower of thick, ugly pipes over a certain location.

Lyons shouldered the SWA-12 and flicked the selector to 3-round burst.

Time to see what the shotgun could do to normal bad guys in close combat.

Thunder erupted, normally deafening, but now a mere rumble over the din of the air-conditioning units. Enemy gunmen blanched at the sudden sheet of death that swept three of their own, buckshot and slugs hammering flesh into spongy pulp with the authority of God's fist. Before the dead even could hit the ground, Lyons was reloading the shotgun and taking cover, rifle fire hammering against the sheet metal and mechanisms of the air-conditioning unit he was hiding behind.

He did a quick mental count. Three down, four standing.

Three more than he was, and those M-16s were great equalizers.

Lyons crouch-walked, moving amid the stones between the air-conditioning units that decorated the hotel roof.

Grimaldi banked his helicopter again, fire lancing out like a tongue from the side door. Lyons peered through a gap between two units and noted that the sweep of 9 mm autofire brought down three more.

Only one gunner remained.

And he was leaving behind the contraption, running like hell.

The Able Team leader dumped the magazine in his shotgun and fed in one of the rifled-slug magazines, hopping over the cover he had. James and Bolan dropped to the roof from the helicopter, tracked the last gunner and popped a short burst into the gunner, who spilled lifelessly to the rooftop.

Lyons reached the bomb first and noted it was on a countdown timer.

He knew nothing about the mechanism, but it was a sure bet it was supposed to be simple and durable, not capable of misfiring while in transportation. He dug his fingers into the timer housing and began to tear, bending metal until his fingers were bleeding.

"Carl, we can get the bomb squad—" Bolan began to say when Lyons finally wrenched the timer housing and its wires free from the missile platform. Wires sparked futilely as they crossed each other in open air.

Lyons grinned.

"Oh sure, just because you get the bombs susceptible to cavemen," James remarked.

He flipped the timer backward over his shoulder, and it landed ten feet away, suddenly popping as some booby trap was triggered by the violent impact inside.

Enough to set off a bomb or tear off his hand at the elbow, Lyons figured. He simply continued grinning.

Just another day for Lyons to keep surfing his wave of luck by nutting up and doing it.

"THERE WAS a full minute left on the timer," Bolan noted, unfazed by the detonation of the box timer.

"And we only got seven bad guys up here dead," James mentioned. "And four DSO dead, too."

"Khwamwang's ranch house had nine people missing," Bolan continued. He checked his watch. "I'm betting Khwamwang wasn't at that ranch house, either. Come on!"

Lyons led the way back to the roof access, and the Stony Man trio was back in the hallway of the presidential suite just as two more gunmen were stepping out of an alcove, bringing up their M-16s.

Bolan analyzed the plan instantly. The two men with the rifles would open fire, blazing into the suite. Bodyguards would usher the prime minister into the secured office and hold them off. The missiles would have gone off, destroyed the roof and maybe killed Xiang.

If that didn't work, the hole would have been big enough to shoot down through to kill him, or force him out into the gunfire of the two killers in the hall.

All this went through Bolan's upper mind in an analytical half second. The Executioner's hands, however, brought the Uzi into firing position and raked the two gunners with a sweep of flesh-shredding Parabellum rounds that were drowned out by the thunder of Lyons's autoshotgun.

Between the three Stony Man warriors, the two Thai hit men were reduced to a puddle of conjoined hamburger in expensive suits and alligator shoes.

Lyons and James paused, but Bolan threw down his Uzi, not wanting a weapon in his hands when he went through the door of the besieged suite.

The Executioner entered into the scene, his reserves of strength having all but run out. Foot throbbing in agony too much to walk on, body hammered with countless bruises and glancing hits on his body armor, head ringing from explosions and thundering gunfire in close quarters, he didn't want to know what he looked like in a mirror.

The look of horror on dozens of faces as they looked up from the wounded in the presidential suite told him volumes, however.

The look of sheer panic on the faces of two men, Thaksin and Khwamwang in particular, as they were manhandling Prime Minister Xiang toward an office, was the priceless image the Executioner had been waiting for....

KHWAMWANG PHATTANA was impressed. After all, it wasn't every day when you needed an entire army to wipe out just one man. However, since the first assault, Xiang Di Hua had lived the blessed life with a small army of protectors who had proved their ability to make some of Khwamwang's best resources disappear.

He received a hasty cell phone call about the farmhouse out in the Virginia countryside. There was gunfire, and the sound of panic in the man's voice before a resounding crash left only dead air on the other end. Rifle fire and grenades still chattered for moments, but nobody seemed to be speaking anymore.

He was glad to have separated the hit squad. He needed to make sure that if the PM left before the explosion was set up, he'd be penned in. Now, from the sounds of gunfire thumping and thundering on the rooftop, he knew his diversion was over. And he wasn't sure, but the thump about ten minutes earlier from one of the stairwells sounded like a grenade.

Someone was here, and they were taking out his men.

It was noisy, but dressed in the grim black of a security man, with a badge provided by Thaksin Sunthonwet, he was virtually invisible among the staff, moving quickly through the suite, making sure everyone was getting ready for the evacuation that was inevitably coming.

Thaksin gave him a nod, and Khwamwang joined him, pulling a small pen gun from his pocket. It was chambered for .22 Winchester Magnum, and pressed against someone's chest, it would be swift, silent and effective. And invisible, since, after all, it looked like nothing more than a pen.

"It's time," Thaksin said. "We're taking Xiang away from here."

Khwamwang grinned. "Very far."

The two conspirators moved swiftly. There was still a chance to salvage this operation. They would be hunted, but better hunted by the law than hunted by Chang. The San United Army wasn't known for dealing well with massive failures. Khwamwang had personally executed people who simply turned and ran from missions for Chang. And he'd killed them slowly, as a spectacle for others.

Besides, Xiang Di Hua was so damned insufferable, he had to die.

The two killers moved toward the Thai leader when behind them a door kicked open. Standing there in the doorway, on rubbery legs, dressed in black clothes marked by rents and tears, face covered with bruises and dirt, was an ice-eyed warrior in black.

"It's over, Khwamwang!" he stated.

Khwamwang swung a Browning Hi-Power from its hiding place under his jacket, snap aiming. "Kill him now, Thaksin. I'll deal with this one..."

BOLAN LUNGED across the room, three strides and a leap, 9 mm bullets skimming his windbreaker and one flicking a sliver of skin off his neck before the 6-foot-3-inch two-hundred pound soldier slammed into the Thai murderer, driving him away from Xiang and Thaksin.

Khwamwang was strong and skilled, though. He swung Bolan around, discarding the gun as an unnecessary distraction in their wrestling match, hands like talons sinking into Bolan's flesh. A head butt had the Executioner seeing stars, but the soldier hammered both his fists under the assassin's armpits, the impacts sounding like drumbeats. With a sickened grunt, Khwamwang's clawed fingers released their torment on Bolan's trapezius muscles, and the Executioner followed with an elbow that crashed his adversary's jaw. A pistoning knee hit Khwamwang in the gut, but the Thai killer slashed Bolan's face.

"I said kill him!" the assassin ordered Thaksin.

There was a deathly pause as Thaksin, looking around at how the whole scheme had fallen apart, took out his gun, pressed it between his own lips and fired.

Khwamwang roared with rage, thumbing Bolan's right eye and snapping a punch into his ribs.

Bolan forced himself upright and swung the Thai assassin around with every ounce of his strength.

Khwamwang tried to squirm out of Bolan's grasp, but in a moment, there was nothing to hold on to, just air. Then his body slammed through a heavy pane of glass that split the back of his scalp and broke both his shoulders before his rocketing mass overstressed the anchoring metal and the glass. Shattering the window, his body tumbled backward, sailing through open space, from twelve stories up.

Ten stories...

Nine stories...

Six stories...

Three stories...

The Thai tried to scream, but by the time he finished taking in a breath to let it out, he hit the ground.

He felt nothing ever again.

BOLAN LEANED on the windowsill, looking down at the shattered corpse of Khwamwang Phattana, lying in the wreckage of what used to be a van.

Lyons grunted, looking at the dead security chief, Thaksin Sunthonwet. "Saves the cost of a trial."

James shook his head, went to stand beside Bolan, then waved Lyons over to look out the window.

"You must have been really mad at either Hal, Ironman or Khwamwang, Striker," Lyons said.

"How so?" Bolan asked, letting the weariness of the past couple days catch up with him, the threat now gone. He could feel that his eyes were puffy and dry from lack of a good night's rest.

"You managed to hit my van with Khwamwang," Lyons said with a laugh.

The Executioner managed a chuckle, then closed his eyes, waves of tiredness washing over him.

"Have Hal deduct it from my baby-sitting pay."

10

"I'm telling you Striker, these long flights are hell on me," Jack Grimaldi said with a wink. Mack Bolan knew that for Jack Grimaldi, every second he spent out of a pilot's seat was a second he wished that he was soaring among the skies, extenuating circumstances for a romantic encounter and a good hot meal excluded.

Grimaldi settled into the reclining pilot's seat of Stony Man Farm's latest noncombat transport, and his favorite new toy, the Bombardier Aerojet Learjet 60. One of the latest of the famed Learjet lineage, the plane could be used by Grimaldi to ferry the Executioner across the Atlantic—well within its 2300-plus nautical mile range—in one fueling.

Bolan didn't mind. After the small-scale war he waged in Washington, he could use the next several hours to recuperate and allow his agonized foot to heal more, his bruises to fade. Between Washington and Thailand, with stopovers, he'd be back to full fighting trim in no time, thanks to Calvin James and his miracle work with bandages, stitches and antibiotics.

He'd have taken the Phoenix Force medic up on his offer to accompany him to Thailand, but Brognola had an emergency mission for both Phoenix Force and Able Team. For this battle, Bolan had only Grimaldi and Michelle Lam on his side, plus a CIA agent promised to them in Bangkok. That made Singer's offer of an ally all the more intriguing to the Executioner.

Grimaldi had taken the Learjet from New York to San Francisco, and was stopping off there for the purpose of meeting a friend of Singer's.

"A real stand-up guy," Singer had said.

Bolan asked Singer what that meant.

"Mick did all eight years for a robbery so someone else wouldn't go in the hole for life."

"A robber."

"He doesn't rob citizens. The real charge was possession of an unlicensed class 3 weapon, an Uzi, and a few pounds of quinine-laced flour."

The Executioner was intrigued. "And so I just show him your 'chop.'"

"Yeah."

"How do you know him?" Bolan inquired.

"Before he did his time, he did some protection for a kid I was representing."

"And how did the representation go?"

"The case ended before it went to court. The other party lost interest. You could say it died out."

Bolan nodded. "I understand. I've had several cases like that."

The cabin of the Learjet was silenced, the airtight cabin keeping out the roar of the jet slicing through the atmosphere at 435 miles per hour, only a thin whistle damped from the shriek of moving at high velocity fifty thousand feet above sea level. It was a time for the warriors to gather their thoughts as they settled down and relaxed.

Michelle Lam, who came along because she would make an invaluable guide and translator, was sound asleep. Lying there, she was angelic, the rising sun gleaming off her skin, making her seem even more doll-like as her face was pure porcelain in comparison to her black silk hair. Bolan took a moment from his research on Thailand and brushing up on the bit of street language he'd learned while on leave during his service in Southeast Asia. Michelle was as fragile looking as a flower.

He remembered other faces, brave women who agreed to help him, because their crusade coincided with his.

Bolan looked into Michelle's face, and thought of the one woman who would walk the rest of his days, ever at his side, at once the comfort of his greatest love and the pain that told him that he could never be anything other than the Executioner, damned to his War Everlasting. April Rose was as much a part of the Executioner now as when she lived, before a bullet in the back, a bullet meant for him, turned him back to the bleak coldness of a world of men without conscience, governments without restraint, terror without end.

Going to Thailand to face a billion-dollar industry that was all too similar to the one that claimed Cindy Bolan, his teenage sister, the Executioner felt a calm that disturbed him.

He knew what the disturbance was, what the strange calm was in him. In Europe, over the centuries, soldiers who marched in perfect cadence across bridges had been known to topple them, crippling armies and slowing their progress as their boots all struck in perfect unison. By breaking cadence from their march, the soldiers didn't provide concentrated jolts, but instead diffused the combined footfalls that otherwise would shatter even the strongest wood and stone. The diffused footfalls became a single harmony, a blanked-out sheet of sound instead of individual tremors.

Bolan could feel the calm formed by his emotions in conflict. The memories of Cindy, what she had done to try to save the Bolan family from Mafia moneylenders, and the fury that drove his father to gun down Cindy, his mother and nearly kill Johnny. The duty he had, to preserve just governments, good leaders like Xiang Di Hua. The numbers listed, numbers like the ages of human beings sold into sexual slavery, and how many of them there were.

The Executioner's eyes closed.

This was a war that had been too long unattended, a side of animal man that had prospered for too many years, untouched.

The whistle of winds shrieking on the skin of the Learjet 60 guided the Executioner to dreamless sleep.

He'd need it for his meeting in San Francisco.

MICK HAYES DIDN'T draw attention with his cowboy boots, complete with pinwheel-style riding spurs on the heels. He was broad and beefy, his flannel shirt hanging over his jeans and exposing a black T-shirt. His hair was tamed by a ponytail ringlet, and his beard covered scars from his long years of hard living.

No, Hayes wouldn't get much of a second glance for his footwear.

Not in San Francisco, the city that flamboyance built.

To tell the truth, Hayes had only been a marginal fan of Westerns and all things cowboy. What he had learned, however, was that a back kick, or a spinning kick with the cowboy boots and their riding spurs, would leave at minimum a twenty-stitch wound. Too many people didn't equate the spurs with offensive weaponry, so he wore them when carrying a gun wouldn't be prudent, or when he wanted just that added extra, unexpected backup.

The big man entered the bar, and even without the bulges of weapons under the long black sport coat, Hayes could peg Singer's friend for nothing less than a blooded warrior. Hayes remembered his days working as a mercenary in Southeast Asia, his first real job after the state decided it no longer needed to care for a juvenile delinquent who was dumped off by some whore.

This man looked as stone-cold ready as some of the guys who ran the shows. Quiet, full of confidence, and always capable of exploding into action at a moment's notice.

Mack Bolan walked to Hayes's booth and sat down without any formality.

"Singer told you what I needed you for."

Hayes was impressed by the voice. "Yeah, I still have contacts in Thailand. You're here on his crusade, aren't you?"

"A coinciding crusade."

Hayes mulled that over.

"Michael 'Mick' Hayes. Also known as Cowboy Mick Hayes. In and out of foster homes most of your life. Thrown into juvenile hall when you set fire to one of the homes you were in, and stayed until the state could no longer legally hold you. Foster family died in that fire."

Hayes said nothing, but stiffened.

"You didn't say anything to the psychiatric staff, nothing that made it on the permanent record, but they abused you. That much could be made out by your subsequent career."

Hayes relaxed. "You're not with the Justice Department."

"I have an arm's-length relationship. We'll leave it at that."

"But you know enough about me," Hayes replied.

Mack Bolan's icy cold eyes met Hayes's. "Trust me. If you knew, the people who sent you to jail for stealing their heroin wouldn't think twice about carving you up."

"All I had was flour laced with quinine."

"That's because you sent the real stuff away with your partners and made a stand to the police. You screwed Tony Lobianco out of his revenge, and out of getting his smack back."

"You know Tony Low?"

"I was there three days before his funeral," the Executioner said.

Hayes shook his head. There were rumors of a marksman's medal left at the scene of the Mob boss's hit. The ex-merc's face remained a dispassionate mask as he did some mental arithmetic. It had to be him.

Bolan slid an envelope across the table. "Your name is Stephen Dallas, and you will meet me in Bangkok. We'll all be staying at the Grand Hyatt Erawan Bangkok."

Hayes felt the envelope. He could feel the outline of a passport book. "Made this ahead of time?"

"When I'm on a mission, I need my assets in motion quickly."

Hayes took the envelope. "Airline tickets in there?"

"Northwest Airlines. You'll have a stopover in Tokyo and get dinner on the flight."

Hayes leaned back. "You're just going to let it go that I'm going to go running around the globe with you?"

Bolan nodded.

"Against the kind of guys who can stage a hit on the prime minister of Thailand in the U.S. No questions."

"You lost your youth to it. My family died from it. I don't see how you cannot want to be a part of this," Bolan stated.

Hayes sighed.

The big man was right.

11

Don muang, or Bangkok International Airport, wasn't much different from any other major international airport. The Thai version of Kanji on the signs, and the piped pop music were about the only subtle differences.

Mack Bolan and Jack Grimaldi were heading into Thailand under the pretense of being United States Marshals on a mission for the Justice Department. Thanks to treaties with the Thai government, and an unofficial nod from the Thai state department, they would be allowed to carry a side arm with them on and off the flight in the airport. Grimaldi knew it was a necessary evil. There was every possibility that the San United Army would be mobilized against them, and the Stony Man warriors were hoping that the two of them were going to be a distraction from Michelle Lam and Mick Hayes.

The odds were even that an attack would happen, and Grimaldi was glad for the SIG-Sauer P-226 in his waistband holster. With sixteen rounds of hot 9 mm, and a double-action trigger, Grimaldi considered the SIG to be as good a gun as any he'd used. He'd rather have a MAC-10, but in an airport, that would be impossible. Bolan went with his .44 Magnum Desert Eagle in a waistband holster, simply because the Beretta 93-R machine pistol, with its sound suppressor, was larger than even the heavy hand rifle. Besides, even for a Fed, a silenced machine pistol would have attracted too much attention. The .44 Magnum pistol was more legal looking. The drape of Bolan's tropic-weight navy blue blazer hung well over even the large butt of the Desert Eagle, and the pleated black khaki pants provided more than enough looseness to cover the six-inch barrel.

Bolan glided alongside Grimaldi, the two of them cutting the crowd, which parted for the ace pilot and the tall, mean wraith, looking for other armed men, as well as their local contact, Alvin Warren, with the U.S. Embassy. Listed as a member of the State Department, he was really with the Central Intelligence Agency, and would allow the two Stony Man warriors access to heavier weapons if necessary.

Warren was easily recognizable as he stood in a photographer's shirt and tan khaki pants. He was about five-nine, about Grimaldi's height and bore a roundness that combined with his shaved skull and round, babylike face gave the pilot the impression of a European Buddha. Red cheeks formed into a smile as he greeted the two men. Though round and thick chested, his grip was strong, and his dark eyes had sized the two of them up quickly and easily.

"Pleasure to meet you, gentlemen," he said. "We've been told to expect you, and I have a vehicle waiting for us."

"Thanks," the Executioner said, looking around, sounding bored and distanced. Most people would have taken such a tone of voice on greeting as rudeness. Instead, Grimaldi was pleased to note Warren's subtle stiffening, his own eyes scanning the crowd.

"I've been looking. There are some hostiles present, I've noticed," Warren said. "Caught the 'printing' of handgun butts under jackets of a couple locals sitting in that café over there."

Grimaldi turned his gaze on the cafeteria, and only saw one man who was sporting an odd, additional bulge. "Where'd the others go?"

"Looks like they're eating in shifts," Warren said.

Bolan was brusque. "Two more coming in to eat. How many have you noticed?"

"About five so far," Warren answered.

Bolan looked at Grimaldi. "They're making every effort not to pay attention to us. We'd better accompany Warren out to the car."

Grimaldi nodded. "No need for a conflict in the middle of a crowded airport."

The trio moved toward the entrance of the terminal, and Bolan noticed that they were picking up a literal parade of followers now. He stopped counting at ten and looked at Warren.

"They've got a good-sized force. At least fifteen," Warren noted.

"Twenty," the Executioner said. He gave the CIA man an apologetic smile. "I can see over more heads than you can."

Grimaldi grinned at the rare display of Executioner humor. "Are you armed, Warren?"

The CIA man nodded cautiously. "You two?"

"Yeah," the Executioner answered. "Anything else in the vehicle?"

Warren sighed. "No."

"Well, stay alive," the Executioner said. "They'll make their move as soon as they have car bodies for cover."

The trio entered the parking lot, and as they reached the cars, the three of them spread out. Grimaldi slid his SIG from its holster and held it down beside his leg, keeping an eye on the twenty-man army spreading out behind them. Warren slid a stainless-steel Beretta from under the jacketlike photographer's shirt, and put his thick body behind a red Toyota pickup truck. The Executioner was nowhere to be found, disappearing like a ghost.

That's when the first gunshot smashed against a Mazda's windshield next to Grimaldi's elbow. Glass spiderwebbed, more gunshots popped and the Stony Man pilot could feel the air cracking around him with nearby 9 mm supersonic bullets.

Raising his P-226, Grimaldi fired off his response to the attempt on his life.

The battle was on.

BOLAN STEPPED from behind the Volkswagen van, lifting the .44 Magnum Desert Eagle and pulling the trigger the instant the front sight blade of the hand cannon bisected the distant torso of a two-gun packing Thai hit man. He flicked off the Desert Eagle's safety and stroked the trigger, a single .44 Magnum round rocketing out the six-inch barrel.

The two-gun kid jerked violently as 240 grains impacted his torso at over 1200 feet per second, shattering ribs and plowing through the gunner's aorta and lung, finally bursting the ribs on the other side of his chest. Death wasn't instantaneous, but the shock spared the Thai consciousness while his chest filled with blood and drowned him.

Stepping sideways, getting the roof of a Mitsubishi under both arms, he'd drawn a lot of gunfire with the snap and roar of the Desert Eagle. The SUA death squad had no compunctions about firing wildly into a parking lot where innocent people were trying to get to their cars, but the Executioner's fire was checked by the fact that a missed bullet, or even a hit through soft tissue would result in a .44 Magnum round possibly punching into the airport terminal and the people within.

Accuracy was essential, and the benchrest of the blue Mitsubishi's roof was going to help in that regard. Bolan hammered a single 240-grain skullbuster into the head of a second gunman who was firing wildly into the lot, his bullets striking a passing automobile that careened out of control into a parked van. Cursing under his breath, the Executioner felt some satisfaction as the massive head wound from the .44 stopped that killer from endangering any more lives.

To his far right, Jack Grimaldi was crouched behind the trunk of a Mazda, having slightly more freedom to open fire with his weapon. He also wasn't getting the same focused attention as Bolan's cannon.

The Executioner put another two rounds at pelvis level into another gunman, watching his legs fly out from under him, smashing face first into the sidewalk in front of the terminal. Bolan took a couple more steps and ditched behind a Toyota as a fusillade of gunfire chased him. Crab walking he hurried to the Volkswagen and popped up to a kneeling position, just in time to see three men come through the aisles of cars, pistols in the air.

One of the SUA assassins was hoping to cut around to Bolan's former position to slide around the Executioner's flank. Instead, he ran right into the unblinking .44-caliber eye of the massive Desert Eagle. At a range of three feet, the Executioner pounded two shots into the gunman, sending him tumbling backward in a bloody, boneless heap. The other two stopped and skidded in midrun, swinging their guns into play.

Palming a fallen Browning-style handgun from the man he'd just killed, the Executioner burned off the remaining 9 mm rounds into the duo. Gunfire plucked at Bolan's back and shoulder in return, but the gunners had been aiming for a standing enemy, and the soldier was on his knees. One shot from the Browning plunked into each of the killers, one dropping instantly out of the fight. Bolan turned his attention against the man who'd taken only a peripheral hit, knuckling down as he tilted tighter against the grille of the van and pumping out four rounds pointfire, arm straight between his eyes and the enemy. Three went into his adversary's chest, and one slipped low into his groin. The gunman crumpled into a ball of twitching flesh.

Bolan took the opportunity to feed a fresh magazine into the Desert Eagle as a chorus of autopistols hammered the van, glass popping and raining over his jacket and down his neck and hair. Pivoting around the corner, keeping low, he spotted another gunman take a trio of 9 mm slugs high and in the chest before watching the beefy little CIA agent retreat behind a blue vehicle. As the gunners turned their attention against him, Bolan stiff-armed the Desert Eagle and put a 240-grain round through the chops of a distracted hit man, his jaw shorn off by the unyielding force of the Executioner's hand cannon.

As the hit men swung at the sound of the massive .44, bullets hammering all around the Executioner, Bolan triggered his weapon at full speed. The gunmen had put themselves in front of the automobiles parked in the lot, making excellent backstops in case a bullet should tear through the soft flesh of a would-be killer. The remaining eight rounds in the Desert Eagle slammed into a trio of gunmen, tearing through flesh and bone, hollow-point lead smashing into a car with resounding thunks.

Then, except for the post-gunfire ringing in his ears, silence.

The Executioner rose, feeding the Desert Eagle its second-to-last remaining magazine, and looked for the others. Alvin Warren was racing to get a Chevy Blazer started up, knowing that having a readily available vehicle hot and running would be paramount to avoiding a snarl of red tape in the wake of the brutal battle.

Grimaldi was nowhere to be seen, and the Executioner jogged toward the Mazda where the Stony Man pilot had fortified himself.

That's when the Executioner saw his old friend, lying on the asphalt, his blood pooling on the black tarmac beneath him.

12

Michelle Lam noticed Mike Belasko, haggard, and with his neck taped up, step into the lobby of the Erawan Bangkok, but didn't see the pilot, Ricardi, with him anywhere. She sat straight up and wanted to rush to his side to ask what was wrong, but Belasko had specifically instructed her not to have any contact with them in the hotel.

A sinking feeling filled her gut, and she settled back into the lobby chair, reading the newspaper and feeling the full weight of how little she knew about her native land. Even the act of reading a newspaper was like listening to a radio station that slurred with static every few seconds. Idioms were slightly different than she knew them. It wasn't so bad speaking, especially once the local talking to her noted the Americanized accent.

But it still ruffled her feathers that she was talked to like a small child.

As soon as Belasko passed by, accompanied by a much shorter, pudgy man who looked like a typical tourist, complete with sun hat, Lam put away the newspaper and went to the elevators.

She'd been in her room for ten minutes before a knock at the door summoned her. She opened the door and was shocked to find a broad, six-foot-plus bearded man who looked like a mountain trapper stuffed into a T-shirt, denim vest and jeans. He smiled cordially and strode into the room to the ringing tinkle of metal on his heels.

"Cowboy boots?" Lam asked.

Mick Hayes simply smiled. "It's a long story."

"Dammit! You men and your cryptic macho crap! You speak Thai?"

Hayes took a step back. "Um...yeah."

"Then the hell with you Belasko! I'm out of—"

The door opened and Bolan looked at her. "Sit down and relax, Michelle."

Lam paused. He filled the universe, a massive presence at once calming and respectful. She went back to the bed and sat down.

"You need to teach me that trick," Hayes quipped.

"What happened to Jack?" Lam asked, impatience breaking her calm.

Bolan nodded. "He's at the embassy. Took a round in the thigh and fell over, splitting his forehead. Bullet went through, but I figured he'd better heal his leg. We'll just be investigating for now."

Lam breathed a sigh of relief, then turned to the man near the door. "Who's this guy?"

"Alvin Warren." He grinned broadly, one cheek sinking in with a dimple. Where Hayes was a huge bear of a man, this one looked like a genial cherub who still lived with his parents.

Despite that image, he seemed to have a rather large pistol secluded under his photographer's shirt.

"My God, what have I gotten into?" Lam demanded.

Hayes sighed. "A lot of trouble, considering who we're working with."

Warren perked up. "Yeah. I'd heard about a guy called Belasko who did some crazy stuff. Seeing you in action, up close, though, that's amazing."

Hayes quirked an eyebrow. "Belasko?"

Bolan nodded.

Hayes shrugged. "Beats a name like Dude Love."

Bolan didn't break a smile, but his grim mood lightened.

Lam sighed. "Mr. Ricardi got shot, and hurt, and you're still joking?"

"Jack has been through much worse, and he's tough," Bolan stated. "But our war council is running a little short right now. That's why I've let Alvin in more on what our mission is here."

Warren nodded grimly. "The SUA is bad enough as a major heroin dealer in this part of the world, without also being a major player in the sex-tourism game."

"So how did they figure out you guys would be at the airport?" Hayes asked. "Unless there was something leaking in the State Department, and your people ratted on Belasko and Ricardi."

Warren shook his head. "The message was to me only. However, Prime Minister Xiang is still in the U.S. with a contingent of assistants and bodyguards."

Bolan made a sound of agreement. "If you run a billion-plus-dollar-criminal industry, you have enough cash to bribe someone. Whoever was working for the SUA had his own tastes that these savages supply."

Lam made a worried noise. "And you left him all by himself with a potential traitor by his side?"

"Not by himself," Bolan answered. "I said whoever was working for the SUA had tastes. Note the past tense."

Lam suddenly realized the meaning of it.

She felt very cold, and it wasn't the hotel's air-conditioning at work.

Han Quo raced to Chang's office. "Sir!"

Chang Chi Fu looked grimly at Han, his eyes, as black as an abyss, boring deep through him, already gleaning the truth. "They failed. Twenty men failed to stop those I told you about."

"They had help," Han offered weakly.

"You were willing to send only six men after these two."

"I did not know," Han said.

"No, you simply did not believe me. Now you understand. I, too, once did not believe that the Americans could fight so well."

"But even seven-to-one odds..."

"I'll tell you how it was done," Chang said. "The Americans

chose their own battleground, and used superior cover and aimed better."

"We do know that one was injured," Han said.

Chang's smile relaxed Han. "Excellent. How many of our men survived?"

"Only five," Han said.

"Did they get arrested?"

"No, they took off once it was determined that most of them were dead or dying. They did let us know, however, the one-armed man was a bloody mess."

Chang rose from his desk and went to the window, looking out over Chang Mai's skyline. "Have our people keep an eye out for the other American. When we get an opportunity, I want him destroyed."

"Thank you, sir."

"Han," Chang spoke up. The man paused, his spine tingling. "I want you to wire more money to our people in Washington. We'll need to hire extra men and firepower to replace the team we lost. There are three new Americans on the scene, and I want to know their names."

"Yes, sir."

Han left Chang's office, glad that the failure he experienced wasn't fatal.

13

"The guy we're meeting is Dandy Chuck Brewer," Mick Hayes told Mack Bolan. "He was a boxer who killed a guy. I met him here in Thailand during my mercenary years. We both settled in Frisco, but when he killed a man, he decided to return to the good life here in Bangkok."

"Why'd he kill the guy?" Bolan asked.

Hayes sized the Executioner up. "The dude raped Chuck's boyfriend."

The Executioner simply nodded. "A fitting end for a rapist."

"Dandy's going to like you."

"I don't see what a man's sexuality has to do with his courage. He went outside the law, which is morally wrong, but I've never been one to pass judgment on that as long as no innocents were harmed," Bolan answered.

"Dandy did it all face-to-face," Hayes said as the two walked into an otherwise abandoned-looking building along an alley.

Immediately, from the presence of *kra-toey* prostitutes and couples holding hands, Bolan knew that this bar was meant to be below the radar of even Bangkok's wild night life. Hayes and

Bolan cut through the crowd, receiving a couple catcalls when they came upon a broadly built, tightly muscled man wearing a black leather vest and jeans. The vest showed off a torso of toned muscle while tattoos obscured the chiseled cut of long, powerful arms. A handlebar mustache swooped off either direction of his upper lip. Brewer gave his companion a kiss on the cheek, a pat on the bottom and shooed him off gently in the pidgin language of Bangkok's backstreets.

"Dandy Chuck, meet Mike Belasko."

"Where did they grow you from?" Brewer asked, not masking the appreciation in his voice.

"New England," Bolan said.

"No indignation," Brewer noted.

Bolan shrugged. "You find me attractive? So have a lot of women. But I turned down most of them. Those women, except for a few cold-blooded killers, didn't make me uncomfortable. Why should you?"

"Point taken. Mick called me and asked if I had any information on the SUA's local sex trade," Brewer said. "I take it you're finally going to stomp something into the ground."

"You don't care too much for Chang's operation?" Bolan asked.

Brewer sat up, crossing forearms as thick as liter bottles. "I have a problem with the fact that homosexuals get a bad rap from pedophiles. The North American Man Boy Love Association loves to cuddle up against the gay and lesbian movement and proclaim they're being harassed by homophobes. Would you find a thirteen-year-old girl attractive enough to want to have sex with her?"

Bolan shook his head. "I know the same applies to a gay man and a young boy. Consensual sex between adults who can choose their partners is not my business. Alexander the Great was anything but a closet homosexual, and he conquered most of the Middle East."

"I told you this guy was cool," Hayes spoke up.

Brewer grinned. "All right, you needed a handle? I've got one for you. There's a guy, Quan Li Ma. He has a floating casino on the Chao Phraya River. Prohibitively expensive to get aboard, a ten-thousand-dollar U.S. cover charge."

"Exactly what you'd need to taste a piece of young merchandise for a night," Hayes noted.

Bolan frowned. "Is it all boys, or a mix?"

"It's a mix. A lot of travelers, especially from the Philippines, are of the opinion that the younger the prostitute, the less chance for sexually transmitted disease," Brewer answered.

"Which, of course, is a lie," Bolan said. "The poor kids continue to get reused until they're useless. What's the name of the river boat?"

"The *Sathorn Current*. It berths along the Sathorn Roads, naturally, in a part of Bangkok called the City of Angels."

"Close enough for the downtown businessmen to pop on down if they're looking for a piece," Hayes said.

The Executioner nodded at that disgusting prospect. "Any idea of the security?"

"About a dozen, maybe two dozen men. Quan has the juice to arrange automatic weapons. Quality weapons, too. Not used AKs."

"No concrete information?" Bolan asked.

"Long-distance observation and some discussion with a few of the oldest girls who had gotten off the ship," Brewer said. "There's not much of a job prospect for a former prostitute in the slums of Bangkok."

"I figured there would be innocents in the field. When does the boat berth?"

"From four in the morning to eleven, and it has a speedboat dock on it to ferry customers back and forth," Brewer answered.

The Executioner set his jaw firmly. "What's the screening aside from the ten grand?"

Brewer shook his head. "You have to have sex, on videotape."

"That's out," Bolan answered. "Mick, how are you at piloting a Zodiac boat?"

"I'm pretty good at it." He patted his slablike chest. "Plus, I have the added bonus of some buoyancy in case I get tossed overboard."

A ghost of a smile drifted over Bolan's face. "We're going to need silenced close quarters automatic weapons."

Brewer nodded. "Mick told me that a guy like you could use some offensive equipment. I happen to have a good supply. Come on to the back room."

The trio moved along through the club and entered a storeroom that was in the basement of the club, behind a cavernous room that smelled of cheap liquor. The first thing that Bolan smelled was fresh cosmoline and dried-out burlap. A single yellowed light popped on with the scrape of a chain.

Arms lockers were stacked sideways on heavy-duty shelving.

"State your preference, Belasko," Brewer said. "I've got the MP-5, but no integral silenced models."

Bolan looked at one chest that had some Ingram MAC-10s and the smaller M-11s. There was a mix of .45-caliber, 9 mm and .380 auto versions in one cabinet. He was well versed in the use of the stubby machine pistols. "I like your MAC collection, but I was looking for something that can be kept quiet, and still be kept down to 800 rpm."

"Those are Cobray M-11s," Brewer said. "Stripped down for display, but I have plenty of accessories."

"Including silencers," Hayes noted, picking up a suppressor. "Why's the bottom notched out on this one?"

"Extended barrel for the Cobray allows the use of an MP-5 K-style forward grip," Brewer said. "But check these out. You familiar with the M-16?"

Bolan caught Hayes's stifled chuckle. "Somewhat."

"Call this an improvement on the old wire stock. Using the Colt M-4s four-stage collapsible tube stock...we have an improvement on the old MAC-10."

Bolan took the weapon and felt the familiar balance of the older machine pistol. The weight of the stock was well balanced by the sound suppressor, and the forward grip was very natural and didn't look as if it would snag on anything. He studied the weapon closer and saw an enlarged cocking bolt for better viewing of large tritium night sights. "What's its rate of fire?"

"It's 800 rounds per minute," Brewer said. "Slow-fire conversion is a cottage industry for 11-Cobray owners."

"I can use grenades, too," Bolan said, taking six of the Cobray machine pistols.

"I figured if you were going to be fighting for the kids, you'd need hostage rescue. Aside from regular high explosives, you have smoke and tear gas, for cover and retreat, and flashbang," Hayes said. "Since I'll be outside the ship covering you,

I'm going to take a bandolier of tear gas and fragmentation with me."

"The Cobrays are also short enough, even with the silencers, to fit into a gym bag easily," Brewer said.

"When does the operation go down?" Hayes asked.

The Executioner looked at his watch. "The ship should be fully under way, with plenty of passengers on board about now, right?"

"But the pass... Oh, wait," Hayes said.

"If they're not prisoners on that ship, they're a party to kidnap and rape," Bolan said, checking the bolt of his Cobray.

Hayes swallowed. "Kill everyone on board?"

"No. Long ago, I learned that putting the fear of God into an enemy makes them three-quarters dead," the Executioner said. "That'll be enough for anyone who doesn't put up a fight."

THE SOUND OF MUSIC and merriment on the *Sathron Current* covered the softer thrum of the Zodiac's motor, but even so, Mick Hayes let the engine go off-line as they got within two hundred yards of the riverboat. It bobbed in the water, gliding slowly to within fifty yards, with the aid of paddling by Mack Bolan, Mick Hayes and Alvin Warren.

"There's a couple nice-looking speedboats there," Hayes said softly.

"I know. That came to mind for extracting the kids," Bolan answered. "Hold the speedboat bay, and we'll be golden."

"How will we know it's you coming?" Warren asked.

"You'll know" was all the Executioner said as he slid into the water.

The big man wore a neoprene wet suit that kept his body relatively warm, despite the rapid cooling of the Chao Phraya with the setting of the sun. Hypothermia was always a potential risk with swimming in any waters at night, and Bolan, dragging a tow bag with shoes and other equipment, slid through the water easily, with only an Applegate-Sykes six-inch double-edged blade in a forearm sheath. A hood would keep Bolan's hair from getting too wet.

That was another difficulty of slipping onto an enemy ship.

Dripping water everywhere made for poor stealth. The wet suit helped keep Bolan from being a sopping mess when he took it off in the speedboat bay. The spongy material held water well, as opposed to a dry suit, which formed a solid barrier between man and the elements but restricted movements and sloughed water off like a duck.

Bolan reached the back of the riverboat, feeling the rush of turbulence beneath him as the screws under the keel pushed the boat at a leisurely one mile per hour. Any faster, and the Executioner doubted he could have reached the ship. As it was, the soldier, despite being in excellent physical condition, hung to the far side of the protective seawall around the small bay, holding on to a lip of the ship's hull. He glanced back and felt the bag's rope slipping from his free wrist. It bobbed on the surface of the water, and with a wild lunge, Bolan grabbed the rope, only to feel it slip away from him again. Swimming without a breather unit, but with a face mask, he was spared the stinging splash of polluted river water in his eyes, but swallowed a hacking lungful of the stuff.

It tasted slightly better than some of the worst sewage he'd had to endure, but the Executioner couldn't allow himself to get sick in the water. The sounds of his vomiting would only draw attention. Bolan felt the bag slipping again, and he snagged it tighter, then looked back. He had lost about ten yards, and was losing more, when he turned and kicked hard.

Muscles burning with the effort, the soldier finally caught the riverboat again, then ducked his head under the water, opening his mouth and heaving his entire body. The foul, gut-churning burning of the river in his stomach disappeared with a flash, and Bolan hugged the speedboat bay again, this time fully armed but even more exhausted than before.

"Getting there is half the fun," the Executioner muttered, sliding beside one of the motor launches. It bobbed and swerved, but Bolan was able to hold it off with his knee pressed against it, using both hands to slice open the waterproof bag that held his gear. Bolan slid out the Cobray and hung the sling over his neck, then shouldered the waterproof bag, crouching low and moving forward again.

A cigarette sailed into the water between Bolan's knees as he slowly circled the front of the motor launch. The soldier knelt back slowly, bringing up the Cobray, and saw the legs of a guard standing on the boarding platform under the sloped prow of the launch. He could see the guard's feet, but the nose of the speed-boat protected Bolan from being seen, especially since the light was toward him, not behind him.

The lapping of water and the thrumming vibration of music and partying on the ship was enough to be felt through the steel of the platform Bolan stood on, but not loud enough to interfere with the fact that the guard was either alone or working along-side a living zombie.

Bolan eased around slowly and visually confirmed that he had only one guard to deal with. The Cobray rose to his shoulder eas-ily, and with a short stroke of the trigger, a trio of rounds smashed into the Thai's lower back, breaking it instantly. Tumbling to the deck, he started to give a strangled call, but Bolan tapped the trig-ger again, and two rounds made his head bounce before the launch bay was silent once more.

It took a minute for Bolan to peel himself out of the wet suit, revealing the blacksuit beneath. An application of combat cos-metics covered his face and hands, and he slid on the rest of his combat rig, complete with shoulder holster for the Beretta and hip holster for his .44 Desert Eagle.

Now the Executioner felt whole and ready for combat.

All he had to do was raise terror and mayhem on a boat, and rescue innocent slaves of sexual predation.

Long numbers for the soldier, yeah.

But the stakes were too high for him not to make the effort.

The cleansing flame of Bolan's War Everlasting had been de-layed too long from this den of corruption and torment.

The Bolan blitz was on.

14

Quan Li Ma had been told of the tall, grim American's presence, but other than calling in more of Chang's men for security work on the *Sathorn Current,* he felt secure enough. He stepped to the fine teak banister that was warm and smooth under his palms and looked out at the casino spread out in rich shades of green and brown. The decor was French colonial, and high-tech cameras and low-profile communications at each table were discreet.

Most importantly, Quan realized, there were wealthy men and women down there, with bodyguards and a desire to share an evening with a slender Thai waif, teenage boys and girls who were bought for a night of taking pleasure in their beauty and youth. That portion of the operation was almost all profit, except for paying the salary of the people who brought the youths into Quan's floating Bangkok Babylon.

Oh, and buying them food. Having his waifs truly starved to death wouldn't make them sexually appealing except to a very select clientele. As it was, once in a while Quan had to dump a body or two into the Chao Phraya after a particularly rough night. That was upsetting to the other cattle in the hold, Quan thought; it made them jumpy and nervous for days, rather than their usual withdrawn and shattered demeanor.

It didn't really matter. The trauma of sexual abuse produced a forlorn look that their users could explain away as the melancholy of youth, making them even seem more angelic and appealing. Lack of a solid diet and good sunlight made them slender and pale, like porcelain angels. All a perfected plan, after years of work, and reaping children who would otherwise starve to death in the poor slum villages around Thailand. Quan breathed in the power of the room; businessmen and politicians from California to Wales were down there, waiting to partake of joys and pleasures that would get them crucified at home.

"Sir," Quan's chief of security, Balsong, spoke up. "I have something to show you in the video room."

Quan looked over his empire once more, then followed silently.

The video monitors were all vibrant with activity, recording images of customers in their rooms, as well as views of the deck and other parts of the boat needing security.

"I already have men in the hallway," Balsong stated.

Quan watched as the man that Chang described, a giant black wraith, finished prebattle preparations and watched for coming guards. Quan leaned closer to the monitor, watching him. "How many men?"

"I've got four on the scene," Balsong stated. "All armed with shotguns."

Quan's lips set in a thin, grim line. "Shotguns would be too loud."

"He's armed with a machine gun, and he knows how to use it well. He only took out the guard already there with a few shots, like a trained professional. We need the shotguns against someone that good."

Quan shook his head, then noted something new on the screen. "Someone else looks to be coming aboard."

Balsong lifted a radio to his lips, alerting his men. There wasn't a good view of what was going on, but both the motor launches were bouncing as if people were boarding. He glanced back and saw that the tall Caucasian had disappeared, then something flickered on the screen.

AS SOON AS Alvin Warren, Chuck Brewer and Mick Hayes rowed into the launch bay, Mack Bolan was moving. Their job was to take charge of the two motor launches and have them ready to go when the Executioner returned with the children.

While he waited, he knew the eyes of the security cameras were on him, having spotted them when he was preparing for battle and knew the only reason why a security team hadn't burst into the launch bay was the fact that they wanted to suck him into a trap. Bolan slid a flash-bang from his harness and pulled its cotter pin, holding down the spoon. With a kick and a low lob, the Executioner whirled out of the way of blazing shotgun blasts through the entry to the bay. A brutal thunderclap and blinding flash issued from the doorway, and voices screamed in terror and pain.

So much for the stealthy approach, Bolan reckoned, and he whirled into action, swinging around the Cobray and ripping off short bursts into the gunmen, who were clutching eyes and ears, gasping and whimpering in pain. Their suffering ended as ripping 9 mm rounds tore through them, their loosely held shotguns clattering to the floor before riddled corpses.

The Cobray was fed a fresh magazine of Parabellum rounds, and Bolan was back in motion, stepping past the bodies strewed in the hallway. He'd made it halfway to a doorway at the end of the corridor when it opened, and a couple stepped through—an impeccably dressed businessman, a European, with an attractive woman on his arm in a spectacular red gown. The two of them bracketed a slender Thai teen who had the gait and stare of a zombie, and were followed by a massive six-and-a-half-foot tall man who was digging under his jacket at the scent of blood and gunpowder in the hallway.

The stock of the machine pistol went to the Executioner's shoulder, and the front sight post was right on the face of the handyman just as the big guy's arm hauled out a big handgun and snap-aimed it. With a gentle pressure, and the sound of doves taking flight, the silenced machine pistol made the bodyguard's face disappear in a mist, his corpse stumbling backward, pistol tumbling to the ground. The businessman was already turning, shoving his female companion and their teenage charge in front of him, racing into the club.

With three long strides, the Executioner grabbed his collar, keeping him from reaching the closing hatch, and with all his strength he slammed the slick, rich European into a bulkhead, watching the gray-painted steel blossom with the blood of a broken nose. Dazed, the man lost all fight when Bolan rammed the sturdy stock of the Cobray into his ribs. Bolan turned, and the woman in red had her face twisted into a cruel snarl, her arm around the Thai girl's neck.

"One step closer and I'll break her neck!" she spit in French.

Bolan looked at the hatch behind him, then back to the Frenchwoman. "Let her go now. I'm not asking you again."

"She's mine, I paid for her. I have friends who will hunt you down and torture you for days until you finally die if you do anything to me," the red-gowned witch stated. "As it is, you'll be lucky to leave alive for what you've done to my Jean-Claude."

Bolan looked down to the faceless man he reckoned was Jean-Claude. "Who is the rag doll?"

The Frenchwoman smirked. "Hired help, actually. I watch. He does."

Bolan narrowed his eyes, then brought up the Cobray, aiming at the woman. "So you're the real devil here."

The woman's look of triumph disappeared into an ugly scowl. Bolan dismissed the fact that the buxom woman would have been stunningly beautiful were it not for her surroundings. She was as much a part of animal man as the lowest street-corner drug dealer. "I'll have your skin flayed off."

"Tell you what. If your friends hold regular seances, you can tell them you died defiant," Bolan stated, pulling the trigger.

He stepped to the Thai girl, who had been shaken from her trance by the spray of blood on her hair and face, her deep almond-shaped eyes meeting Bolan's ice-blue ones. She started to recoil in fear, but the Executioner had stepped aside for Sergeant Mercy's compassion. Warm, gentle hands rested on her shoulders as Bolan's piercing gaze never let her attention wander. His voice was deep and reassuring as he spoke in Thai, haltingly, but still understandable even to a shell-shocked kid.

"Head down the hall and join the men on the boats," he told her. "They will protect you."

She nodded, then seemed to shake out of her stupor. "They keep us in a long room. On the left side of the boat," she said in the most basic Thai she could for the big American.

"How far above the water?" Bolan asked.

The Thai girl thought. "The water splashes our windows a lot."

"Right on the waterline," Bolan said in English. He patted her on the shoulder. "Go to that man."

Alvin Warren was down at the end of the hallway, past the bodies on the floor, waving to the girl to come to him.

"But..." the girl protested. She'd switched to halting English. "Show you where."

Bolan shook his head. "Too dangerous."

But those dark, haunted eyes bored into his soul. They spoke more eloquently than their limited understanding of each other's languages. The girl had chosen to end her life as a fighter, if it was at all possible to rescue her friends the same way she'd been spared horrors from this evening.

"Tranh," the girl said.

"Mack," Bolan whispered.

She managed a smile, using muscles not worked for months.

ALVIN WARREN COULDN'T believe that Belasko was taking the girl, but he figured that the girl knew her way around the ship better than he did. In his heart of hearts, though, the stocky little CIA agent hoped that the big soldier knew that kid sidekicks weren't as immune to bullets in real life as they were in comic books and movies. Keeping the Cobray clenched tight in his fist, he looked back to the motor launches, which were rumbling lowly.

Brewer had taken the boat on the left, while Hayes was working the one on the right, both of them more than skilled enough to handle a motor launch.

When Belasko returned from his mission, they were going to split up the freed children, and each be the rear gunner on each boat. For that purpose, however, Warren insisted that they be supplied with something that had more punch than the little 9 mm machine pistols.

Belasko hadn't made a fuss over that decision. It was likely that there would be other speedboats ready to leap to the *Sathorn Current*'s defense, and they'd be armed with more than ill intentions and harsh words. Brewer was able to arrange something to satisfy them both, so Warren could forgive the momentary knots in his shoulders from handing up twenty-five pound M-60E machine guns, and the belt-filled canisters of ammunition for them.

Warren stepped from the hatch, waving for Hayes to move to the prow of his launch and kneel, covering the entrance with a Cobray machine pistol, while he walked to the edge of the platform. The stocky little agent had many fears in his life, and one of them was the uncontrolled quality of standing in even calf-deep water. He felt the rush of waves pulling at his legs, and knew that one misstep could pull him into the Chao Phraya, which was a deep inky black, seemingly ablaze with the jeweled reflections of Bangkok's downtown lights.

But someone also had to keep an eye out in case the bad guys were calling in reinforcements from shore. There was room for another pair of smaller boats to slip in; after all, that's how they got the Zodiac aboard.

Just the thought, though, of floating in the inky, eternal blackness of a river at night sent chills through him that made him wish that a speedboat would come buzzing past, assault rifles blasting and chopping angrily.

Men, he could fight, and despite the fact that Warren had learned to swim in spite of his fear of the water, rivers and oceans were unfightable. The high-pitched whining buzz of an engine filled the air, and Warren cursed the gods of war, knowing he'd called this on himself.

It wasn't a speedboat's motor he heard, though. With a quick glance, he saw the skating forms of men seemingly skipping along the water like growling banshees.

"Jet Skis!" Warren hissed, dropping to one knee. "We've got company!"

"Crap!" Hayes grated. "Alvin, get back to the hatch. We'll take the big guns!"

The CIA man was about to protest, but realized the flannel-wearing bear-man was totally correct. The bay had to be protected on both of its vulnerable fronts. An attack from the rear would be an ideal time for the ship's own security to move in and try to take the trio right then and there.

Turning, Warren scrambled, slipping and hammering his knee on the raised platform. The Cobray would have been sent skidding out of his reach if it hadn't been for the shoulder sling that Belasko insisted be put on all the autoweapons they were using. As it was, the stocky little fighter spotted shadows moving frantically in the access doorway, bringing up weapons.

Throwing himself flat on his stomach, Warren opened fire. Unable to raise the weapon to aim at their chests, he simply swept a whole magazine at ankle and shin level, listening to screams of pain as bone and muscle splintered, bodies tumbling to the unyielding floor that he shared with them. Then the Cobray cycled dry, and one angry face glowered, pulling a handgun to avenge his horrible injuries at the hands of the stocky American.

TRANH MOVED SWIFTLY despite her apparent fragility. Bolan followed the black silken halo of her hair as the two of them cut through corridors with a speed born of desperation and need.

Alarms were going off as they raced down service hallways and Bolan knew full well that the security cameras were going to be tracking their movements. Tranh seemed to understand his need for haste, and she poured it on as the two charged through the ship at a ground-eating pace.

Reaching the hold where the others were barracked, Tranh stopped, breathless. Bolan realized that they were around the corner from the guards who were keeping the youths hostage on the ship, and he patted Tranh to have her move aside. Letting the

Cobray hang under one arm, the Executioner pulled his Beretta 93-R, knowing the need for accuracy and speed. Then, with his free hand, he palmed a grenade, leaving the pin and spoon untouched.

A soft lob, and the deadly egg clanged off one wall and clattered on the floor. The two guards leaped from the doorway, racing down the hall in the opposite direction, not bothering to look too closely at a grenade tossed almost in their laps. That was all the time Bolan needed to bring the machine pistol to target acquisition and pump a single subsonic 9 mm round into each of them.

The two Thai gangsters had struggled to outrace death from a dead grenade, but couldn't outrun the bullets that cut them down and ended their careers as slavers.

Tranh ran to the door while Bolan raced to the two dead guards, removing keys from one of their belts and kicking away their handguns. Heavy footfalls pounded up the hallway.

With a glance, the Executioner saw Tranh holding the unexploded grenade. She held out her hand. The two traded, the tossed keys landing in Tranh's hands while the Executioner caught the grenade and with rolling grace, popped the pin and the spoon. He lobbed the bomb so that it rebounded off a wall and rolled into a hallway where the ship's defenders were rushing to confront him.

Bolan turned away, opening his mouth and shutting his ears, yelling. The explosion shook him anyway, but when he brought his hands from his ears, no sound of a charging force resounded over the ringing in his ears. He glanced to Tranh, who was holding her ear and wincing, but still working through the keys. She saw the concern on his face, gave him a thumbs-up and kept going.

The little Thai was a fighter, without question, the Executioner reckoned. He swept the Cobray into both hands, checking around the corner and seeing that dead men formed a shield for wounded and angry gangsters who were trying to sneak back toward Bolan and the children in the hold.

The Executioner held down the trigger, the Cobray making little sound in the confines of the ship's hallway, much to the relief of Bolan's ringing ears. However, just because it was relatively quiet didn't mean the machine pistol didn't make a shredding impact on the stunned San United Army thugs. Bodies were chopped and heads cored by an onslaught of Parabellum slugs.

Gunmen went to the deck or tried to push themselves behind doorways for the slightest cover, some returning fire haphazardly, their rounds slamming into the bulkhead behind Bolan as he turned himself into a sliver of a shadow against the corner of the hallway. Snapping another magazine into the hungry Cobray, the Executioner pulled a tear-gas grenade, armed it and lobbed the bomb into the hallway, the choking clouds gagging the surviving Thai gunners.

"Mack!" Tranh called.

The Executioner whirled and spotted the first of two SUA troopers swinging around the way they had come and ripped off a figure eight of 9 mm shockers into the pair of hunters. They were slammed to the deck as a third gunner shrieked, receiving a single bullet through his forearm, making him drop his gun. More gunners kept rushing out into the hallway, and the storm of lead forced Bolan back toward the force he'd crippled with machine pistols and grenades.

Tranh had opened the door to the hold and was slamming it shut behind her when a stern-faced Thai reached out to grab her. Bolan let the Cobray fall free and drew the Desert Eagle from quick-draw leather and hammered the Asian gangster with a 240-grain warhead that smashed him against the bulkhead, both of his lungs and several ribs ruptured in the path of the devastating hollowpoint.

Gunfire rang out and the Executioner dropped back, left hand plucking free a fragmentation grenade and letting it drop after thumbing the pin free. Down the hallway that Bolan had ducked, the Thai gunners were recovering from the stinging clouds of riot-control gas and were starting to react to the huge form in black.

The explosion was deafening, the soldier neither having the time nor the inclination to cover his ears. Not when he had a crew of gunners, blinded and wounded, but still armed and dangerous, facing his unprotected flank. He stiff-armed the Desert Eagle and planted .44 Magnum coffin nails in the survivors of the squad that he'd dealt with, then rammed home a fresh load of 240-grain hollowpoints.

His head ringing, his balance slightly off from the thunder of the grenade and the Desert Eagle, he turned back into the hallway and saw the door where Tranh had taken cover was still firmly closed, no shrapnel having penetrated it.

Thai gangsters twitched and struggled on the bloody floor of the hallway, and Bolan passed by, pumping mercy rounds into the heads of those who were still moving.

The Executioner knocked on the door, and Tranh opened it a crack, then her face lit up as she saw the big man. "We're going."

Tranh looked pensive. "There's..."

Bolan nodded, understanding. "All right. But I have to get you out to the boats first. Get these kids to safety."

Tranh nodded.

The Executioner looked at the kids. Thirty of them. The launches would be loaded to the maximum, and many of them didn't even look as if they could run.

Tranh held out her hand, following Bolan's eyes. The girl wanted a gun, but both of the Executioner's side arms were too complicated for a new user.

"Know how to use one?"

At her nod, Bolan looked around and found that some of the dead Thai gangsters had Glocks. Small enough for Tranh's hands and devoid of complicated safety levers and a light trigger, the Glock pistol was perfect.

"Cover our backs and start shooting at anyone following us," Bolan said swiftly, handing her the Glock and several magazines.

Tranh studied the weapon intently, pressing the magazine release and noting what it did. The only other lever was the slide release, and she pulled hard and checked the chamber. She smiled with satisfaction, stuffing the magazines into her tied-off T-shirt. She popped the Executioner another thumbs-up, and Bolan scooped a particularly spindly youngster into his arms, nodding for the others to follow him.

15

Wiping the blood from his forearm, Mick Hayes blinked more of the stuff from his eyes. After he'd put a burst of 9 mm rounds into a guy about to cut down Alvin Warren, a burst of gunfire had sent the big guy diving to the deck of the motor launch before he was perforated by a stream of gunfire, where he split his forehead and cut up the skin on his arm. With a grimace, the ex-mercenary rose again and spotted one of the offending personal watercraft, triggering his Cobray and sweeping the rider off with a shrill death scream.

"This is one plan that's going wonderfully!" Brewer yelled. Like Hayes, he'd decided to leave the M-60s in reserve until the heavier 7.62 mm firepower was needed against harder enemies. As it was, the Jet Skis, with their mobility and the fearless riders firing wildly on them, were pressuring the pair.

"No plan ever survives enemy contact!" Hayes spit. He looked behind him and saw another flash-bang grenade go off in the hatchway.

Warren had been fighting a tense pitched battle to keep the boats in friendly hands. From the sound of it, the CIA agent was conserving his machine pistol's ammunition by cutting loose with the loud and thundering clatter of the 12-gauge shotguns used by the ship's crew.

Back and forth in the close quarters of the bowels of the ship, the 12-gauge shotguns were truly deadly, spreading .36- caliber balls through the air like swarms of scything bees. Hayes didn't envy Warren's position, and swung the Cobray in his fists to burn off half a magazine before swatting a Thai gunner off his ride, weapon tumbling in the air and falling to the water away from him.

"What kind of idiot goes water-skiing at night?" Brewer snapped, his own weapon downing another of Chang's improvised navy.

"The same kind that attacks a riverboat full of gangsters and heroin dealers?" Hayes asked.

"Point taken," Brewer answered, reloading his weapon. "Where is—?"

"Start firing up those big guns! We need coverage!" Warren bellowed.

Hayes whirled and saw that Warren was at the hatch's entryway, Cobray held to his shoulder. The gaunt, slender, ghostlike forms of Thai youths huddled behind him. When they were in his view, Warren tapped off short bursts at gunners who were passing behind the boats.

"All right! Fire it up!" Brewer roared. His rippling muscles easily hoisted the M-60, but he rested it on the back railing. As he triggered a long burst, the Jet Skis suddenly realized they were outgunned. Two more went down with Brewer's salvo, but the others were retreating.

Hayes took a quick tumble out of the boat, waving Warren past him to provide more cover. The big guy took a child in two hands, finding him deceptively light, and loaded him aboard Brewer's launch. Warren's Cobray burped and fluttered, granting cover fire as Hayes kept loading kids aboard.

"That's enough!" Brewer shouted. He spoke quickly in Thai, telling everyone to hug the deck, then jumped from one launch to the other, reaching down and taking kids from Hayes's hands.

The pace was hectic, but the kids were at most one hundred pounds, a third of Hayes's weight, and Brewer's strong arms worked with equal speed and precision until the other launch was nearly full.

Hayes looked back and saw a slender young woman, cradling a Glock in both hands, looking back into the boat. He ran up and climbed onto the platform, racing to her side, switching to Thai to speak to her.

"What are you doing? It's time to go!" Hayes said.

"Mack, he is getting the rest of us, from the casino," Tranh answered.

A figure appeared in the hallway, holding a pistol, and Tranh opened fire, missing with two shots before tagging him with three others. Hayes kept his Cobray tight in both hands. "Get on a boat. I'll cover for him."

"No," Tranh said. She wasn't changing her mind.

"We can't leave anyway!" Warren shouted. "Boats are coming in!"

Hayes shook his head, his heart pounding. "Hurry it up, Belasko."

THE TIME FOR STEALTH had long since passed, so the Executioner slipped the Cobray's sound suppressor. Stuffing a 50-round snail-drum magazine in the bottom of the machine pistol, he entered the casino proper with a mighty kick, hosing the ceiling with a burst of gunfire that raised screams and sent well-dressed people scurrying and diving for cover.

He let the Cobray drop on its sling and hurled his remaining flash-bang grenades with all his strength to the far ends of the large converted hold, letting the thunder of explosions stun some and panic most. A gunman on a balcony drew aim on the soldier, but he stepped behind a wooden post, letting it absorb a pair of bullets before he swung around and zipped him open with the machine pistol.

The Executioner spent another moment to pull the pin on a smoke grenade, then sent it tumbling, gushing black smoke.

With purpose, he made his way through the casino. He paused wherever he saw a kid, herding them along with him.

A bodyguard rose, moving to tackle this black wraith who ruined his master's evening, but Bolan drew the Desert Eagle with one fluid movement and backhanded the thug across his face. The heavy nose of the .44 Magnum pistol smashed bone and tore skin, and sent the hard man tumbling backward with ruined features. Bolan paused here and there, firing the hand cannon into gambling equipment, or tagging an in-rushing SUA soldier with a 240-grain hollowpoint before the gunner could fire.

"You bastard! Kill him!" a voice shouted.

Bolan turned and saw an announcement speaker. The Desert Eagle spoke again, forever drowning out whatever else the speaker would have to say.

A short-haired girl put her hand in Bolan's and looked up at him, instinct telling her that this giant would protect her from anything. "Is this everyone?"

She nodded.

Bolan pointed toward where he'd entered, and where Alvin Warren was frantically waving and pushing innocent kids along.

She ran to Warren and past him to safety as the little CIA man raced up. "We've got company. Boats, and they look pretty heavy."

"All right. Get back and we're moving," Bolan answered.

The two Americans raced back toward the motor-launch bay and heard the sound of whimpering kids and a thundering M-60.

"'Bout time you guys showed up!" Hayes roared over the din.

"Alvin, relieve Brewer of that M-60," Bolan ordered. "I've got Hayes's barge."

Bolan grabbed a railing and hauled himself up and over. "Get the lines!"

Warren nodded, turned and took out an SOG Tiger knife, slashing the mooring line, before running to the stern where Brewer was laying out sheets of 7.62 mm deterrent. Bolan's own Hell's Belle bowie made the same short work of a mooring line as Hayes deftly tossed him the Maremont M-60. Making sure the canister was secure and the belt link unkinked, he slung the big cannon over one shoulder, braced it to his hip and targeted a boat that was sending gunfire flickering and hammering into the roof of the bay.

With a pull of the trigger, the Executioner felt all the recoil and power of the cut-down machine gun, but didn't let the jump and kick of the weapon keep him from spreading fifty brutal rounds of 7.62 mm NATO machine gun ammunition across the bow of one of the boats and into its passenger section. The flickering muzzle-flashes from that speeding missile blinked out instantly, and Bolan followed that boat, hammering out more gunfire, spearing the rest of the 100-round belt into the out-of-control vessel until it burst into flames and veered away to slice through the inky night.

He looked at Alvin Warren, who was using his weight to keep the M-60 under control, and watched as the other vessel swung off. Bolan quickly hung another canister onto the Maremont, closed the breech on a live round and added his own stream of machine-gun fire to Warren's efforts. Twin blazing fingers of heavy fire walked onto the enemy craft.

The launch lurched under Bolan, and Hayes let the big motorboat slip into the Chao Phraya. Brewer did likewise, but Warren was sent tumbling to the deck as that boat dropped harder into the water. Hitting Reverse and spinning backward until they were facing away from the *Sathorn Current,* Hayes and Brewer couldn't have been in better synchronicity.

Bolan looked up, and SUA gunners were still in action, sighting on the motor launches. He swung up the M-60 and triggered a withering blast. Another stream of autofire ripped from Warren's weapon, bullets snipping and snapping into the water below and behind them. By the time the launches reached their full speed of twenty-five knots, however, they were well out of danger.

That didn't keep Warren from firing until the barrel of his M-60 was so hot he could see the glow of individual bullets pumping down the barrel of the big gun.

"We're clear!" Bolan shouted across to him.

The stocky little American looked at the frightened, haggard young people in the boat with him, then voiced the question with his eyes. After seeing what these poor kids were like, were you ready to stop fighting?

Bolan set down his M-60, reassured by the sight of Tranh giving comfort to some of her fellow ex-prisoners.

No. The Executioner wasn't ready to stop fighting.

But this skirmish in the war against Chang Chi Fu and his sex-slavery trade was over. Time to see how the enemy reacted.

16

Night retreated from Chang Chi Fu's window, and the rising sun painted his world a pale orange, making his tired eyes ache. Rising, the general of the San United Army felt his head pounding from the alcohol he'd consumed the night before. He looked at his watch, and could barely focus on the numbers, but figured the time from the position of that burning torch that was attempting to sear his eyes from his skull.

He'd spent too many years rising with the sun, on the run from his enemies and drilling his small ragtag force into a military power. His body was ingrained, despite long, late nights and the numbing of alcohol, to rise with the sun, and he pulled himself from the bed, picking out a pair of khaki slacks and a white shirt for the day.

It was his usual uniform, the outfit of a rich man who conducted business out of his palatial spread in central Chang Mai. It was a long way from when he was fighting tooth and nail, hopping the borders between Myanmar and Thailand and fighting all comers, bringing the San United Army scratching from the depths of obscurity to a power that could set up businesses in the towns, taking over from local gangsters.

He remembered the setback, though, years ago, when he allied with the Communists and the Chinese. They had five hundred tons of heroin, and an army ready to help supply the power needed to crush the Thai government. But the deaths of four DEA agents had drawn someone's attention.

That someone sent a small group of men, highly trained fighters, armed to the teeth, capable of fighting off any means of attack. They tore their way through Bangkok and beyond, eventually hunting down Chang and his coconspirators, all the way to where their heroin train was loading up, ready to make a multimillion-dollar sale. They had been poised to conquer a country, and a small group of men blew it all away.

Only Chang had managed to go to ground, hiding in the weeds, watching the faces of the warriors who smashed his world. His eyes had been burned with the image of them, never to forget them. One day he'd have the opportunity to hunt them down and gain revenge for having been bloodied and driven into hiding.

All that work.

Destroyed.

But Chang still had his remaining men. He had access to old supplies and routes of heroin that hadn't been committed to the scheme.

And he had one more option: the untapped villages along the border to Myanmar. There was money in taking children from families so poor that they were willing to sell their daughters for the cost of a bowl of rice on the table. It was even cheaper when his men put a few bullets into a resisting father or brother and just loaded the cattle onto one of his troop trucks and drove them to Chang Mai and then on to Bangkok.

The slavery network branched out, following the lines of Chang's older heroin networks, finding business in the same alleys where his men were dealing out smack to locals and tourists. He'd even been able to export the kidnapped young women and girls to places as far as the Philippines and Hawaii.

And the money, which first started as a trickle, became a flood. A bloody flood, one that washed away most of the pain but none of the indignation of Chang's original loss. He forged ahead, with a nationwide control of both illicit sex and drugs, until he reached the point where he was once more a target.

He cursed the fact that his attempt on the upstart prime minister failed, and that failure brought with it the return of the one-armed man.

There was a knock at the door.

"Come in," Chang said, buttoning up his shirt, broken from his reverie.

Han Quo entered the room. "The *Sathorn Current* was attacked last night."

Chang shrugged, letting the fabric fall looser over his barrel chest, looking at Han in the mirror. He spent a moment polishing sweat from his bald head, then turned and looked at his chief lieutenant. "Is Quan still alive?"

"Yes, and the ship was not sunk," Han returned. "But he took them."

Chang frowned. "The cattle?"

Han nodded. "He took them all from the boat."

"Alone?"

"He was alone in the bowels of the ship, but a smaller force was performing a holding action at the motor-launch bay. We'd sent out forces to help cover them, but they were too heavily armed and kept our men from the shore reaching them."

Chang frowned. "That's a lot of lost revenue."

"There was also some losses among the clientele," Han stated. "Some were panicked and trampled to death. A couple were shot down."

Chang's voice was menacing. "Send a message to all our friends in the police. There is a two-hundred-thousand-baht price on the head of the American. To the people on the street, make it five times that much."

Han blinked. Chang had nonchalantly put a huge price on the head of these attackers. The local law enforcement would only hear about a lower bonus, but it was still more money than the average Thai would see in five years of work. "We're not using our own forces in Bangkok?"

"I'm not going to waste our people," Chang stated. "I'm going to show this American thug that when he comes and interferes with my business, he incurs the wrath of a nation."

Han nodded.

"Dismissed," Chang spit.

The general had phone calls of his own to make.

If the American thought he was ready for a war, he was mistaken.

MACK BOLAN'S ENTOURAGE learned Tranh's full name, Choi Tranh, and that she had been sold by her parents to the soldiers of the San United Army when she was only nine years old.

Now she slept, cradled in the reassuring, gentle arms of Michelle Lam. The American crusader herself was emotionally worn-out from taking a look at the underbelly of her ancestral homeland, seeing and hearing things, learning about atrocities that made her blood run cold.

Tranh slept fitfully, but comforted by the warmth of a compassionate human being. She'd been through that hell for the past seven years. For her first three years, after the SUA had purchased her from her starving family, she'd been put to slave labor in the poppy fields of the Chang Mai province, where the sun burned her skin dark, and now, her shoulders were freckled and scarred with pockmarks from removed melanoma.

But it was Tranh's description of the past four years as a toy for the wealthy elite and morally depraved that made the Executioner's belly burn.

Bolan checked his watch. He'd only gotten three hours of sleep, but he knew that to close his eyes now, his attempts at rest would only supply him with more dreams that even his years of facing atrocities couldn't hold from his conscious memory.

This mission had crept under Bolan's skin, and was turned into a fractured nightmare in his subconscious mind.

Choi Tranh didn't deserve this, nor did the thirty other youths whom he'd freed from the *Sathorn Current*.

Nor did an entire nation of young people, whose only crime was being too undefended, too beautiful, considered not valuable enough to be protected from sexual predators. A good man back in Washington, D.C. had asked the Executioner for his aid, and was risking death, battling political enemies in the employ of the wealthy flesh peddlers, and Bolan was here to give as good as he always gave.

Jack Grimaldi limped into the room. "Couldn't sleep?"

Bolan looked up at his friend. "You shouldn't be walking on that."

Grimaldi simply shrugged. "It only hurts when I tap-dance."

Bolan simply didn't have the energy to chuckle, and the Stony Man pilot plopped into a seat next to the soldier's chair. "How's the tour going?"

"Michelle hates us for having ruined her dreams of a beautiful Thailand," Grimaldi stated. "But I keep reminding her that there is beauty still in this land."

"We're just here specifically to wallow in its ugliness," Bolan agreed.

Grimaldi nodded. "While I've been out, I've been catching some hairy eyeballs. They know what we look like."

"That could be a problem."

"Not really. I'm tempting bait, Sarge."

"Yeah, but a lot of the time, bait gets swallowed."

Grimaldi shrugged. "Who lives forever, big guy? Here. I came in with this."

Bolan accepted a fax sheet. He saw a grainy, transferred video image, himself in blackface, and an all-points bulletin. "Two hundred thousand baht?"

"The rough equivalent of forty-thousand U.S. dollars. Depends on the exchange rate."

Bolan put down the sheet.

"Chances are, you're higher priced on the street."

"So everyone on both sides of the law with anything more than a peashooter is going to be gunning for me," Bolan stated.

Jack Grimaldi blinked, and a look of surprise was on his face.

"What's wrong, Jack?"

"Your face just broke into the biggest smile for a moment."

The Executioner felt an enormous weight slide off of him, déjà vu setting in. "Being hunted by the law and the underworld. A price on my head. An enemy whose tentacles are wrapped around the soul of a nation."

Bolan paused. "It's just like old times, Jack."

IT WAS LATE AFTERNOON when everyone finally was awake, got cleaned up and ate. Alvin Warren was still munching on a packaged snack cake while they were en route to Casey Michaels, the man who was the chief officer of the embassy and the ambassador's right hand man.

"Warren," Michaels spoke up.

Warren continued chewing, but obviously was giving Michaels a bemused attentiveness. Then he stopped chewing, licked his upper lip and waited for Michaels to say something.

"Get rid of that piece of crap!" Michaels grunted.

Warren shrugged and popped the rest of the cake into his mouth and smirked, still chewing.

"Pig," Michaels grunted. He turned his attention to Mack Bolan, trying to give him an intimidating gaze. "You."

"I've read about my APB," Bolan answered. His face was impassive, his voice low and controlled.

"I don't think you truly understand how deep in shit you are, boy!" Michaels spoke up. "I have the police asking me if I've seen you. There was a terrorist attack last night!"

Warren gave a low belch and drew Michaels's attention. "Sir, I was with Agent Belasko last night. There was no terrorist attack."

"Then why are there thirty kids now running around the embassy, and why did you come in at nearly four in the morning?" Michaels asked.

"Belasko and I went out partying. Seems we knew each other back from when he was first stationed here in Southeast Asia. One drink led to another, and we went out and found all our illegitimate kids."

Bolan's lips tightened to prevent a smile.

"Well...at least all the kids he had here in Thailand. I'm not saying anything for the rest of the world."

"Warren," Michaels growled.

"I'd like to have twelve travel visas for my little munchkins to journey back home."

"Goddammit, Warren, you're only thirty!"

The man simply shrugged. "We age quick in my family."

Michaels turned away and growled in disgust. "The President says to give you some help, but we can't have you associated with the embassy in any way. We had an important French businesswoman die on that boat last night."

Bolan folded his arms. "She was going to watch as this girl was raped. She's only sixteen. Maybe you don't think that's worth a death sentence, but then, you've probably never had a member of your family raped."

Michaels whirled, his face turned red. "Do you know what you've just admitted to?"

"Taking out the garbage? Pest control?" Warren offered.

Michaels's face darkened even more.

"Get out of my office. Get out of my embassy. If I see you again, I'll have the Marines empty their rifles into all of you, dig graves for you, drop you in them, then shoot you all over again."

"I thought this was the American Embassy, not the Cambodian," Hayes said to Michelle Lam loud enough for Michaels to hear.

Bolan was the only one unmoved to laughter.

"What, are you as stupid as you are homicidal?"

"I need a secure base of operations," Bolan stated.

Michaels sighed. "I just said that I can't help a known terrorist. Not with this kind of pressure on me."

"So who's trying to put the pressure on you? Who's specifically telling you to flush me to where they can get a shot at me and my people?" Bolan continued.

"Nobody's saying that you're here," Michaels said, his face starting to drain of blood.

"He's lying," Warren spoke up.

"How do you know?" Grimaldi asked, his voice full of mock innocence.

"Thanks for the straight line," Warren said. "His lips are moving."

"Always a pleasure," Grimaldi answered, smiling.

"The SUA doesn't have heat on you, but they have heat on people who can try to push you or the ambassador around," Bolan noted. "You're clean, but I need a name."

Michaels lowered his head. "And if I tell you?"

Bolan nodded to Hayes.

The bear of a man grinned. "Arrangements have been made for us to be gone by sunset."

"Duprey. He's a close friend of the ambassador's and is part of the French Foreign Office," Michaels said. "He knows that you're here, and if by midnight you're still present, he'll inform the Thai government that the Embassy is sheltering terrorists."

"Duprey was a customer?" Bolan asked.

Michaels snorted. "Yeah. He's a known cradle robber."

"And a friend of yours," Bolan stated. The temperature in the room dropped twenty degrees.

"We're associates," Michaels answered. "Besides, he's friendly to our government."

Bolan locked gazes with Michaels, chilling him to the bone. "Maybe your version of the government still endorses slavery and sexual abuse."

The Executioner left Michaels's office with his allies, but the chill remained with the shaken embassy chief.

17

Andres Duprey poured himself another snifter of cognac and swirled it gently in the glass, careful not to bruise the delicate mixture. With a single sip, he felt the smoothness burn through his mouth and down his gullet, filling his body with warmth and a feeling of comfort in this godless land away from his civilized home.

Of course, Duprey admitted, the first sip from this glass didn't match the first sip of the day, which had come when Quan had phoned to notify him about the loss of his favorite boy aboard the *Sathorn Current*. The first sip of the day was a sensation that cleared the palate and always tasted the best, because you had nothing else that numbed its flavor, you were clean until that moment and this was your first exposure, your first sweet breath of air.

The second snifter had been consumed in one solid gulp when Chang's man telephoned him to let him know that it was time to start putting pressure on the U.S. Embassy to disassociate itself from the investigators who had come to this country to help handle the conspiracy that had tried to kill the prime minister. It didn't hurt that Chang Chi Fu knew of Duprey's preference for Asian teenage boys, and mentioned more than once a willingness to expose Duprey's escapades on videotape to more conservative members of his government.

The sheer silk curtains blew, flying like ghosts with an uncommon evening breeze, and Duprey spun toward them.

Just the wind, he reminded himself.

Nobody would be foolish enough to move in on the French embassy. Not with its tight security. Duprey felt safe and comfortable. Nothing would touch him here, unless he wanted it to.

Duprey looked back to the window and went to close them when a big hand clasped his over the doorknob. The Frenchman paused, his eyes wide, and looked up at a face greased over in black, the only color being the icy bullets of a man's eyes, stabbing deep into his own.

"I'm here to send a message to Chang Chi Fu, Duprey," the man said.

The Frenchman tried to pull his hand free, but the grip was stronger than stone. Callused fingers, moist with black greasepaint, held his soft flesh firmly. Terrified eyes looked to the merciless ice that trapped him.

"Then say it, say whatever you want," Duprey whispered, his throat constricted with fear.

"The message isn't verbal. There's also a message for you, Andres. Or should I say Naughty Father?"

Duprey's bowels turned to ice at the mention of the name he forced his young lovers to call him. He squirmed and twisted, and swung a pudgy fist at the tall wraith's head, but a forearm cracked across his wrist, snapping all the momentum out of the punch and sending numbing jolts of pain down his arm.

Duprey noticed something in his attacker's hand, an impossibly long-barreled handgun. Its butt chopped down on his shoulder, and the Frenchman went to his knees with a whimper, tears pouring down his face.

"Please...please...I'm only trying to give them the love I was shown as a boy myself. I meant them no harm. I paid good money to have them protected," Duprey said, choking back bile as nausea swept him.

Those cold eyes bored into him, cruel drill bits. The blackened face's features were a gargoyle's mask of barely controlled rage. "I asked Pham Luc, and you know what he said to me?"

Luc, beautiful young Luc, who had been his truest love, who took refuge in his arms, as Duprey had sought to escape the pressures of being a political stalker, seeking secrets for his nation's government. Now he was being punished for finding love?

"Luc told me that he had all the love he needed before SUA soldiers blew his parents to ribbons with AK-47s. Luc told me he didn't need your love, he just needed a family," the Executioner grated harshly, bringing the long barrel and putting it in Duprey's mouth.

"But..."

The sound suppressor of the Beretta 93-R stopped up the pedophile's mouth.

"Luc didn't love you—he feared Quan. He'd have been shot and thrown into the river if he refused you. But no one can rape him now."

Duprey spit out the barrel, shaking his head. "Who are you to judge me?"

A single 9 mm round punched through Duprey's right eye, sending his brains geysering out the back of his skull. The Frenchman was dead before he even hit the ground.

"I am not your judge," Mack Bolan, the Executioner said, "I am your judgment."

LAM STOOD AT THE DOOR of Quan Li Ma's home, her hands clasped behind her back, showing off her small but perky bust. Long, gently curled black hair spilled over her bare shoulders, and she felt more than a little pensive at Mike Belasko's plan. The three armed guards behind her, with their wicked-looking weapons, were grim-faced warriors who looked like they were begging for an excuse to pull the triggers on their Uzis or whatever they had.

The door opened and a bald giant of a Thai stood there. His right eye bore old scars, and for all the world he reminded her of some kind of monstrous enemy from a cartoonish video game. His good eye, the one not turned blue and pale, lifelessly staring ahead like a gleaming laser, looked her up and down. There was a mild appreciation breaking the cruel line of his lips, taking in the way that her gentle, subtle curves complemented the blue silk gown. According to Dandy Chuck Brewer, this beast of a man, as tall as Belasko himself, was named Balsong, and was Quan's chief of security.

The scarred mask returned to sternness, as he spoke a single word of dismissal to his troops. "Follow me," he added in his thickly accented English.

"How did you..?"

"You're too fat to be Thai," Balsong growled. "As young as you are."

Lam gasped. She looked down at her figure and didn't think she would be considered fat. In America, she was even considered fairly skinny.

"Fat," she whispered.

Balsong turned and grabbed one of her breasts, giving it a cruel squeeze, and his scar of a mouth turned into a hideous smirk. "But fat in a good way, little one."

She yelped in pain, the hand twisting her flesh pulling her to tiptoes.

"Enough!"

Lam turned to see the man who spoke with a clipped, slightly French accent.

The hideous giant released Lam, and she stepped back, struggling to adjust herself in her dress. Her heart hammered until her ribs hurt, and she'd breathed so fast, her throat dried out.

"Why, Miss Lam, we were just looking for you," the Thai with the French accent said. "My name is Quan Li Ma."

Lam narrowed her eyes. Somewhere inside of her, she'd suddenly dropped all of her personal indignation and found a coiling viper of rage deep in her belly. This was the scum who represented all the terror and horror that ECPAT was fighting against. The personification of the scum that, until now, was just an abstract entity. Her aching flesh forgotten, she managed spiteful growl. "Were you?"

"You and the old man you're with, the one-armed man, have been paying visits to our places of business. I don't think that the two of you were interested in purchasing our wares," Quan said.

"I wasn't."

Quan smirked. "And so you decided to come and visit me?"

"It's a social visit, Quan. I even wore my best dress for you. Though, it's pearls before swine."

Quan chuckled. "I like your fire. Balsong, you may have her. Whatever's left, you can hand to the off-duty guards."

Lam's eyes flickered to the giant, whose face first split with a smile.

"Did you hear that, Mike?" Lam asked.

"What?" the flesh peddler and his monster hardman asked in unison.

A window shattered, and in the same instant, so did Balsong's hideous face, his skull rupturing in an explosion of gore that sent his corpse smashing across some of Quan's wall tapestries, turning them into soaked rags. Lam ducked as Quan screamed, watching the volcano of blood that used to be his top protector.

Lam hadn't been sure that Mike Belasko would be able to provide her any protection, but he had explained to her that the rifle he had, a Savage 116FSS, would provide the kind of power necessary for protecting her. He'd placed a .338 Winchester Magnum round in her hand, and she was shocked at the relative weight of the bullet. It was huge and missilelike in comparison to the slender, puny .38-caliber bullets she put in the Smith & Wesson Bodyguard that Singer had given her. He explained to her that this round fired a 250-grain slug at over 2600 feet per second, and produced two tons of energy at the muzzle.

"How about three hundred yards away?" Lam had asked. "How hard does it hit then, because that might be how far away you are?"

"Only about 2400 pounds of force," Belasko told her. He smiled wryly. "That's still about twelve times more powerful than your .38."

"And you're a good shot?"

"It's been confirmed a few times," the Executioner mentioned.

Now, as Lam looked at the devastated chunks of skull sprayed across a tapestry, she felt an odd detachment. Her anger had disappeared, and though she normally felt revulsion and terror when she saw scenes like this in the movies, this was different. This was the satisfaction of seeing a stinging wasp smashed underfoot with force and a splash of goo.

Balsong, his head a hollowed-out chunk of wreckage on a neck, stumbled a moment, then fell across Quan, who shrieked even worse, crying out like a child. Lam turned, hearing the thump and thunder of the rifle, and she swiftly dug under her dress and pulled out an earpiece. "Mike?"

"Get to his phone," Bolan ordered. "I'll keep their attention."

"Okay."

"You know what to do?"

"Yeah," Lam said, breathless now. She raced toward the office that Quan had come out of, passing through the doors and looking around.

The desk phone sat on a large mahogany desk covered with papers and she swung around it. With a satisfied smile, she noted that the phone was as modern as any, complete with a crystal LED to display incoming and outgoing numbers. She pressed the redial button, and instantly a telephone number appeared on the screen. She memorized it, then jotted it down on a small pad next to the phone, pressing each of the speed-dial buttons.

Making sure she didn't wipe clean the last number dialed, she hit it again, then spoke quickly. "Jack? What's Chang Mai's area code here?"

She noted the sound of weapons fire changed outside. The .338 was no longer booming in response to the M-16s of the troops at Quan's home. Instead, she heard the constant chatter of rifles.

Grimaldi spoke a number first, obviously distracted. "You find Chang's possible number?"

"Yup."

"Right. Mike's coming in now."

"Thanks." Lam ran out to the pair in the hallway. Quan was still trying to get out from under the knot-muscled tree of a corpse that had crashed across him, pinning him down. She set her jaw and began patting down the muscular bodyguard's dead form, eventually finding a hefty handgun. She looked at it for a moment, studying it. The name of the gun on the slide was HK USP 45. It had a hammer on it, which she was glad for, and she tried pulling it back to cock it, finding that it wouldn't move.

"Right, safety on," she muttered. She immediately looked along both sides of the gun, finally seeing a lever that didn't follow the sleek lines of the gun, pushed out of place. She thumbed down the safety on the Heckler & Koch USP .45 and tried cocking the hammer again.

"Success," she whispered, when the door crashed in. Lam swung up the handgun, taking a moment to see if it was Belasko. But these men were short, wearing khaki uniforms and carrying rifles, looking around to see what was going down.

Lam, kneeling, fired a shot into each of the two guards, surprised at the loud thump but gentle kick in comparison to her usual tiny .38 belly gun. One of the guards went down as a .45-caliber slug tore through his belly, bounced into a rib, then severed his aorta. The other man spun as his biceps were torn by Lam's second shot. Holding the USP tighter, she fired repeatedly, pointing the gun vaguely at center of mass, concentrating more on her target. The man went down after the fourth shot, slugs having punched into his body and slamming him against the wall in a boneless heap.

The woman turned back to Balsong, pressing the muzzle of the gun into Quan's face as her free hand groped the corpse for more magazines for the pistol. The Thai flesh peddler screamed as hot metal cooked his skin, and finally, Lam was rewarded by a pair of box magazines. She idly looked at one of them and saw it was marked for twelve shots.

"Twelve .45s?" Not being a tall woman, she was surprised. The gun was a little big, but she'd have expected such a huge weapon to be unshootable. And here she had defended herself against two armed killers.

"Michelle!" Bolan called. The American social worker whirled and saw the big man with the cold blue eyes, carrying a huge double-barreled assault rifle, perched in the window. "Time to go."

Lam looked down at Quan. She was still pressing her .45 into his face, sneering. "It'd be so easy to execute him."

"Could you live with yourself?" Bolan asked her.

Lam thought back to the children, how sick they were, weak and starved, and most of all, the shock and emptiness of some of their eyes. Abuse had shattered some of them, maybe even irreparably. And for what?

Quan's home was lush and beautiful. His hands were finely

manicured. His Armani suit was impeccable, even with the spray of blood and brains across its lapels.

The four-pound pressure on the cocked HK's trigger disappeared, and in the same heartbeat, so did the center of Quan Li Ma's face.

"If I can't live with myself, I'll go see a therapist," Lam told him. "But I think I just settled a few nightmares."

Bolan nodded. He wasn't smiling, but he was accepting of the woman's decision.

The pair raced across the grounds of Quan Li Ma's mansion to where Jack Grimaldi and Alvin Warren were ready to pick them up after providing covering fire.

18

There were times when Jack Grimaldi wondered. He thought about a life he had spent, without the prospect of settling down and raising little flyboys and flygirls, having given up anything resembling a normal existence to follow Mack Bolan blindly on his crusade. The old Catholic school teachings bouncing around in his mind came forward—when Bolan entered his life, Grimaldi dropped everything like an disciple being chosen to follow the Messiah. Jack thought about why he felt the need to take such drastic action, then Tranh stirred, her black silken hair spilling down his shoulder as she awakened from fitful sleep.

She spoke in French, haltingly, the language that she shared, to her delight, with Grimaldi, a man who learned the language training to be a *savateur*.

Tranh stroked a lock of black hair back over her ear. "We are nearing my village?"

The launch that Bolan and the others acquired chugged its way up the Chao Phraya, and they had gone nearly 175 miles north of Bangkok.

"We're near Nakhon Sawan," Grimaldi said.

Tranh blinked, noticing the dark stain where she'd drooled on his shoulder. "Oh... I didn't mean to..."

The Stony Man pilot grinned. "You were tired."

"Thank you," Tranh said, smiling.

She'd come a long way from being the sullen, frail shell of what had once been a beautiful girl. Now, after a few days of healthy eating and drinking, medical attention and, what was more, true affection from all involved in the Executioner's Thailand crusade, she had become stronger. Her slender arms had actually put some mass onto them, but most of all, her eyes showed a light within them that still hadn't been seen in some of the innocents rescued from the *Sathorn Current*. Jack realized now what had made him drop everything and follow Bolan.

It was a just crusade, a cause worth following.

But what drew people to him was the fact that Bolan *cared*. And that caring allowed for a personal healing, which was in stark contrast to the wars he waged. Burning down evil, tearing out the weeds so that new growth may enter. To some, that was a lightning rod that attracted an ex-Mafia pilot and former child prostitute to cast their fears aside and face the hordes of hell with an icy-eyed man who laid his life on the line every day.

Tranh moved to the railing, overlooking the brown churning waters of the river and to the distant shore. "We're nearing where I worked...the fields."

Tranh pointed to a hill that she recognized, and Grimaldi studied it closely. "This is our first stop. We'll come to your home soon enough."

Tranh's dark, almond-shaped eyes met his. "Mack is going to destroy the field?"

"It's his job. We're making the man in charge of your suffering pay," Grimaldi answered.

"I want to help him. I know ways around the fields," Tranh said. "I tried escaping several times, and know the area."

The pilot frowned. She was only sixteen, but the look in her face made her older than he was.

"I can't follow you two in French as quick," Bolan stated, "but I can get her meaning. She wants in."

"Forgive me," Tranh said, switching to clumsy English. "But I must help, as well."

"You've helped enough, Tranh," Bolan told her. "I can't endanger your life."

Tranh's glance changed to an ice-cold darkness that shocked even Grimaldi, and she spoke swiftly in Thai. Some of what she was saying jolted Bolan like a 9 mm bullet into chest armor; he could understand some of her language, and his grim mask melted some.

"Your life is worth living," Bolan said softly, standing before her. "It's not worth risking."

Tranh's fury didn't fade with the soldier's soothing words. "And them?" She waved her hand at the shore, sweeping, taking in hundreds of children that they were here specifically to rescue. "You saved me. Now what?"

"You live your life."

"My life!" Tranh spit. She lapsed, speaking in Thai, her voice angry.

Bolan put his hands on her shoulders, looking to further dissuade her, when Grimaldi tapped him.

"I understand what she needs. You're not going to stop her any more than you could stop me from being your personal chauffeur across the skies."

"I can fight," Tranh said in English. "You saw me."

"She also knows the way to the plantation," Grimaldi added, expecting guilt to shut him up, but finding none. "A native guide would be helpful. Sarge, she's one of us. She's a child of pain. She's choosing her path."

Bolan gave Tranh's shoulders a squeeze. "You just guide."

Tranh nodded. "No shoot. Just aim. You are my gun."

The Executioner managed a smile. "That's right."

FOR MACK BOLAN, it was business as usual. Like countless other jungles, it was full of savages, not primitive indigenous tribes who had their own ancient form of civilization, but true savages. Animal man, the enemy of all things good and true, predator upon the helpless. In these jungles, be they made of tropical fauna or urban concrete, the Executioner had brought the torch of his cleansing flame time and time again. Would this be the time the doomsday numbers rolled against him?

If they did, it wouldn't bother the soldier. Years ago he had made peace with the fact that he would die in battle, even before he began his crusade against the Mafia.

Now, here he was, fighting an enemy so close to that original pack of demons he had stocked the halls of hell with, cruel scum who stole youth and innocence through sexual slavery. Reapers of blood money from the poison of the poppy fields that would be transformed into heroin and sent rushing through veins worldwide.

No nuclear weapons.

No ideologies based on racism or hard-line religion or dying economic strategies.

This was the same enemy that had made the Executioner what he was, just with a different skin color, a different language spoken, a different environment for him to call the killzone.

Ruiners of human life, who broke almost everyone with whom they came in contact.

Almost everyone.

Choi Tranh was beaten and pounded, but she was pushing to recover from her wounds. She had the salve of human affection healing her, but something else kept her moving, kept one foot going one in front of the other, with slow certainty and the instincts of a night cat as they slid through the darkness. It was a strange mix, partly a need for vengeance, but the drive was something deeper.

A calling.

Bolan knew the call.

Tranh had felt pain deep to her soul, a pain so profound that it forged her into something more than she had once been. Into a being who had the compassion for those who did suffer, and the will and duty to prevent anyone else from suffering that same pain ever again.

Even armed with nothing more than a Glock that Brewer had affixed with a sound suppressor akin to the one on Bolan's own Beretta 93-R, Tranh was a soldier in spirit, if not in skill.

Tranh was his ally here in the field, sister by default to the one-man army that the Executioner was.

Tranh came to a halt and lowered to the ground, the soldier's instincts kicking in and locating exactly what she had spotted.

Her senses were acute, or perhaps she had the scent and sound of these men from spending too long under their cruel mastery.

As it was, two of them were sharing a cigarette at the base of the small road that they were working parallel to. The Executioner slithered, careful not to disturb the bushes they were in, sliding his catlike bulk past Tranh, his hand pushing her gently to the ground. The girl understood, going fully prone, but still able to watch, her eyes sharp and dark, seeing all.

A wraith in black, his face, like Tranh's, blacked out under a layer of greasepaint, and his sleek blacksuit making him a ghost in the shadows, he slid until he had the bulk of a tree to shield himself from view, resting his wrist against the bark. The long snout of the silenced Beretta immediately took target acquisition, and Bolan held his breath, letting it out in tune with the press of the trigger, sending a round chugging as Tranh, on the ground, suddenly let loose with a sharp whistle.

One of the guards turned at the sound. The other tumbled lifelessly, sprawling on the dirt road, a pool of darkness spreading from where his head lay on the tire-rutted dirt.

The Executioner adjusted by only a slight degree and pumped the next Parabellum pill into the suddenly confused Thai gangster, the pencil of fire coring him through the forehead. Bolan looked at Tranh, who rose slowly, looking pensive.

Bolan nodded, and she moved swiftly, helping him slide the lifeless men into the bushes at roadside, covering them with the broad leaves of the massive ferns. She gave him a glance for reassurance, then borrowed a rifle from one of the dead men, slinging it over her shoulder. She was supposed to be a noncombatant, but there was no stopping her.

On the boat, Grimaldi and Bolan had given her the same crash course in rifle marksmanship that the Executioner had learned long ago provided the best results. Tranh wouldn't be ready for the kind of commando work that Bolan had planned, but the heavier weapon would help when she had to break and retreat into the jungle. For now, she cinched it tight to her back and stayed low, keeping in Bolan's line of sight.

The two of them kept moving along, slow and low, the Executioner a leopard, Tranh with the grace and agility of a house cat. It took another couple moments for them to finally reach the edge of the rows of poppy plants that stretched away under the silver-blue light of the moon.

Easily five acres were spread out on the low rolling hills.

Tranh glanced at Bolan, then pointed toward one path along-side a low, one-story, barracks-style building. The soldier nod-ded. That had to be the building where the children were kept, because of the fencing around it, a spool of razor wire around the top and two grim guards stalking back and forth like caged animals. The tension was in the air, and the Executioner realized that it was Chang Chi Fu's directive that had put them on the de-fensive. The soldiers and managers of this plantation were sta-tioned in a two-story, French-styled mansion easily one hundred years old.

Let the kids rot in a prison compound, while their oppressors lived in the lap of classic old-style luxury.

The Executioner had Tranh take cover behind the thick trunk of a tree, letting the tall roots provide her with a bench rest for her rifle, as well as providing a shield against enemy gunfire. He held up his finger, and she nodded, understanding the unspoken message.

Stay put and cover me.

Bolan trusted her implicitly. She wouldn't jump the gun and she knew when to shoot, when to run away and, most of all, when to be quiet.

Surviving a living hell of rape and slavery had given her a gift. A gift not to be cherished, but a gift that would keep her alive for her devotion to this cause.

Keeping his body low and against the dark green backdrop of the forest, Bolan kept on his course toward the barracks build-ing, walking toe-heel so he could feel the presence of anything he'd step on before he set his entire weight down. Finally, mus-cles aching from his slow crawl toward where the captive chil-dren were kept, he paused, crouched low against the wire fence. Again the Beretta filled his hand, and the luminous green dot of the tritium front night sight rose to the Executioner's line of sight. He took a lingering fifteen seconds to line up the silenced pistol on the farther guard, pursed his lips to a tight, grim line and pressed the trigger gently.

The cough of the Beretta coincided with the sudden halo of

spraying mist under the amber cone of light on the pole outside the barracks. The guard jerked, then dropped to the ground, hollowed of whatever was left of his black soul, tumbling into a heap of wretched meat. His partner swung toward the fallen man, at first too shocked to say anything.

Bolan flicked the Beretta swiftly to 3-round-burst mode and tapped the trigger, ripping a trio of 9 mm slugs into the back of the second guard. All three rounds smashed bone, breaking ribs and severing spine, and the slaver crumpled nervelessly to the ground, gurgling as he tried to scream through lungs flooded with blood. The Executioner switched back to single-shot mode and put one final mercy round into the Thai child abuser.

More mercy, no doubt, than the guard had ever granted to a kid hunched over, fingers ripped raw from harvesting opium, back roasted to peeling by the sun. Bolan remembered having been forced into slave labor, harvesting the raw material for heroin, after being shot down in pursuit of closing off a drug pipeline. The Executioner had finished off that harvest, but not before being submitted to slavery and abuse himself. He sympathized with the children, and when he opened the door, bodies scurried awake, confused to be roused during the night.

They saw the big man with empty hands, backlit by the lamp outside.

Bolan repeated a phrase that Tranh had taught him.

"We're going free."

The children shut up and began gathering their clothes with silent swiftness. They knew instinctively what to do, and they assembled around him. Bolan turned and killed the lamp that illuminated the barracks door with a single round, then pointed the first child to where he knew Tranh was crouched, ready to give cover fire at a moment's notice. The first pair of children moved off quickly, quietly, but surefooted among the very field that they roamed daily. The next pair followed immediately after, and Bolan took the time to make a head count, counting nearly forty kids.

According to Tranh, they had eighty kids toiling in these fields.

"Where are the others?" the Executioner asked in French.

One of the children pointed toward the other side of the fields where a flurry of activity was now visible to him. Guards were loading children onto a pair of trucks, and the Executioner felt his gut go cold. He brought his communicator to his lips.

"Warren, I've got bad news. They're moving the kids."

"Is there anything we can do?" Alvin Warren asked from the motor launch.

"Yeah, be ready for the first batch of kids. This is going to get noisy," the Executioner growled.

Mack Bolan raced into the darkness as fast as he could.

19

Tranh watched Bolan race from the barracks, her eyes following his darting path and seeing nearly one thousand yards away a pair of massive diesel trucks. Small and large bodies were gathered around the vehicle, and Tranh almost darted from her hiding place, but realized that the Executioner had entrusted her with a mission.

Don't let the kids down.

Already the former slaves were reaching her, and Tranh's slender arm brushed them to the sheltering shadows of the road, her other arm holding the bulky weight of the AK-47 ready. Despite the sling taking an edge off the total nine-pound weight of the rifle, her biceps and forearm still ached from holding the chopper in one hand. She knew full well that it would require both hands to use the big gun.

Hurried questions were whispered her way, but Tranh silenced them with a short command, her hand going low to inform the children that they had to keep down.

"Get moving," she whispered. "Up the road. It's safe. We have a boat for you."

Frightened faces looked up to her, white ovals reflected in the moonlight, their fear dissolving into awe at the reedy young figure in black who stood, part of the force that was rescuing them.

"Your father, he is going to get the others," one said.

Tranh looked back across the field and saw moving shapes heading toward the barracks, now that its light had been knocked out mysteriously. She swallowed, then thought for a moment.

"He is not my father," Tranh said.

"Then who is he?" the child asked.

Tranh smiled. "A brother."

The faces watched her in awe, then Tranh nodded for them to go. They raced on obediently.

A few more freed.

A generation of victims to go.

The soldiers were shouting now as they got closer to the barracks. The kids who still hadn't made it to the relative shelter of the road stopped, seeing the armed SUA men, confusion and doubt stopping them and leaving them easy pickings for these human vultures.

"Get moving!" Tranh called sharply. The children spun, seeing her, and so did the SUA assassins.

No choice.

Do or die, Tranh thought. If death came, at least she was giving someone else a chance at a longer, happier life.

She clamped the rifle to her shoulder and tapped the trigger, sending a burst of 7.62 mm rounds into the silhouette of a Thai thug before he could bring his weapon into play. He jerked out of the way as if smashed by a war hammer, and Tranh felt the spike of recoil slam into her shoulder. It hurt, but it wouldn't hurt as much as a bullet smashing into her.

Swinging the weapon back and forth, she kept tapping the trigger, sending out short squirts of autofire that rippled and popped after the initial thunder in her hearing. She knew that the noise of the gun somehow had dulled her sense of hearing.

No matter, all she needed to do right now was see.

And she saw the two other Thai gunmen moving, avoiding the deadly hornets she launched at them, too busy to return their own fire. That wouldn't last long, only until the magazine ran dry.

And that was coming up quick, Tranh figured.

She shot a glance toward the children, moving to the cover of a tree, then felt a flurry of gunfire hammering at the trunk she stood behind. Wood splintered and stung her cheek as hot rounds tore into the tree. Tranh was shocked, dropping to the ground, then looked up again. The last of the kids was a racing white ghost in the swallowing tunnel formed by the forest's canopy and the road.

"Reload, reload," Tranh whispered, fumbling and finding the lever that released the magazine. Mack had given her a few quick pointers on the weapon, which looked like his own main weapon for the assault. However, his rifle looked more complex.

That was all right. Tranh had only to add one of the curved banana magazines to her rifle and get back into action. With a sharp clack that signaled her hearing was clearing up, Tranh looked for the enemy killers, and looked right down the cold, merciless barrel of an assault rifle inches from her face.

"Time to die, little girl," the San United Army thug growled.

The explosion of gunfire was deafening as Tranh was knocked hard to the ground.

Jack Grimaldi stood above her, his Cobray smoking from the stubby barrel, the figures of Alvin Warren and Mick Hayes racing into view, their own weapons seeking targets.

"Thought you could use some help," Grimaldi whispered in French.

"Thank you, Jack," Tranh said, still dazed from the point-blank exposure to so much gunplay in the past few moments.

He flashed her a brief smile, then looked worriedly across the field to where the Executioner was engaged in his grim work.

BOLAN WAS NO SUPERMAN, but after his years of War Everlasting, he was still an outstanding athlete, the very nature of his way of life tightening his muscles and driving him to physical excellence with every moment. But as fit as Bolan was, it was still a tiring race loaded down with weapons. His body was drenched with sweat under his blacksuit, and his muscles screamed for mercy.

No mercy for the Executioner this night.

Angry shouts erupted, and suddenly gunfire ripped the darkness behind him. Bolan gave a momentary pause, and his muscles surged with relief. Tranh was having problems, but from the sound of it, disciplined fire was being put out. It wasn't Chang's heroin-dealing gangsters doing the shooting, but the young girl.

Not the best option in the world, Bolan thought. He'd hoped that Tranh would be quiet and stealthy enough to keep low and out of the way. That's why he didn't bring the rest of the crew of the launch along. A full-blown force would make too much noise, and possibly endanger the very children they were racing to rescue.

But now, they were moving the kids.

Doomsday numbers were tumbling, and the way things looked, the Executioner had to pull a miracle to even hope of saving the kids being loaded onto the two trucks. The weapon in his hands, a Kalashnikov AK-47 with a modified M-203 grenade launcher attached under the barrel and a 3X night-vision scope. The gun was made lighter by replacing the original wooden stock and pistol grip with an imported black fiberglass version, but it was still a hefty and awesome weapon.

Bolan decided to slow things down.

He dropped to one knee, raising the stock to his shoulder and bringing his hand forward to trigger the M-203. Bolan sized up his options and let the 40 mm minibomb go hurtling into a tree trunk in front of the two trucks, hoping the explosion would shatter the tree and block the road. The thunderclap of the missile sent the SUA gunmen whirling, aiming their rifles down the road, spitting lead from their weapons.

Good distraction, the Executioner reckoned, letting the Kalashnikov hang on its sling, drawing the Beretta again and lining up the silenced machine pistol on the backs of his enemies. He was gunning them down in cold blood, but this wasn't Hollywood where the hero always escaped from the first barrage of gunfire by the villains. He fired out four 3-round bursts from the 93-R, its muffled messages swallowed by the thunder of Type 56s and M-16s scything blistering storms of autofire down the road.

All four bursts were at head and neck height, over the tops of the children who had thrown themselves to the dirt already. The bursts connected and three men whirled, chopped by the hot

Parabellum sizzlers, dying soundlessly. The fourth man whirled, his ear torn off and shoulder cored, but still alert enough to shout a warning about the man in black attacking from behind. Bolan's last silenced burst ripped a trio of 9 mm slugs into the survivor's throat, sending him tumbling into hell before Bolan reloaded.

The doomsday numbers were evening up, but there were still three gunmen armed and ready, and a military-style jeep was growling its way up the road toward the two trucks. And who knew how many men were manning the two vehicles.

As if to answer Bolan's unspoken question, one of the trucks spewed out its load of SUA employees. The driver and a shotgun rider were in the front, and a lone gunman in the bed of the truck, their weapons tracking the warrior as he dived for cover, feeling the hot lance of a single round slicing through the flesh of his shoulder.

On the ground, the Executioner was able to shoot upward, and he rolled enough to bring his Kalashnikov into play, milking the trigger to send out a fireball storm of devastation that chopped two Thai child-slavers to ribbons.

Two down, four to go, and the second two-and-a-half-ton truck was growling to life, its diesel engine spewing black smoke from its tailpipe.

Clear out the last of the guards and get onto that truck before it left, the Executioner analyzed. Kill four men in a few seconds, without harming innocent children who were scattered, crying in terror all about them, and race to a vehicle that had at least one cold-blooded killer in its bed.

Bolan shoved himself to his feet, blood soaking his blacksuit's sleeve, and he raced toward the remaining soldiers on foot, ripping off a figure-eight of 7.62 mm steel-cored slugs that crucified another couple of gunmen, smashing them to the ground as gunfire hissed at his back and heels. Another round sliced at the Executioner's flesh, this time nicking the triceps of his arm.

That's okay, Bolan mused. Let them concentrate on the one arm. I know how to shoot with my left hand.

The Executioner, however, was still in the heart of the battle, letting the Kalashnikov fall on its sling, heavy weight slamming the nylon strap into his neck as he ripped the .44 Magnum Desert Eagle from its quick-draw leather. One of the gunmen was curs-

ing and struggling to reload his pistol when Bolan snap-aimed
and put two .44 Magnum skullbusters into him, rupturing his rib
cage and shredding his lungs. The last rifleman looked at his
friend swatted aside by the thundering .44 Magnum pistol and
its blazing muzzle blast and was caught flat-footed as Bolan
hammered one last, blistering slug through his face, the 240-grain
round spraying brain and bone matter in a great cloud of devastation.

The Executioner had done half his work, making sure these
thugs weren't behind him to terrorize the children on the
ground. But there were youths on the truck, and it was wheeling around the wrecked tree, starting to pick up speed. Running like a madman, the Executioner plowed on, racing to
catch up with the truck. All the while, the enemy jeep was
rolling closer and closer.

XAN MAK GON HEARD the body slam into the side of the truck
and leaned out, looking at the arms and legs of the scrambling
intruder. His pistol, a Browning Hi-Power clone built by Pinidad,
was secure in his fist as he swung out and around, aiming the
slender muzzle at his foe.

A big boot came lashing out and smashed Xan glancingly off
his forearm, but he still held on to the gun and the side of the
truck, both of them gripping the canvas cover ribbing. The SUA
thug, however, triggered a shot that went sizzling into the road,
away from the truck, and clanging on the hood steel of the jeep
racing up on them. Xan recognized the shouts of Meng and Li
as his bullet peppered the jeep, and moments later, autofire
started ripping savagely at the bouncing truck.

Xan went to the floor hard, hearing the thumps and cracks of
high-velocity bullets tearing into canvas and bouncing off steel.
Children were screaming all around him, but they went nowhere
near the Thai slaver. They had learned to fear him for his rages
and appetites, and anything that frightened the monster who
ruled their universe was worth being equally scared of.

Heavy thumps suddenly filled the air, six rounds of rapid fire,
the autofire slacking off from the jeep where Xan could see it
over the tailgate of the truck. He turned and fired wildly into the

canvas covering of the vehicle, emptying out the pistol, hoping he hit the mysterious figure clinging to the side.

Xan lifted his head above the tailgate and saw that Li was still struggling with the jeep, but Meng was nowhere in sight. Lifting his head farther, he then noticed a body bouncing out the open doorwell of the jeep, a ragged lump being dragged along and torn slowly to pieces by the merciless pace of the chase and the rugged road.

Li shouted, waving wildly, and Xan ducked back behind the tailgate, literally vaulting backward when a thunderbolt split the air and struck the bed of the truck right where his head would have been. The intruder had a massive hand cannon, and would have decapitated him were it not for Li's warning. The SUA slaver struggled to pry the empty magazine from his pistol, clumsily groping for a replacement as he saw the ruthless black shape of death swinging around over the tailgate, gleaming cannon swinging toward him. Xan screamed, when the truck suddenly lurched wildly.

Mack Bolan was jarred from the back of the truck, his .44 Magnum Desert Eagle tumbling from his fingertips and his other hand releasing the fistful of canvas that was the only thing between him and a short, lethal flight under the wheels of the jeep. With every ounce of energy, ignoring the pain of a bullet that sliced the flesh of his hip, he threw himself to the safest flat surface he could find, the hood of Li's jeep.

With a shouted curse, the Thai driver tried to swing the wheel. The Executioner's fist wrapped around the wheel before the man could react. The truck started edging ahead as in the back of it Xan was slowly gathering to his feet, ramming home another magazine. Bolan cursed and gave the driver an openhanded slap with shocking force.

Distracted, the driver hit the brakes, and Bolan spun on the hood, boots crabbing for every ounce of additional traction he could. With a hard lurch, he crossed the rapidly increasing distance between the grille of the jeep and the truck's tailgate with the length of his fingers to spare. Xan's bullets sizzled between his legs, but instead, they were pounded by road, boots bouncing and being kicked by ruts and lumps at sixty miles per hour.

The Executioner pulled hard, yanking on the tailgate, and

swung himself up farther, knowing he was facing a loaded gun. Still, he'd have a chance against a gunman with the drop on him. Road rash and the upcoming jeep would turn him into chowder, with no guarantee of a quick death.

Xan looked over his sights at the Executioner's black-painted face, his arms squeezing over the tailgate. Ice-blue eyes stared hard at him, a moment of cold anger being transmitted with pure, righteous force, and the SUA man started to squeeze the trigger.

The bouncing truck made even the point-blank shot swing wild, and Bolan grimaced, his biceps grazed by the 9 mm slug, rather than his skull.

Suddenly small bodies lurched and leaped onto Xan's back, screaming at the man who had shown a moment of fear. Bolan heaved himself up, his boots barely rising above where the crumpled grille of the enemy jeep hammered the rear fender of the truck once more. Scrambling in, the Executioner pulled the Beretta and popped up. With the sleek Italian machine pistol on burst mode, he hammered a half-dozen rounds into the driver. Moments later, the jeep was swerving and veering, slamming hard into the impenetrable wall of trees on either side of the cruddy excuse for a road. Crunching steel and rapidly receding flames told Bolan all he needed to know about the status of that particular enemy.

Spinning, bringing the Beretta up, Bolan was faced with Xan, who was busy taking out his rage in the form of a brutal pistol-whipping of a ten-year-old who was clawing at his leg. The first impact was the last one, as the Executioner let the Beretta drop to the floor, his big callused hands grabbing the Thai slaver by the neck and hauling him bodily away from the child.

Xan cursed and screamed, but Bolan kept swinging, sending the killer tumbling backward out of the truck, grabbing his ankle as he flopped over the tailgate.

Bolan held the slaver's ankle for twenty seconds, but he only screamed for ten. A nearly headless lump of human flesh went tumbling down the road as the Executioner let go and retrieved the weapons he dared not fire in close proximity with the children.

There was an uncomfortable silence, the children looking up

at the huge man-monster, his black greasepaint cut by rivulets of blood, cold blue eyes scanning each and every one of them for injuries. Only one, the ten-year-old, was bleeding from a gash on his cheek, sobbing softly. Bolan knelt by the kid and pulled a piece of gauze from his war harness, sprinkling antibiotics on the cut and pressing the gauze tenderly to the wound. The kid, despite the sting, held the gauze to his cheek, giving the soldier the freedom to tape the field dressing to his face.

"You'll be all right," Bolan whispered, giving the kid's shoulder an affectionate squeeze.

He looked around and the children's fear diminished.

Sergeant Mercy's tenderness had won them over.

Bolan rose from his crouch and peered through the door to the cab, seeing the two Thais in the cab watching the road anxiously. It made sense, because at the speed that the truck was bounding along, one mistake could mean death.

The Executioner growled a curse, knowing that they wouldn't slow until they were miles away from the battleground they assumed was behind them. But doing anything to the cab would be suicidal, and cost the lives of Bolan's charges. He pulled his knife and cut a slit in the fabric at the side of the truck, grabbing a pipe rib and swung out on the driver's side, keeping his body tight to the vehicle.

Even so, branches slashed and slapped at the Executioner's face and body. Where his battle harness didn't protect him, and especially where his injured shoulder and biceps were exposed, he was pummeled mercilessly. Still, the warrior summoned the strength to hang on, gripping his Desert Eagle and aiming it at the driver's-side mirror.

The driver caught the movement and saw the wraith for an instant in his reflection before the .44 Magnum slug tore through the metal and ripped the mirror free. The truck immediately began grinding down through its gears, brakes squealing as the driver was caught in a state of panic. Bolan himself grunted in agony as the mirror bounced off his bleeding hip, adding to the white haze of pain that was threatening to have him drop to the road and sleep forever.

The truck finally finished grinding to a halt, and it took every ounce of the strength in the Executioner's left arm to keep him from being ripped clean off the truck. He was thrown to the running board of the cab, and face-to-face with the San United Army slavers who gawked at the bloody, black thing with the ice-cold death stare. The shotgun rider, packing a pump shotgun, struggled to swing the barrel of his cannon across the dashboard, but the Executioner shoved the Desert Eagle's muzzle into the cab, letting him have it point blank with three .44 Magnum contact shots. A shredded corpse tumbled out the passenger-side door, and the driver screamed hideously as hot brass bounced into his face.

Bolan let the Desert Eagle drop onto the passenger seat, his big hand grabbing the driver by the shirt and hauling him out through the window, both the Executioner's long arms entwining the Thai wheelman's head. Throwing his 230 pounds off the running board, a resounding crack filled the night, and the battle for control of the truck was finished.

Faces peered at him from the darkened back of the truck.

The mission may not have gone as quietly as it could have, Bolan thought, but the children were now safe.

That was all that mattered.

20

Sonya Getter looked as if she belonged on a catwalk modeling clothes rather than running a camp in Southeast Asia for runaway children and other victims of Thailand's struggle to save its future. At more than six feet, with long red hair, she had a complexion that looked almost ready to give itself over to freckles, but somehow managed to come up short. Instead, she managed a slight redness that she tried to keep under control with a wide-brimmed safari hat that was truly for practical purposes. Her arms, when they weren't covered in lightweight cotton sleeves, often peeled badly after a day in the sun at the camp.

Skin care was important to the former teenage beauty contestant, but care for the human race won out over whatever discomfort she felt. Sometimes she felt like throwing everything in a bucket and heaving it over the small rope bridge to the river below, but she managed to bite it off. Getter frowned and looked down at the river, where two heavily laden boats, each sporting a rifle-wielding man on the prow, chugged laboriously along.

Trouble?

Getter's eyes focused tighter, and she got a good look. The

motor launches were heavily laden with children to the point of capsizing. She raced off the bridge, making her way to the river-bank, a desperate scramble down a steep slope. At times like this, she wished that she had taken the UNICEF security chief major Kevin Peters's advice to carry a side arm.

Gunmen were one thing that her skills at speech and barter-ing could prove next to useless against.

"Hold it!" Getter yelled.

The lead launch rumbled to a laborious halt, the man on the prow, taller than she was, with piercing blue eyes, regarding her with the precision of a machine. Bandages covered his forehead and arm, but he still stood, the biggest rifle she'd ever seen propped against his hip.

"We need a safe place to off-load," the man said in a voice at once calm and full of weight and importance. She was taken aback.

"We're a peaceful United Nations installation," Getter replied. She was determined to convince him to turn away. So far, no waves of hostility came off him, which shocked her for one so large and full of power that he could easily walk over her, even without a rifle.

"We know," the man said. "My name is Mike Belasko. United States Justice Department."

He jumped off the prow of the boat and landed on the shore with the grace of a panther and moved toward her, slinging his rifle and extending a large hand. Over Getter's life, there weren't many men who made her feel physically small, but Belasko wasn't just physically bigger; there was some enormous weight around him that she couldn't quite place.

"Why come here?" she asked, her voice resigned for now.

"My recommendation," a familiar voice called down.

She looked up and saw the shaved head of Alvin Warren pok-ing over the railing. He gave her a grin, and Getter felt her stom-ach turn.

"The CIA and the Justice Department?" she asked with a sneer.

Warren's grin disappeared in an instant, and he began setting up a ramp.

"Where did those kids come from?" Getter asked.

"Rescued from the San United Army," Bolan stated matter-of-factly.

"You didn't—"

"We did," Bolan said. "Still want to deny them help?"

"General Chang Chi Fu is a cold-blooded murderer. He'll send a thousand men here looking to get back any losses," Getter snapped. "How dare you?"

"There was nowhere else to take them," Warren said weakly. "You were the only person I knew to turn to."

Getter glared at Warren. Her height advantage over him made his shrinking from her blistering stare even more obvious. "Really."

Bolan looked at the two of them, studying the moment. "You have a history."

The way he said it, it was as if he'd already read their life stories except for a few missing pages. Now he wanted to know what was said on those pages.

"Your friend Alvin, or whatever his name is, was originally assigned to us as our chief of security in the camp. Turned out he was actually using his post here to spy on Communists or drug dealers or whatever threat of the week there was for the CIA," Getter stated.

"I couldn't bear not to come clean with Sonya. I was falling for her, and I told her the truth."

"You told me after you'd gotten everything you wanted," Getter said. "What more did you need? You had sex with me." Sonya hissed.

Bolan sighed. "Look, I'm trying to make sure that Chang and the SUA don't hurt these or any other children again. You can give me a little wriggle room."

Getter glared at Warren, who was scratching the back of his head, his lips drawn tight.

"No lies?"

"Just my name," Bolan answered. She could tell immediately that he was being honest.

"And what about you?" Getter asked Warren.

The CIA agent's dark eyes looked up to hers. "I intend to make amends."

"Sure...now that you need help and you're in the area."

"Sonya, I said I'm sorry once. What does it take?"

"The truth." She turned and headed back toward the camp, helping Bolan and his people guide the kids to shelter.

HAN QUO WATCHED Chang Chi Fu's face turn into a grim mask. As the Bell UH-1 swung low over the plantation, still in flames from white phosphorous grenades set off in the night, Han knew full well that the general was inches away from snapping like a twig.

Chang looked down at the smoldering fields, doing mental arithmetic, and simply sat back, closing his eyes. He remained still and quiet, his face unmoving.

"Fifty million U.S. dollars for the crop alone," Chang said with a strange softness. "It happened again."

"We have forces all across the countryside now. There was no way we could have anticipated—" Han began, but Chang's raised finger stopped him.

"This type of man stopped me once," Chang said with an unnatural calm. "The previous team did enormous damage. They must pay."

Han nodded.

"There is no way they could move eighty children off this plantation. Not with trucks, and not with the boats they took from us," Chang stated.

"But they could have rented other—"

"No, they could not have," Chang said, cutting Han off. "My men have been watching for any boats large enough to carry a hundred people being rented. None has been taken out, but the two launches we had stolen from us haven't shown up yet."

Han looked below. "The Nakhon Sawan plantation is close enough to the river."

Chang's glare cut across and burned Han. "It's also in Thailand. They can't escape."

"Sorry, sir. Just trying to think."

"Thinking is the job of the general. You are simply to hunt and kill," Chang growled.

"Yes, sir," Han said, defeat shrouding him. Any future failures, even of etiquette, would be the end of his life.

The UH-1 landed and Chang disembarked, looking at the soldiers already on the scene. On the porch of the manor, seven ragged soldiers paced like caged cats, looking nervously at the stocky little general.

"Those are the men who let the American take the children?" Chang asked.

Major Zho Luk gave Chang a sharp salute and nodded. "They stated that the launches proceeded up the river under retreating fire."

Chang swiveled his head at the soldiers. "How many dead?"

"We lost twenty-five men, and one jeep was irreparably damaged and, of course, the crops," Zho stated.

Chang rubbed his chin. "Those seven men survived?"

"You can even see the section of shoreline where they took fire and lost another man," Zho stated. "I investigated it myself."

Chang nodded. "Tell them that they will be reassigned."

Zho gave Chang a sharp salute and turned away to the porch. Han swallowed. "Sir..."

"See, they didn't think. They withdrew, but they came back and kept fighting."

Han stiffened.

"They were soldiers. They did their best to hold the ground and fought the fires to save as much of the crop as possible."

"Up the river, there's a UNICEF camp," Han said softly.

Chang smiled. "Now you're starting to prove useful."

"I can assemble a small team, and we can perform a reconnaissance on the camp. Nothing to attract their attention," Han stated.

"I'd say yes, but I have another plan," Chang stated.

Han sagged.

"Do not worry, you've proved yourself more than enough times, and you just proved your usefulness now. But why risk any more of my own men? We have an entire government looking for the terrorist who murdered a foreign national," Chang said.

Han blinked.

"You may make the phone call."

"Yes, sir."

21

Casey Michaels picked up the telephone on the second ring. On the line, it was the voice of a Thai national, and the sinking feeling in his gut hit full force with the sound of his words.

"They found the American, Belasko."

"Who did?"

"We're thinking Chang. I'm not sure. All we know is that there was an anonymous tip dropped off at Security Force HQ."

"Where's Belasko?"

"Nakhon Sawan. Actually fifteen miles east. A UNICEF camp."

"Jesus."

"Local security forces are going to be descending on the camp within a few hours."

"All right. Just keep your ears open. Thanks for the tip."

"The least I could do. I hate Chang and his baby rapers as bad as you."

The phone went dead, and Michaels replaced the receiver. He got up. There wasn't going to be much he could do to help Belasko, but if he somehow managed to get a message out...

He picked up the phone and held it to his ear.

"I know you're listening," he said. "You probably also heard about what was happening to your boy. Can you contact him?"

There was an uncomfortably long silence. Long enough for him to doubt whether playing inside the rules against a bastard like Chang warranted the lives of dozens of men and women and hundreds of children.

"Rest assured, Michaels," a gruff voice growled. "Now quit breathing on an open receiver. You're giving me a headache."

Michaels set the phone down and sighed.

He could get used to playing outside the rules.

Stony Man Farm, Virginia

AARON KURTZMAN CHUCKLED as he killed the connection to the embassy. Called "the Bear" because of his massive build, and confined to a chair thanks to a sniper's bullet, he was still an indispensable part of Stony Man Farm's operations. Never an actual physical force in the adventures of Able Team, Phoenix Force or the Executioner, his brain and mastery of computers allowed him to give the fighting men of the Farm dominion over their enemies. But all the brains in the world couldn't stop a bullet. Over his shoulder, Barbara Price was already looking at their options.

"Phoenix Force has already assembled back at the Farm, and Able Team is going after the leak that let the Thai contingent get hold of the Dragon missiles," Price stated.

"Gotta admit, we have plenty of options, but none that can be there in less than ten hours," Kurtzman said. "However, I'm working on getting a link up through to the UNICEF phones in Nakhon Sawan."

"Chances are, the Thai military isn't going to raise any hell for just finding a few extra kids at a UNICEF relief camp," Price agreed. "Mack's good at disappearing into the forest."

"Striker's been in tighter spots before."

Price looked at Kurtzman with disbelief. "Tell me the last time Mack has had to fight both sides of the law when an entire nation was gunning for him."

Kurtzman looked at her incredulously. "Do you want the time before he met April, or after she died?"

"My mistake," Price said.

"No, Chang's mistake."

Price turned and looked over the situation map on the wall. "How soon until we hook up?"

"Ringing now."

"Who am I talking to?" Price asked.

"Sonya Getter. Teenage beauty contestant who stated she wanted to really help kids. Joined UNICEF and learned the world was a real son of a bitch," Kurtzman said. "So she went to the son of a bitch's asshole, Thailand, and decided to keep kicking ass until things got better, or she got permanently retired."

"I like her already."

The room's speaker's clicked, and an uneasy voice answered. "Hello?"

"Hi, Sonya Getter? This is the U.S. Justice Department," Price said into her headset, so she wouldn't sound as if she were talking from the bottom of a trash bin.

"Uh-huh, and Belasko is a cop," Getter answered.

"We really do work for Justice. We never said we were cops," Price said frankly. "Is Mike there?"

"Yeah. Give me a second."

"You might not have a second. The Thai National Security Forces are alerted to the fact that Belasko's hiding out with you."

"Shit," Sonya answered.

"Just tell Belasko that the good guys are coming. It's time to lay low."

"I thought you were the good guys."

"We are. We just pissed off the wrong people."

A beat of silence. "I know what you mean. All right. I'll chase down Belasko."

Price smiled. "We'll make sure that the camp receives some assistance in exchange for what you've done for us."

"You don't have to do me any favors."

"No, we don't. But I also didn't have to hang my best man out to be hunted down by the law."

"All right. I'll hurry."

The phone link disconnected.

Price breathed softly, "Please do."

MACK BOLAN SAW Sonya Getter jogging up to him and knew something was up. He began assembling his gear, despite protests from the crusade's entourage.

"Belasko," Sonya called, "you're leaving?"

"I kind of figured something was up."

"They know you're here," Getter stated. "I don't know how much time you have."

Bolan winced as he cinched the pack over his bullet-torn shoulder. The dressings were holding, but the wound hurt like hell. "I'll take any incriminating equipment with me."

"I'm coming with you," Michelle Lam spoke up.

"No, you actually would have a legitimate reason for being here. And nobody has equated any of you, except for Jack, with me," Bolan said with a grunt.

"You're hardly in any shape to travel alone," Grimaldi said. He began loading himself down as heavily as he could.

"I'm coming, too," Alvin Warren added.

Tranh silently gathered her weapons, her face an emotionless mask.

"You're not coming," Bolan grunted.

"You need someone who can speak the language," Tranh told him.

"By the time you finish arguing..." Getter began.

Kevin Peters, the UNICEF security man, came racing toward the group. He was hard to miss, even with the debate, well over six feet and a mountain of ebony muscle. "Guys, I've spotted Thai military helicopters in the area. They're gunships."

Warren cursed.

"Listen, Chuck and I can help Mike, Tranh and Jack move. None of them are in top condition right now, and we're not exactly in-country legally," Mick Hayes stated. "You, Alvin, are going to be needed to help cover for Michelle, who's not cut out for jungle humping."

"Jungle humping?" Lam and Getter asked simultaneously.

"Hard hiking through the jungle," Bolan explained as Brewer strapped some of his gear across his broad, rock-hard shoulders.

"And the launches?" Getter asked.

"Mick and I took one of them a few miles back downriver and scuttled it with the more incriminating stuff we couldn't carry," Brewer stated.

Bolan looked at Peters. "What's the fastest way to sneak out of this camp?"

"I'll take you myself. I've got a jeep on hand, and I'll do a Chicago stop to let you guys off," Peters said.

Getter sighed deeply. "I don't need this camp being raided. These kids are scared to death of soldiers and guns as it is."

Bolan grabbed the rest of his gear and looked at Warren. "I'm counting on you to make a good smoke screen. Got it?"

"If I don't see you guys again, it was a pleasure working with you," Warren said.

"Good luck," Bolan told the stocky little CIA man.

"I'd accept it, but you need it more."

Bolan nodded, and as they raced to Peters's jeep, he knew that right now, they were busy making their own luck.

He stopped and turned to Grimaldi. "Jack, take the launch and head back to Bangkok as fast as it can take you."

"But it'll be hours—"

"Jack, you can help by bringing Dragon Slayer. I'll stay alive until you get back, and then we can do some serious damage," Bolan ordered.

Grimaldi looked at the tree line, and then at Bolan, who was getting into the jeep with the giant Peters. "I'll be back fast."

"I know you will, Jack," Bolan answered. "You've never let me down."

The jeep tore off down a dirt road, dust flying from the spinning of tires. Grimaldi tried to convince himself the sting in his eyes and lump in his throat were from the dust cloud. "And I hope I never do."

22

Alvin Warren's heart was thumping in his throat as he walked beside Michelle Lam, pointing out various bits here and there as the helicopter came down, its rotors hammering the air and sending jolts of pressure through his head. He paused, watching the big bird set down, then looked to her, shrugging.

"Got to make this look good," Warren told her.

"How nasty are those things?" Lam asked, looking at the ugly craft that circled the camp.

Warren glanced up. Two Hueys were still circling overhead. Hanging off their sides, outside opened doors, were the unmistakable barrel pods of artillery rockets, and the ugly insect limbs of some form of machine gun he was too far away from to see. It didn't matter, though. If they were mounted on the wing pylons of a modified Huey, they had at least a one-mile range, and could turn a human being into a cloud of vapor with a sustained blast of gunfire.

And knowing technology, the Hueys also had the ability to even see through a forest from a mile up and put down a deadly wave of accurate fire. Having done inspections of the Thai security forces' aircraft and equipment, he knew that they had forward-looking radar and infrared that would make tracking humans in jungles relatively easy. And their orbit was growing wider and wider, as if to try to ring in the Executioner and his fellow escapees.

"Very," Warren answered in a voice more somber than he wished.

"There must be about thirty men getting off those two helicopters," Lam whispered.

"There will be more being dropped off elsewhere, maybe even fast-roped into the jungle," Warren answered.

"So they'll catch Belasko?" Lam asked.

"Hard to tell. He's hurt, but he also looks like he was born in a jungle. I don't think that a few injuries would keep him from leading the gang to safety. Those guys will be on him like white on rice, but I have a feeling he's been shot up and chased through more jungles than you and I have been to McDonald's," Warren said.

Lam patted Warren on his stomach. "If that's the case, it should be a cakewalk for Belasko."

Warren smiled. "Come on, let's go see what our visitors want."

FOR FIFTEEN MINUTES, Mack Bolan marched hard, his gunshot wounds flexing and moist under their dressings, combining blood with sweat under his jungle fatigues, making him itch worse. Certainly he'd had the time to wash up and dress his injuries, but at the pace he was moving at, with Tranh taking the lead and deciding the pace, he was nearly as hot, wet and miserable as he'd ever been in his life.

Hot, wet and miserable, however, outside of handcuffs and under hostile guard. Tranh paused ahead of him, drenched with sweat, as she propped against the trunk of a tree.

"Left Hayes and Brewer behind," Tranh said in her halting but improving English.

"No," Mick Hayes answered. "But hell, you did a good try at it."

Brewer came up swiftly behind Hayes, sweat drenching his hard-cut muscular form. "We're being followed."

Bolan nodded. He felt ready to vomit, exertion taking its toll on him, as well as on the other men. "Tranh, as soon as you have your wind..."

"I go now," Tranh answered, taking off like a gazelle through the undergrowth.

"Helicopters," Brewer said, looking up and around.

"Once we reach the riverbank, we'll be able to hide in the mud from their FLIR," Hayes mentioned.

Suddenly the bull roar of exploding tree trunks and shattering wood filled the air. The Executioner spun, slapping both hands into Hayes's chest, throwing him forward, leaping and following. Behind him, a deadly hail of devastation filled the universe, a wall of flying shreds of foliage and belching thunder shattering the tranquility of the jungle. A .50-caliber round strayed and smashed the ground between Bolan's feet as he hustled along, the explosive impact on the log he was leaping over sending him sprawling facefirst into another tree trunk.

Hayes brought up his AK and started to open fire on the helicopter when Bolan grabbed the barrel.

"Don't shoot!" The soldier hissed.

The ex-mercenary nodded sagely, then looked back at the wreckage of the helicopter's passing. Trees that had stood on either side of their path no longer were there. It was as if a giant foot had fallen from the sky and smashed everything flat, grinding it under a heel.

Bolan didn't want to think of Brewer, alone back there.

And most of all, Bolan didn't want to even contemplate Tranh being snuffed out.

Hayes grabbed Bolan and helped him to his feet, and the two warriors began charging along.

Again, the warning rotor slap of the helicopters thumped in the air and the crusading duo picked up the pace, racing along.

This time, explosions started hammering from the sky.

Bolan and Hayes split, and the Executioner listened as the ex-merc's body went sliding down the riverbank, hitting the water and going deep just before a 2.75-inch artillery rocket came sizzling out of the sky and hammered the ground thirty feet beside him. The concussive force lifted Bolan like a child's toy and sent him pinwheeling against a tree, hardwood smashing against his ribs and his head bouncing off the rough trunk. Dropping to his knees, the Executioner clawed to get up and saw that the Thai helicopter had zoomed past, and was swinging around for another run.

Behind him, the chattering of twin machine guns shredded along the riverbank, and Bolan felt the icy cold of loss as he wondered where Hayes was.

These were soldiers of the same side, sent to hunt and destroy him simply because he had killed someone protected by the law. No matter his pain over any losses, he couldn't bring himself to fire on the two helicopters, so he lunged deeper into the jungle, one foot plodding painfully in front of the other, each step sending agonizing spikes of pain through his rib cage. His dressings had been torn by the explosion and he was seeping fresh blood from his unclosed wounds, and from dozens of new tiny cuts and lacerations.

Pain enveloped the Executioner as he kept plowing along, his body sluicing through dense undergrowth at a relentless rate, cutting this way and that, making sure the thick bodies of tree trunks came between him and the sensitive FLIR lenses of the hunter-killer helicopters.

Machine-gun fire and artillery rockets flashed and thundered, hammering a brutal swath through the forest as both helicopters made yet another pass. But Bolan was outside their blast radius. He'd managed to elude them, and taking cover in the long, tall roots of a tree, using the hollow barely under the trunk to tuck him away, he'd disappeared from whatever sensors they had.

Like two hungry dragons, the helicopter gunships swooped and thundered, roaring and spitting their devastation intermittently, seeking the flesh of their last morsel of prey, until finally, after an eternity, they swung off lazily, bobbing on air currents as their rotors carried them away.

The Executioner pulled himself from under the thick roots, his body shaken, bloody and battered. A quick inspection revealed that he was missing his rifle, but he had the holsters for his Beretta and Desert Eagle. The Velcro pouches holding all but two reloads for each weapon were missing, as were most of his other supplies, torn away in the explosion and impact against a tree.

Dazed and stunned, Bolan pulled himself back to his feet and checked his balance and strength.

He could walk. He could move his limbs without agony, except for the deep scoring on his arm and shoulder and hip.

The Executioner was alive, alone, low on ammo and weapons. He was bleeding and out of medical supplies in enemy territory.

People he cared about were dead or missing, the victims of a faceless predator.

No...not faceless.

Mack Bolan, half-crushed and stumbling, had a face. A name. General Chang Chi Fu.

The bastard had won a skirmish against him, but judgment day was coming.

It was time for the San United Army to face the cleansing flame.

MAJOR KEVIN PETERS, Canadian army envoy to the UN, watched in disbelief as the two helicopter gunships swooped mercilessly out in the forest. He turned back to Colonel Trang Li, who watched with detached interest.

"That's a lot of firepower for a handful of people," Peters growled.

Though Peters was a mountain of a man, it was as if a child had been talking to Trang, who pulled a pipe from his breast pocket and simply pinched in some tobacco. "When you are dealing with terrorists and insurgents, it is best to act with swiftness and decisiveness."

"They had no weapons as far as I could tell," Peters replied.

"My gunners reported otherwise," Trang answered. "Now, if you will kindly forgive me, I will take my prisoners and be on my way."

"Prisoners?" Peters asked.

"Alvin Warren and the Lam woman. They have no legitimate reason for being in this camp. However, they will be interrogated and released once we have checked out their stories," Trang stated.

"All you have is circumstantial evidence."

"And we have circumstantial evidence that you were harboring suspected terrorists who have killed foreign and domestic nationals on Thai soil. If you persist in interfering with my investigation, we can always take a look into your personal affairs, Major Peters."

Peters, used to feeling out of place, growing up a football-linebacker-sized Haitian in Montreal, felt his skin heat underneath. No redness of embarrassment crossed his features. His skin was dark enough to hide the flush of blood that came from the hot fury building in him.

"Trang, this is United Nations territory. Warren is formerly with the UN," Peters stated.

Trang laughed and walked away, leaving Peters to fume.

Total dismissal, and with the two gunships hovering in the sky, depleted on ammo, but not so depleted that they couldn't kill twenty-five people easily in one rolling sweep, Peters couldn't reach out and snap the man's neck. So the big Canadian fumed.

The soldiers were prodding Warren and Lam into the side of the helicopter. Warren's eyes met Peters's.

The two of them had been friends since on a joint operation in Bosnia, working on an intelligence operation to support peacekeeping forces. Now, Peters watched as a good friend was getting carted off, perhaps even sold to General Chang, and couldn't lift a finger.

Not if he was to uphold his vow of keeping an eye on Sonya Getter, being her guardian angel while keeping an eye on the San United Army.

Kevin Peters took a deep breath and watched the helicopters lazily crawl into the sky, slowly swinging away toward the city of Nakhon Sawan.

Toward a fate unknown, but stinking of dread.

CHUCK BREWER WAS GLAD that he couldn't feel his right arm. Not anymore. But then, the arm was nowhere around, lost somewhere after being cleanly shorn off by a single .50-caliber slug that struck him in the elbow.

All he physically wanted to do was lie down and bleed to death, let it all end. He didn't care anymore. He was floating beyond pain, and his mind was wandering, but he remembered the weight against his shoulder now. He glanced over and saw the bearded jaw resting against a blood-slicked shirt. Above the bushy beard and mustache, Mick Hayes's face was a bloody mask, his forehead split open.

That's right, Brewer thought, get Hayes to some medical attention, save the life of a man who was stand-up.

Brewer's legs were rubber as he continued hauling the 260-pound mass of Hayes through the jungle, back toward the UNICEF camp, knowing full well that he might be walking into a trap.

Hayes started to slip out of his grasp. It was impossible to hold on to the big man with only one hand.

But somehow, the corded muscles of Brewer's left arm grabbed Hayes's belt and hauled him back up, yanking him against his body.

"Dammit, Mick, I'm trying to save your life. At least learn to walk," Brewer growled, stumbling along.

They managed another several minutes—or was it hours?—of walking before Brewer's blood-slicked grip broke on Hayes's belt, and the big man tumbled to the ground.

Brewer stumbled to his knees and remaining hand, coughing and vomiting.

It hurt, but he had a life to save, even if he was bleeding to death.

He wasn't about to fail.

He'd run from hellholes before, but he'd never failed at doing what he wanted to do.

A shadow loomed across his vision, and Brewer reared back, fist cocking.

"Goddamn, you do look a mess," Major Kevin Peters said before darkness descended upon the wounded merc.

23

The Executioner hurt, but it was nothing he'd never felt before. His limbs moved, painfully, but none of their motion was limited. He could walk, and most of the blood that was in his mouth was from a painful deep bite on the inside of his cheek. It was healing, puffy, and starting to taste tangy, a sure sign he needed antibiotics. His balance was sure again, and when he closed his eyes, there was no flash, no starring.

When he coughed, it was because of a trickle of blood from his broken nose that was sliding down the back of his throat. Bolan had reset the nose, and it was excruciating, but by far, it was the sharpest sting.

Which didn't say much when you had hundreds of such stings in a matter of minutes.

No, Mack Bolan was no Superman.

But he knew that having brought along too many people had exposed them to unnecessary danger. From here on out, the Executioner had to go to war alone against the scum who were trading in child slavery and prostitution.

He hurt with every step, inside and out.

What had the others lost?

Was Jack dead after all this time?

No matter how he tried to dismiss the idea, he couldn't. The thoughts of his compatriots, dead, burst apart by a government that had asked for his very help in this crusade, filled his stomach with the single deepest wound of all, a wicked shot to his conscience that would either kill him with grief or kill him as he drove deeper and harder against his enemy Chang.

No more, the Executioner decided. If the war was getting this costly, it was time to start fighting this battle the way he fought when it was every man's hand against him, when there was only a hint of help, if any.

Bolan knew full well where he had to go, and according to his sense of direction, which was unaffected, he was on his way. By the position of the sun in the sky, he reckoned he was only an hour away from where he needed to be, and there would be a half hour left of daylight by the time he got there.

Perfect.

The Executioner didn't want to hit an armed enemy camp in full light. Getting back to the plantation where he had been the night before, he would take a two-and-a-half hour rest. That would help him to refresh his strength, and give him time to watch, from a distance, just how well Chang was working on reorganizing the place.

Keep a torch burning for me, Chang. Your Executioner is coming.

TRANH SPIT OUT a mouthful of the dank river, and looked up the shore. The air strike had driven her along faster than she'd ever run before, and suddenly she was in midair, feet bicycling over empty space before hitting water. She knew almost instinctively that if she wasn't struck by shrapnel or stray rounds on the way down, she had it made.

But there was Mack to worry about.

"Mack!" Tranh called. Her voice sounded weak, and she cleared her throat of river gunk and spit once more. The taste of that swill in her mouth made her want to bend over and empty her lungs and stomach, but she held her breakfast.

Mack might have been hurt.

No, if she didn't see him, he might be dead.

Tranh looked up and saw that there was no grass or other foliage on the steep slope to the river, which made climbing up the muddy slope, digging in with a twisted ankle, difficult. It took her all of five minutes to climb fifteen feet of blasted, mud-slicked slope, plenty of time for an otherwise treatable wound to turn into a lethal bleed-out.

She clambered, flat onto her gut, and looked around.

"Mack?"

Shapes moved, like ghosts in the high grass, then a moment of temporary darkness.

The girl remembered coming to and recovering, hearing the helicopters leaving.

Did they leave enemy troops behind?

She felt around, and all she had was a knife. Her hand slid to it, then she saw the big black Canadian, Kevin Peters, carrying Chuck Brewer's limp form as if it were a child. Tranh also saw Hayes being walked along, and lowered the blade, staggering along, making an effort to follow.

Peters turned and spotted her, making his way to her side. He sized her up. Tranh imagined what she looked like, drenched in mud, and one eye swollen shut with what she knew would be one hell of a black eye for the next few days. "You're okay?"

Tranh nodded. "Almost. I fell in river."

Peters couldn't keep his laugh of relief quiet.

Tranh began to curse a blue streak in Thai, but the blue-helmeted UN security men swarmed over her before she could even think of taking any kind of hiding place. They immediately broke out what little medical supplies they had with them, and began tending to the girl's cuts and contusions.

Luck or happenstance allowed for Tranh to stumble into medical assistance. Peters watched over her by her side, but she kept looking around.

No Bolan.

"Have you seen Belasko?" she whispered when she was sure only Peters would hear.

Peters shook his head. "I went looking, but there are no bodies."

"Then he made it." Tranh sighed with relief.

Peters managed his own weak smile. "He should be back soon, no?"

Tranh's face paled, and she spun, looking around the tree line. No. He wouldn't stop. He'd continue fighting all by himself. Without any hint of aid, not even realizing that people were left behind in trouble.

"I must go to him. He no stop."

Peters reached for her, but under Brewer's weight, his leg nearly gave out. The other UN security men spun and tried to stop her, but they tangled in a massive heap with Peters topping it like a gigantic ebony cherry.

The young Thai girl was gone, bounding into the woods like some elf, disappearing amid the forest.

Peters lowered his head and groaned.

So much for getting this group back together.

SONYA GETTER DIDN'T EXPECT, when she woke up in the morning, that she'd have to be supervising dealing with an amputee and a major head trauma.

Getter shook her head and silently cursed Alvin Warren, then realized that he was missing.

Not missing.

He was taken away at gunpoint by a man who had the heartlessness to sweep a jungle, seemingly with all the guns in Thailand. The thunderstorm that Colonel Trang had unleashed was horrific and merciless, and that there were survivors, however tattered and ragged, was a miracle.

Even Brewer would live.

Blood transfusions would help him, but he'd lost his arm right at the elbow.

Broken ribs from falling across a tree also plagued Brewer, and Mick Hayes.

One entire side of his scalp and face were hamburger now. There wasn't even a shell of an ear left over. Not much to reconstruct, and she bit her lower lip.

"Why did they do this?" she asked.

Peters rested his big hand on her shoulder. "They did it because there's some bad motherfuckers out there that need the stopping only they can provide."

"And this is why the girl and the other guy went for a walk in the forest?"

"Hayes said that she was going to try and continue the mission and find Belasko," Peters said with a shrug. "But the mission bears some weight."

"I don't see why. There's no national interest...."

"It's human interest. Why are you here?"

Getter looked down. "I'm not killing people, or getting killed."

"You've been threatened. That was why Alvin came for you the first time, and that's why he asked me to look out for you," Peters told her.

Getter looked up, feeling as if she were punched in the gut.

"You knew Alvin?"

"We're both spooks. But we're spooks who still have a soul."

"He sent you to protect me."

"Alvin knows that Chang looks at your camp as just an impediment. You're taking away good child labor from him. We started watching his ass because he was becoming a dangerous political force, dealing heroin and all that. Then, it suddenly turns out he's whoring kids out...and we both decided that you needed protection. Major protection."

"And so Alvin's going to be executed."

"You don't know that."

"I do know that," Getter said. "I have this feeling. He's going to be handed over and killed."

Peters grimaced. "Sonya, I'm going to make sure that doesn't happen."

Getter looked up, sadness in her eyes. "How?"

"My American connection said he was going to arrange some help," Peters said. "I just hope it's enough."

"Then I'll take care of things here."

Peters gave her shoulder a squeeze. "I'll get him back for you. But only if you promise to give him another chance."

"You do that, and I'll give the whole world a second chance."

24

Mack Bolan watched the plantation for three hours, and he assessed the situation while his body's aches slowly faded and strength came back to his limbs. Squeezing leaves for moisture, he gulped down water to replenish his body, to replace the fluids lost from sweat and blood. He'd also packed his few lacerations with mud or taped them over with a roll of duct tape that somehow managed not to be torn from his assault vest. The mud would plug the wounds, not the most sanitary choice, but it was better than bleeding out.

He'd even managed, on the walk toward the plantation, to use his Beretta 93-R to snag a spider monkey, which he skinned with his Applegate-Fairbairn knife and ate raw. He was starved, and he was hurting, and food was important. Even without the benefit of a nice grill and dining utensils, food was food. Raw meat was still protein and replacements for the blood he lost and the energy he'd expended. It wasn't a perfect solution, and he knew there was the possibility of simian-borne diseases that could threaten his health later on, but without the fresh meat, he'd be a corpse.

Strengthened, nourished and his eyes having adjusted to the darkness, Bolan's pain grew more distant with each passing moment, his resolve as iron as ever.

He had the Desert Eagle, which would only be his last resort, as the muzzle-blast would alert every soldier for miles. The big .44 Magnum pistol was tucked snugly into his hip holster, and would only come out when the need for silence was over.

Instead, the head weapon on this particular mission was going to be, by default, the suppressed Beretta 93-R. The weapon was set to single shot, which was quieter than the burst-fire mode that increased its versatility in the Executioner's arsenal. Even that particular weapon wasn't going to be intended for anything more than self-protection.

This penetration wasn't for body count, not even to spread death and destruction.

Bolan was here for a single man, someone whom he could use as leverage against Chang. He needed harder information, and he needed a wedge in the door. Whoever would be left in charge of reconstructing the plantation would possibly give him that edge.

Keeping his body low, the Executioner moved almost on all fours, keeping himself no higher than the tallest burned stalks among the rows of burned opium plants. The ruts that had been worn by the feet of countless youthful opium pickers provided the Executioner not only with a hiding place, but with further burning rage that seethed in him.

A burning rage that would stoke the cleansing flame that would wash the San United Army from the face of the earth.

The crunch of scorched plants alerted the soldier to the presence of a patrolling guard and he slowed to a slothlike stillness, not looking directly at the figure that stood in the dark, carrying his AK-47 at waist level, eyes scanning the darkness. In the lack of light, Bolan had a clearer image of the guard than the guard would have of him simply due to anatomy. The peripheral portions of the human eye were more capable of processing colorless imagery, such as would be evident in low light, while direct color vision wouldn't register an indecipherable shape in the darkness, especially if it was pressed to the ground and didn't look humanlike.

The Executioner was a phantom, and he held his ground. Bolan began his career in similar spots like this, as a Special Forces sniper scout specialist who had the uncanny ability to disappear, even three feet away from an enemy.

The guard was six inches from Bolan's prostrate form, looking around, puffing deeply on a pungent cigarette, his eyes scanning far when he should have been looking toward his feet. But it was for the best. Had he looked down, the Executioner would have had to put down another enemy. He stayed still as death, just another patch of ground underfoot. The SUA guard turned and began pacing back toward the mansion.

Bolan counted the long, tortuous moments. Subjectively it felt as if the whole night had been wasted. But by the luminous dial of his watch, only ten minutes had passed. The stress of waiting, the stress of being so close to a lethal opponent, had threatened to drain whatever excess strength he'd acquired in the wait to make this penetration.

Slithering along, quiet as a snake, with equal grace and just as much of a profile, Bolan took a winding course through the ruined crop, his entire body caked with dirt, his face grimed with ashes from scorched opium plants. The soldier didn't mind. Every bit of mud added to his camouflage here in the field. And by sliding through the mud, he was making sure that nobody would see his bulk crawling along the ground. His muscles ached, and his patience was thinning, but he knew that if he got to the edge of the field, he'd have a way to get into the main house.

The big man paused and made sure his holsters were secure. The Beretta dug into his ribs with each forward push along as its 20-round extended magazine pushed against the ground. He dumped the magazine and fingered the feed well, and brushed off the clip's shell. Nothing got up into the action, so he fed a 15-round magazine into place and rolled onto his chest. The Desert Eagle, in its quick-draw leather, was plugged with mud. Bolan cursed, but knew that he wouldn't need the big .44 pistol, and he couldn't keep it from getting fouled with crud until then.

His weapon options were limited, at least until he dropped a gunman and grabbed a rifle.

Provided things went that far.

Bolan reached the edge of the field, and just inches outside the spill of light from the lamps around the old mansion and the porch lights on the front he observed the building and its guard force.

Not too many men, about thirty. Bolan had penetrated harder spots, and these guards, while on edge, had grown tired and perhaps a little complacent.

Maybe they heard about his adventures with a couple of hostile gunships.

The Executioner scanned the building. Too many lights made it hard to sneak up on from the front.

It took Bolan forty-five minutes, crawling outside the sphere of light, keeping low so he wasn't silhouetted to a guard in the field, to get around to the side. The lot there was only seventy-five feet to the nearest part of the forest, protected by a ten foot chain-link fence topped with barbed wire with a gate, and a brick wall of similar height, but with no obvious wire above it. Bolan couldn't see the top, but he knew full well that if there wasn't wire, that meant broken glass or nails had been mortared to the top of the wall to provide anyone seeking an easy exit a set of painful lacerations. Had the Executioner a pack or a blanket, he might have made an effort to go over, but he didn't need more injuries to nickel-and-dime him to exhaustion, making him an easy target.

Against the wall, steeped in shadow, however, Bolan was free to move in a half crouch, himself a shadow among shadows as he slid along the back wall until he reached a point where both the wall and the grounds dropped off. He paused, kneeling against thick cinder block, looking out over a back lawn and garden with a hedgerow maze, as well as a patio built large enough to hold a dinner party for two hundred people. A fountain lay stagnant where once it would have been the centerpiece of a gleaming column of lights. There wasn't any light out among the grass, and only a couple of spotlights among the back wall, illuminating a thirty-foot area of raised concrete steps and ornate railings. Six men were on roving patrol, and Bolan looked along the back for a possible route past them.

Checking around, Bolan spotted a heavy-trunked tree, its bark covered in thick and heavy knots, easy to grab on to or step on to climb up. One branch reached over the wall, and was a tempting option, but there was the possibility that he'd be spotted coming in over the wall.

He still made the climb and eased out onto the branch, which was as thick as his waist, and over to the stone wall—which he noted was topped in broken glass. Bolan scooted along, checking the side of the mansion.

No guards.

Poor lighting.

The ground also looked soft and full of grass. He wasn't quite certain in the half darkness.

Bolan kept moving, but slid around the branch, his fingertips holding him up as the soles of his boots balanced on the bare edges of the top of the wall. Balanced precariously, waiting until one guard turned and headed back to patrol the light, he pushed himself forward, bending his knees to absorb the impact of his drop.

As it was, both his knees felt as if they'd been smacked with a hammer, and his foot turned sideways in the soft wet earth. It took all of the Executioner's strength and will not to cry out in pain, and to dive toward the front of the mansion, so as to keep out of sight of the guard force in the back. Flat on his side, he winced at the tenderness of his left ankle and felt it straining and swelling against the inside of his boot.

Pain was no stranger to Bolan, however. And the swelling wasn't rising that quickly. It was a minor ache, and he got to both feet, no sudden jolts of agony driving him to his knees. He hobbled toward the window, gaining more strength under the hyperextended ankle as he walked on it.

Pressing against the windowsill, he looked both ways, then slid his fingers along the woodwork, feeling for any electronics. Nothing met his touch, and Bolan tested the window itself.

It was locked.

No problem, Bolan thought, sliding his roll of duct tape out and carefully, silently pulling off foot-long strips and slicing them with his pocketknife. He created a giant eight-legged asterisk of dull silver tape on the windowpane, then pulled the Desert Eagle, using its weight as a hammer to pop out the darkened window. Getting the top half free, Bolan reached in, having wrapped his hand in more tape to protect from cutting broken glass, and pulled it out, tapping more and more until he had more than enough room to slide his arm in and feel along not only for the latch, but any more alarm wires that would be hooked up inside.

No alarm wires. He flipped the locking latch and slid the window up, pushing through the window and sliding inside. The windowsill was streaked black with soot—there was no way to avoid them knowing he'd entered this way—but Bolan was in, and he slid the window down again.

A small light clicked on and Bolan whirled, his hand going for the Beretta in its shoulder holster, then froze, seeing the unblinking eye of a 9 mm Browning facing him.

Han Quo looked the Executioner in his eyes. "I've been waiting for you, Mr. Belasko."

The Executioner was caught, dead to rights.

JACK GRIMALDI WAS impressed with the big Canadian as he went about setting up the UNICEF camp for his absence. Patrol perimeters were set up, and a few nasty surprises were being left in the event of Chang Chi Fu's attempt at making a run on his former slaves. He was exhausted from running a motor launch's engines to near burnout, sliding the sleek boat into dock and getting a taxi to Don Muang Airport, where Stony Man Farm had arranged for Dragon Slayer to be delivered the day after they touched down with the Learjet. Charlie Mott had taken the jet back home after supervising the delivery of the deadly sky beast.

"Glad you made it back, Ricardi," Major Kevin Peters said, looking the pilot up and down. "We're not sure Belasko's alive."

Grimaldi grinned. "You don't know Belasko like I do."

"He's survived worse than a couple gunships ripping apart an entire jungle?" Peters asked.

Grimaldi nodded. "I'd say it was getting to be a bad habit with him, but even he doesn't like it."

Peters shrugged. "My men will have the camp sewn up tight, so I'm free and ready to contribute to whatever effort needed to not only get your man back, but my friend."

"I could use the help," Grimaldi said, putting out his hand. It disappeared in the massive Canadian's dark paw, but the grip was gentle, nontesting.

"Colonel Trang has a military base about forty klicks to the south of here, and he's very protective of his airspace. I'm not certain about the air power, but there are at least two gunships and two transport ships that have machine guns on pintle mounts," Peters said.

"Hopefully we can do the kind of search we need without giving any reason for them to launch their aircraft," Grimaldi replied.

"Well, you're going to work on the ground?" Peters asked.

Grimaldi smiled and shook his head, pointing to the aircraft that he'd rode in on. At first, Peters had assumed that it was a variant on the Black Hawk helicopter, but on closer inspection he noted many differences. It was obvious some form of wing mounts had been removed from the sides of the reptilian aircraft, and its bulbous nose suggested a suite of sensors the equal of any surveillance craft Peters had seen in the Canadian armed forces. The undercarriage also seemed buckled, and he thought he noticed the bulge of a hatch underneath.

"We can take a quiet look-see right now," Grimaldi said, moving toward the helicopter.

"Even though it's dark, Ricardi, they're still going to hear the rotor slap of that big bird. Helicopters aren't exactly built for stealth," Peters commented.

"This one is," Grimaldi answered, climbing into the pilot's seat.

Peters stuffed himself into the copilot's bucket, his long legs stretching out as he snuggled down. Grimaldi made a mental note of thanks that the Canadian was only an inch or two taller than Mack Bolan, for whom the copilot's seat had been built. Though thicker in the hips than the big guy, he fit tightly, but not uncomfortably so. "You have speakers that broadcast the sound of the rotor slap at right angles to the original sound."

Grimaldi nodded. "I take it you've heard of the technology."

Peters nodded. "Here and there."

"Just so we know where we're both coming from," the ace pilot answered.

Dragon Slayer, Stony Man's premier combat aircraft, rose like a great floating dragon into the sky, crawling lazily along before finding its direction, tilting forward and speeding off at well over 100 miles per hour, a leisurely pace for the night.

Grimaldi slipped down the night-vision device on his helmet and motioned for Peters to do likewise. The world went from pitch-black to crystal clear green, much better than the fuzzy imagery that he was used to when the first NVDs for helicopter pilots were available. The Stony Man pilot shut down the external and internal lights, switching all the control dials so that they could only be viewed by someone wearing night vision. Peters gave an appreciative whistle and Dragon Slayer throttled up even faster, going a full 180 miles per hour, swooping low over the treetops, occasionally slaloming sideways to avoid the tops of those taller than the usual forest canopy.

Within eight minutes, Grimaldi had brought Dragon Slayer from full speed to a mere crawl of thirty miles per hour, switching on the stealth baffles and gaining an altitude of 1200 feet, swinging around in a lazy circle around Trang's base. Peters, who until now had been enjoying the ride, was now all business, quickly taking in the camp.

"There's a Little Bird on the deck getting ready to take off," Peters said.

Grimaldi swung Dragon Slayer around, spotting, amid a blossom of light, the bulblike form of an OH-6 Bell helicopter. The Little Bird had gone through several designs since its inception in the sixties, with avionics and engine upgrades, while the same general shape, three-bladed rotor and teardrop hull remained the same. It was a popular light helicopter, and was capable of holding six to eight people, depending on how tightly packed the passengers needed to be kept. It was also relatively slow for a helicopter. Depending on the model, it would do 130 to 160 miles per hour, tops.

"You can click the third button from the front on your helmet to activate the zoom on your NVDs," Grimaldi mentioned.

"I don't need zoom to recognize Alvin," Peters stated. Grimaldi could tell by the ashenness in his voice that the two Americans who had been helping the Executioner were being loaded aboard the Little Bird. "Two guards, pilot and copilot."

"Packing it tight," Grimaldi said.

"All the better to hold on to a prisoner," Peters grunted. "We can keep up with that thing...."

"Oh, yes," Grimaldi answered. "We'll hang back two miles and let them lead us on."

Peters chewed visibly, even in the darkness, on his lip.

"Don't worry, big guy," Grimaldi said. "We'll be able to lend a hand."

Peters nodded. "You've got weapons on this crate?"

"Enough to end a war," the Stony Man pilot said.

"Good," Peters growled. "Because I intend to do some ending tonight."

25

Mack Bolan had been in this position a thousand times before. Each time, he knew the answer to survival was keeping still and calm, biding his time until the man who had his gun on him grew careless or could be convinced, somehow, that he wasn't a threat.

But standing before the right-hand man of the San United Army, with a cocked 9 mm pistol aimed at his stomach, his own hands empty of weapons, the Executioner knew that not every throw of the dice would come up in his favor. Bolan relaxed, hoping Han Quo would follow suit.

As if reclining in a chair, legs crossed, taking a sip from a tumbler wasn't relaxed enough.

"Care for a sip, Belasko?" Han asked.

"No, thanks, I'm driving."

Han grinned and set down the tumbler and the Browning. "Sit down."

Bolan blinked in surprise.

"I think you might have had some intelligence that my name is Han Quo. A mercenary who a decade ago had been part of a Myanmar death squad," Han said. "Sure you're not interested in a drink?"

"Not on duty," Bolan answered. "Who are you really?"

"Li Quo," the man answered. "Thai security services. I know, it's a huge mess, everybody's spying on everyone."

"Your infiltration seems pretty good," Bolan said, looking around the mansion.

"It's shit duty, Belasko. Chang is sick and tired of me being the almost bumbling fool," Li answered. "He left me here knowing that maybe I'd be good enough bait for you."

"The enemy of my enemy isn't necessarily my friend," Bolan returned.

"No, and I don't blame you. If I kill you, my cover suddenly becomes rock solid. And I get a lot richer," Li stated. "One small problem with that, though."

"You can't sleep at night with the taste of Chang's ass in your mouth," Bolan said.

"You catch on quick," Li said. "Heroin, I could almost live with. Child prostitution?"

Bolan nodded, understanding.

"You speak English pretty well," the Executioner noted.

"University of Seattle," Li said. He chuckled. "I was there for the grunge movement. Speaking of which, you look a little grungy."

Bolan shrugged. "I've been to Seattle, too."

"You look like someone who gets around," Li stated. "What makes you go one-on-one, looking like you got run over by a stampede, after Chang? You're outnumbered."

"I have a job to do. Just like you do."

"I don't think this job's lasting much longer, and to tell you the truth, I'm glad of it. I'm sick of this whole damn mess," Li spit. "Chang's getting ready to swat you like the annoying bug you are. And he pretty much has left you to swat me."

"I wasn't here for that. I was here to put pressure on you to help me nail Chang," Bolan admitted.

Li nodded. "I wasn't worried so much about you as about Chang. Though I was hoping that the prime minister might have told you about me."

"No, he didn't, but thanks for the vote of confidence."

Li shrugged.

"Any idea if Chang intends to kill you if I don't show up?" Bolan asked.

Li smirked and patted the Browning. "I was hoping that there were no such orders, but it's closing on midnight."

"A deadline," Bolan noted.

Li nodded.

"Then let me clean up my other pistol. Got anything heavier than the Browning?"

"Chang wouldn't let me have anything," Li said.

Bolan grimaced.

"But I know that he keeps some heavier artillery in an upstairs closet," Li said.

Bolan nodded and began fieldstripping the Desert Eagle. As soon as he was satisfied that the big hand cannon would operate, he reassembled and reloaded the cannon. "Lead the way. I'll be right behind you."

"And if we run into guards?" Li asked.

The Executioner pointed to the 93-R's suppressor.

"I can dig it," Li answered. "C'mon."

The two men left the office, ready for anything.

Once more, the doomsday numbers were tumbling.

But for now, Bolan had the advantage of surprise, and a little extra help.

ALVIN WARREN WOULD have loved to rest his head like Michelle Lam was, her lithe body curled against his. She lifted her head, and those big dark, almond eyes regarded him with a hint of doubt and confusion. They didn't speak, Warren having told her that any speech would provoke a violent attack from the guards, but he fully understood her discomfort and fear.

To tell the truth, Warren felt as if he were packing his shorts himself. Pressed to his side, a Beretta double-action pistol was cocked and he didn't care for that. As limber and agile as the OH-6 Little Bird they rode in was, it wasn't a smooth ride, and at every jostle of air currents, he expected the explosion of the Beretta, plunging a 9 mm round deep into his belly, tearing at organs that would leave him slowly dying.

Worse than that, his body would be no impediment if the Beretta was loaded with hardball. The bullet would slice through his body and punch into the helpless Lam.

He tensed, willing the gun not to go off, making sure not to make eye contact with the San United Army thug who was holding him at gunpoint. He gave Lam's hand a squeeze, and she squeezed his hand back. Just a little strength, a unity that made this trip more than a little bearable.

If death decided to take him now, he wouldn't feel that bad. Especially lately, he had fought the good fight, strove against injustice. To not see the fall of the San United Army would leave him somewhat empty, but Warren believed totally in an afterlife, and he hoped to see the downfall of the men who would have him killed. He just wished that an innocent woman, a social worker whose only crime was caring enough to fight against injustice in Thailand, wouldn't die with him.

Death would come, and he couldn't fight back, simply because it would be futile to fight. To start a brawl in the tiny little torpedo that sliced the sky would be to toss it upside down. The pilot's controls were too far away to reach, and he wouldn't be able to fight off both pilots for control of the craft, especially with guards at his back. Warren grimaced and kept considering his options.

To fight on the ground would give him some hope.

But still, they'd chop him down at the knees, and he'd probably be dropped off in the middle of a death squad.

Lam sighed and squeezed his hand again. She was strong, but the hopelessness of the situation was just looming too heavily on them. Something would snap, and it would have to be the will of the two prisoners. Warren growled and looked at the guard.

"Put that gun away," he snapped in Thai.

The butt of the gun came flashing up and smashed Warren across his face, splitting his upper lip and crushing his nose with one blow. Blood flowed, but Warren, even though his hands were free, didn't dare strike back. Not when the guards would be able to execute the two of them.

"Don't speak," the guard said. He dropped the hammer of the Beretta with his thumb, then holstered the piece.

Warren held his split and gushing upper lip, feeling his teeth through the huge gash, then felt his hand go sticky with his own gore. He looked at Lam, who went from frightened to angry.

Good, he thought.

Anger was what would keep their spirits up.

They would survive. They wouldn't give up.

Warren fanned the fury in his heart, letting it well up and burn away the chilling fear deep in his chest.

Survival wasn't an option.

It was a mandate.

LI QUO WAS FRIGHTENED, his heart hammering, but he kept his emotions under control. Fear, he'd learned, was good. Panic was bad. Fear kept his mind open that he was in trouble, and it acted upon his body to increase metabolism, strength, blood flow. All of which helped him avoid getting hurt or avoid going into shock when he did get hurt. One time, Li had been knifed in a fight, but he was in such a state of fight or flight that he hadn't felt the fourteen-stitch wound until he had triumphed over his opponent.

This was the same case now. He was sure that if he got shot, only adrenaline would bleed out.

Belasko was hot on his heels as they moved to the cache of weapons he'd assembled. Throwing open the door to the bedroom he'd acquired, he rushed right to the closet. Li moved the lone jacket and couple changes of clothes aside on the rod and pulled at the duffel bag he'd stuffed with weapons.

"It's not much," Li said, taking the bag and dumping the contents onto his bed.

Bolan picked through the weapons. A rusted SKS carbine with a simple pipe as an optical sight was present. The pipe had two pieces of baling wire soldered to the front, providing a crude metallic crosshair. He shouldered the weapon, and nodded. "Works for me."

"Not an ideal tool," Li answered.

Bolan picked up a second of the four weapons on the bed, an old Thompson 1918 submachine gun. He checked it over. "No tools are ideal. I've just learned to make do with what I have. Besides, the SKS and Tommy might be older than we are, but they were built at a time when weapons were meant to keep working for years. Not a lot of wear and tear on this one."

Li nodded and took up one of the two Vietnam-era M-16 rifles he had. "You think we'll have a chance?"

"We're going to need to get to some transportation, and then you're going to show me how to get to Chang," Bolan said, slipping the other M-16 into the duffel. "Take the ammo for this M-16. Just in case."

Li nodded. "Okay, we're prepped, now what?"

"I'm going to provide a distraction. You get the wheels," the soldier said, slinging the Thompson and feeding a stripper clip into the SKS.

Li swallowed. "All right."

"Don't shoot anybody and keep the M-16 slung, even when I start shooting. Make them think you're still on their side. I'll do my best to keep them from thinking too hard."

Li nodded and felt his heartbeat increase. Dizziness assaulted his senses, and he had to grip the bed, swooning a moment.

"Let it pass," Belasko said reassuringly. "I need you together, and I need you alive."

Li nodded, gritting his teeth and intentionally hyperventilating himself until his pulse subsided. He was floating on an oxygen-adrenaline high, and guessed that his pupils were dilated. "Thanks."

"Good. Remember, adrenaline is your friend now," Bolan told him.

"Adrenaline, and a lot of flying lead," Li mentioned.

Bolan grinned. "That's always been my feeling."

The warriors clasped hands, then turned, moving on to their battle stations.

JACK GRIMALDI KEPT in the shadow of the Little Bird, Dragon Slayer knifing through the night skies, straining to keep up and still keep back and out of sight. Beside him, Major Kevin Peters reached into his combat pack and drew the second-biggest stainless-steel hogleg the little Italian ace ever saw.

"What is that?" Grimaldi asked, returning his attention to the teardrop-shaped helicopter.

"Arcadia Machine and Tool Automag IV," Peters said. "In direct lineage to the original Automag, designed by Harry Sanford. Holds eight rounds of .45 Winchester Magnum."

"Doesn't seem like a Canadian military pistol," Grimaldi said, sideslipping Dragon Slayer so that he could be on the outside of the other copter's upcoming turn. It was swooping low and quick into a valley, and Grimaldi was taking Dragon Slayer along at treetop level at their blind spot.

"No, but then again, I'm in a country where we have wild water buffaloes and tigers," Peters said.

"Uh-huh," Grimaldi returned. "Doesn't hurt that your paws happen to be too big to hold a normal-sized 9 mm pistol."

"That, too," Peters answered. He slipped a magazine of seven big 230-grain hollowpoint hunting loads into the well of the hand cannon. "Where the hell are those idiots going?"

"They're checking to see if someone's following them," Grimaldi answered. "Evasion techniques."

"Damn, so they're on to us," Peters growled.

Grimaldi's face set sternly, lit by the luminous dials of the controls. "Not necessarily. They might just be moving quick to avoid being followed by anyone they pick up. If they spotted us, they'd really be pulling the hard Gs to try and avoid us."

"And can this bird keep up with them?" Peters asked.

Grimaldi bit his tongue, sweeping Dragon Slayer around on the OH-6 helicopter's tail, keeping them exactly one mile distant, always within sight of the remarkable gunship's scanners.

"I'll take that as a maybe," Peters said. He settled back into the shotgun seat as the helicopters continued their shadow dance amid the midnight skies over Thailand.

26

The Executioner learned long ago that wars weren't won with shiny, high- technology silicone and plastic toys. It was the man, the flesh and blood. Not even that; it wasn't the raw strength but the intelligence and endurance, which weren't merely contained by corded muscle and rugged, powerful limbs.

Sure, the Executioner had availed himself of the latest computer technology and communications as an outlaw during the Mafia wars. As Colonel John Phoenix, he had an entire high-tech base of operations with access to everything from the latest precision-tuned machine pistols to the SR-71 Blackbird. More than once, when operating with Phoenix Force, he'd used nuclear warheads to annihilate a foe. He'd even ridden into space.

But here was where the wars were won. Not even in the trigger pull of the rifle with two crossed wires intersecting the body of a wandering San United Army guard in the floodlit perimeter of the mansion.

It was in the mind. The ability to endure while you sapped your enemy's endurance and will.

Bolan had endured wars with the Mafia and the KGB. The

SUA was impressive, yeah, a cancerous octopus that had grown in wealth to encompass an entire nation in suffering of child abuse and heroin addiction, but every enemy could be brought down. This was business as usual for Mack Bolan.

The Executioner had duct-taped a length of PVC pipe torn from a washroom fixture around the muzzle of the SKS carbine to act as a flash suppressor. The carbine wasn't a long-range precision killer. It was chambered for a middle-powered 7.62 mm ComBlock cartridge that had 300 to 400 meters tops in terms of instant-killing power. But for the 200 meters that Bolan could see in the darkness, it wasn't only more than enough, it was perfect.

It was perfect because it was all a trained soldier had on hand.

Easing out onto the balcony of the mansion, he slipped behind a tall, slender Thai gunman manning a floodlight.

Nobody expected an intruder this close to the mansion, and the one scuffing footstep brought a grumbling acknowledgment in Thai that Bolan was late in bringing him his coffee.

The Executioner moved forward in a sudden flash, his big, callused hand clamping over the mouth of the SUA guard and wrenching his head back. The Applegate-Fairbairn folding knife was in his other hand, slicing deep over the man's hip, carving through kidney and causing lethal renal shock that paralyzed the Thai. With a savage slash, Bolan brought the knife forward, then wrenched harder back on the man's neck, listening to tendons pop, then plunged the spear point of the blade into the side of the gunner's throat. He whipped his blade savagely forward, severing the guard's carotid artery. The body went lifeless in his arms, and Bolan lowered him gingerly to the ground.

A quick search added a new-looking M-16 and another Browning Hi-Power to his growing arsenal, which the Executioner stuffed in the duffel bag provided by Li. He slid the Thompson and its spare magazines out of the bag and tapped the first magazine firmly into place.

The SKS went to Bolan's shoulder, and he turned to the mirroring balcony where the shadowed form of another guard was squinting to see what the hell had happened to the other floodlight.

Bolan lined up the crossed wires and milked the trigger, feeling the recoil of the rifle against his shoulder and watching a spray of blood fan out from the SUA light man. Swiveling as the gunners below were starting to react, he took advantage of the two-second pause as the guards were trying to figure out where that first shot had come from, and if it was an attack. Bolan pumped out six more rounds, each shot a hit on a Thai terrorist, steel-cored bullets smashing flesh and bone.

The screams of the wounded cut through the night as wild gunfire sprayed the mansion wildly. Nobody had directly noticed the Executioner as of yet, and he dropped down, letting the SKS clatter to the ground as bullets chewed the walls above his head and smashed glass. The floodlight exploded in a clatter of raining glass, and instants later, the other floodlight was gone, as well. A lull occurred in the shooting, and there were calls out to check and see who was okay and who was dead. Injured men sobbed and begged for help, and in the silver moonlight, Bolan noticed the gunners gathering in a tight group around the wounded.

The .45 caliber Thompson in the Executioner's fists taught the SUA soldiers the folly of bunching up when an enemy had the high ground. Cutting loose at 600 rounds per minute, 230-grain thunderbolts rained down on the shadowy forms below. Three seconds of sustained gunfire ripped and tore into flesh, once more sending men diving, tumbling or just collapsing to the ground as they were chewed to lifeless meat by the merciless skull-busting payload of the tommy gun. Flickers of gunfire flashed in the darkness and Bolan rolled sideways, moving to the other side of the floodlight. It wasn't that far a move, but it was away from the fireball of devastation that had marked his position and signaled the deaths of their fellow gunmen.

Feeding in a fresh magazine of .45-caliber hardball, the Executioner swung the WWII veteran Thompson over the rail of the balcony at the forest of muzzle-flashes that were still blasting at where he had been a moment ago. He took the next magazine more conservatively, pounding out short 3- and 4-round bursts that sought out flesh and destroyed it with merciless efficiency before ducking back from the railing. Gunfire wildly burned the entire balcony now, and was chewing through the stonework of the rail, but the Executioner spared a moment to grab up his spare gear and ducked into the bedroom leading off the balcony.

As he barreled into the room, the door was kicked in by a pair of grim-faced Thai gunmen who were filling the door and framing themselves perfectly to be cut down. Bolan fired the Thompson from the hip, one-handed, the recoil murderous on his forearm. But on the other end, it was positively lethal as the shredding discharge of the big blaster sent the SUA killers' corpses tumbling backward in lifeless heaps. The magazine was empty, and Bolan loaded his third and final into the Thompson.

The SUA gunners had figured out that the Executioner was in the house, and they were going to kick him out.

LI QUO HEARD the first fusillade of shots, and nearly jumped out of his pants, but held his cool, gripping the M-16 tighter to his side as he made his way to a jeep. SUA soldiers were running all over the place now, and he didn't realize that forty men could seem like so many when panic came to shove. As it was, the thunder of autofire splashing inside and outside of the mansion was hard enough to make his ears hurt.

This wasn't something he was accustomed to. Violence wasn't anything he was afraid of, but the sheer volume of firepower was heart stopping. The vibrations shook the air and lit the front of the now darkened mansion with an eerie flickering, as if madness itself had cracked the Earth's crust and let loose the strobes of hell.

Li shook that mental image and began his search for a jeep with keys in it.

"Mr. Han?" one of the soldiers asked.

Li spun. "Yes?"

"You got out, good," the soldier said, breathless. "We think we have the American trapped in that house."

"You mean all that shooting and you didn't get him?" Li asked. "What kind of idiots—?"

More gunfire resounded inside the house. SUA soldiers who were perched by the door were falling away like puppets with their strings cut, heavy fire slamming into them as they tried to rush into the mansion. Li knew what reaper was scything his way through their lot.

Nothing less than death turned human.

"He's making a break! You have the keys to any jeeps?" Li asked.

The soldier nodded. "That one. What do you intend?"

"He can't hit us if we're moving fast enough. We'll engage him on the run. Have the soldiers hold back. I'll drive. I trust you can shoot well enough from a moving vehicle," Li snapped.

The soldier nodded. "Sir! Brilliant!"

There was the sharp barking of commands as Li, keys in hand, slid behind the wheel, resting his own M-16 against his thigh. The SUA thug climbed into the shotgun seat and loaded a full magazine into his AK-47.

"I am ready, sir," the soldier said. He braced himself and turned toward the mansion as Li gunned the engine and began driving at full speed up the walkway toward the porch.

Li held until the last moment, then hammered his forearm into the base of the rifleman's spine and hit the brakes, skidding to a halt in front of the mansion. The SUA soldier succumbed to lethal physics as he not only smashed across the dashboard, making an ugly crunching sound with his legs, but also skittered down the hood, head bouncing into the dirt road before the jeep bounced and lurched over his soggy, frail mortal coil.

Li pulled the Browning from its holster, looking to see how the soldiers would take it.

They were agape.

"Drive!" Bolan growled suddenly, pressing the Desert Eagle into the man's temple.

Li blanched and looked up in horror at the huge wraith that suddenly appeared by his side. The Browning was slapped from nerveless fingers, and only seconds later did he realize that this was an act.

He tromped the gas and began driving as stunned soldiers held their fire.

Li looked at the big Executioner and breathed deep again. "We made it."

Bolan slid the Desert Eagle back into its holster. "They'll give pursuit."

"But we're alive," Li said. "I didn't think we could make it."

"Sure, you did," Bolan said. "Otherwise, we wouldn't have made it at all."

"So it's not unbecoming to give a war whoop?"

The big man with the ice-cold eyes nodded. "Just don't steer us into a tree while you're doing it."

Li Quo let loose a victory cry that drained off the tension and terror of the past half hour.

But the big man was right.

There was still work to do.

MICHELLE LAM GAVE Alvin Warren a squeeze before the SUA thugs pulled them out of the helicopter and separated them. A squat, gruff goon in a general's uniform looked them both over.

"So, you must be Ms. Lam," the man she recognized as Chang said. She felt terror slice into her gut like a carving knife.

"Yeah?" Lam asked, trying to bring more menace into her voice than she ever possessed. It didn't come out particularly strong, but she was at least working on defiance.

Chang chuckled and looked over Warren. "And you're the infamous CIA man who the Americans had originally watching me. What went wrong that they had to bring in Belasko?"

Warren smirked. "I'm only assigned to observation. Belasko is the exterminator."

Chang laughed. "The Exterminator? Sounds like a trashy action movie."

"Hey, that was a darn good movie," Warren said.

Chang laughed again, and Lam felt a little bit of comfort seep back into her when suddenly the shaved, stocky bastard turned to the American and backhanded him. Blood flew from a torn cheek, and Warren collapsed to the ground, where his two guards started to kick and stomp on him.

"Stop that!" Lam yelled. She lunged forward, but iron-strong hands grabbed her wrists and held her back.

Chang smirked. "You've watched too many movies. This pitiful little fuck-head thought he could defy my will. Thailand will be mine to control, and you and the rest of the world can only sit back and watch."

The guards kept kicking and stomping as the stocky American curled up, trying to protect his vital organs.

It seemed to last an eternity. The slap of boots on flesh and the grunts of Warren as he suffered and coughed up blood from his injuries were almost as bad a torture as if they'd been hammering on her.

Almost as bad.

She thought there could be no way he could survive such a beating.

At a hand motion from Chang, the beating stopped, but Warren kept rolling, covering himself, blood oozing from broken lips, his face a train wreck from those kicks that smashed into his mouth and nose and forehead. He was whimpering and coughing, each cough bringing a frothy bubbling to his lips.

"You fucking bastard!" Lam growled, lashing out again, and this time one guard's hand slipped and her fingers raked across the cheek of the SUA general.

Chang stepped back, feeling his own blood trickling down near his eye, then looked at Warren and Lam.

"What's wrong? Can't fight back?" Lam asked. "Need your thugs to do your killing?"

Chang pulled his pistol from its holster and leveled it at Warren, slowly cocking it. "What did you ask, American bitch?"

Lam saw Warren shaking his head, his eyes imploring her to keep her mouth shut. But the unwavering pistol leveled at him told her otherwise.

"I said, you cowardly sack of shit," Lam spoke up, mustering all her strength. "Do you need your thugs to do your killing?"

Chang smiled, then swung the pistol at her.

Lam watched the ugly hole of the muzzle at the end of her nose, and she tried to step back. She took a deep breath, knowing what would happen next. But she had done what she needed to do. She'd saved at least one last life.

No regrets.

"Because, bitch, I do not need anyone to do my killing for me" were the last words she heard over Alvin Warren's anguished cry.

ALVIN WARREN LOWERED his face to the dirt, his eyes clenched shut, blood pouring from tears in his forehead, stinging his eyes, but not stinging as much as the pain of watching the limp form of Michelle Lam lying lifeless next to him in the dirt.

It hurt to breathe, but the knives of agony were numbed compared to the coldness in the center of his soul as he realized that he'd failed her. His glib tongue had gotten himself an ass-kicking that he could have survived, but there was an innocent life that wouldn't go on anymore. Michelle Lam had been executed by this sick bastard who dealt child-rape and heroin.

All because he couldn't keep his mouth shut.

"Well, you get to live, thanks to the American bitch," Chang said in English for Warren's benefit.

Warren tried to speak, but he only spat out blood and pieces of his teeth. He felt one arm gone completely dead, curled against his side.

"Not so glib now?" Chang asked.

Warren shook his head.

Chang chuckled and pressed the gun under the CIA man's chin.

"Feel like dying?"

Warren's eyes opened, staring into Chang's.

"Just do it," Warren managed to say around ruined lips. The muzzle was stinging hot, something he only peripherally noticed.

"Maybe later when Belasko shows up. It looks like he survived one of my traps and is on his way here to the rescue," Chang stated.

Warren let his chin slump to his chest. "Belasko isn't going to be scared of you. You've heard of his reputation from your buddies."

Chang laughed. "And you know mine. It'll be a fun face-off, no?"

Warren spit a gob of blood into Chang's face. The general pulled a handkerchief, wiping his face off with it.

"You should have taken more than a beating for her," Chang said, nodding toward the corpse.

Michelle Lam was lying there, crying out for vengeance, and Alvin Warren was left helpless to do a damn thing.

JACK GRIMALDI FELT his stomach turn to a knot as he watched the murder of Michelle Lam and was about to fire up the weapons systems on Dragon Slayer when Kevin Peters gave a whispered curse.

"We can't do anything," Peters said. "Alvin's still alive."

Grimaldi looked at the scope, then shook his head. To start a firefight now would be to sacrifice a good man's life, and from what he'd seen, from Brewer's loss of an arm to Lam's death, there'd been enough sacrifice on the side of the good guys.

"I'll fast-rope in and make the rescue," Peters said.

"No. There's only two of us," Grimaldi said, his mouth tasting of ashes. "We need help."

"Belasko?" Peters asked. "We're not even sure he's alive."

Grimaldi narrowed his eyes, checking the scanners. "There's always a chance that Striker made it."

"Striker?" Peters inquired.

"His nickname," Grimaldi answered.

Peters frowned. "We can't wait long."

"We might not have to. Look," Grimaldi said.

The infrared was picking up a heat source, a jeep, racing up a road toward Chang's camp. It was moving fast, but with purpose. It was two miles away from the helicopter, and about four from the camp, but slowing down.

Grimaldi swung the cyclic around and brought Dragon Slayer back to treetop level, swooping low over the road, powering toward the jeep. There was a chance, slight, that it could be Bolan. If that was the case, then the Stony Man ace could inform the Executioner of what happened.

He didn't particularly care for the job, but Dragon Slayer was underarmed for the mission of destroying an entire camp.

All there could really be, right now, was the one weapon that was intended for this bloody campaign in Thailand in the first place.

The Executioner himself.

27

Mack Bolan listened to the news of Michelle Lam's death. Outwardly his composure was rock solid, but to any person who knew the Executioner, it was only the calm before a cleansing storm.

He'd learned of Alvin Warren's beating after his capture, and knew that Grimaldi had done right. An explosive fusillade from above by Dragon Slayer would have only served to kill someone who could be saved, and simply disperse Chang's army.

But too many who had joined in the Executioner's crusade had paid.

Grimaldi had already taken his lumps; that was to be expected.

Hayes had lost an ear and some vision in one eye from a head wound.

Brewer had his arm amputated.

And Michelle Lam...

"Belasko? You still with us?" Li Quo asked.

"Yeah," Bolan said. He'd had a chance to raid the arms locker of Dragon Slayer, managing to find a new blacksuit for himself.

Peeling the old one from his skin, he discovered how torn up he'd been by the attack by Trang's gunships. "Just getting cleaned up and ready."

"You don't look in any condition to fight a war," Kevin Peters commented.

"I've fought tougher with worse injuries," Bolan grunted, tugging into the blacksuit, flipping its turtle collar high on his neck. The formfitting suit was an old friend of the Executioner, and just putting it on was a revitalizing process. Water from Grimaldi's survival stores also gave him renewed vigor to fight.

Jack Grimaldi took Bolan by the arm and walked him to where Li and Peters couldn't listen.

"Sarge, we've been here too often before," his longtime friend told him.

"And I'll take care of these savages, like I always do," Bolan answered.

Grimaldi nodded. "It's just...this mission seems to have gotten under your skin."

"I've thought about Cindy more this week than I have in the past ten years," Bolan said. Grimaldi's face changed, and Bolan realized his voice sounded as old as he felt when he said it.

"You get careless, you'll die," Grimaldi stated. "I sure as hell didn't sign on for all this time just for you to lose it because this has gotten personal."

"It's always been personal, Jack. You know that. Every drop of innocent blood has been intimately mixed with my own."

"I know your dream," Grimaldi whispered.

"Blood River...not the blood of my enemies, but the blood of my friends," Bolan said. "I've worried about losing you more times than I care to count, and I know you've held in there when it's been me on the line. So you're going to lose trust over this?"

Grimaldi met the Executioner's stare. When they'd met seemingly a hundred years ago in Las Vegas, Bolan posing as a deadly mob enforcer making a hot escape to the Caribbean, Grimaldi being a flyboy for the Mafia, it was a case of two strangers turning their lives around. Bolan was freshly into his war of avenging his family against the Mafia, and Grimaldi was just trying to scrape by, taking jobs from anyone, even killers and drug dealers for money.

When the Executioner met his future partner, it was under false pretenses, but eventually they came to trust each other. When Stony Man Farm fell to savages the first time, there was no doubt to Grimaldi that even though he was assigned to ferry Able Team and Phoenix Force around the globe, there was one outlaw that would always get his aid with the slightest call. The two men had shed enough blood in each other's defense to kill a dozen men.

"You know better, Sarge. I'm here, and I have your back."

"Thanks, Jack. I never was so clear in what I had to do than right now, so trust me. I know you couldn't fail me even if I told you to," Bolan said.

"I'm not that perfect, Striker. Just the best on the planet."

Bolan clapped one of his oldest living friends on the shoulder. "Come on, before we have to stage the assault using your head as a hot-air balloon."

MAJOR KEVIN PETERS WANTED more than anything to be going down the rope, but there was a more important job for the big Canadian. The ebony giant finished strapping himself into the door of Dragon Slayer, then made sure the pintle-mount for the XM-134 minigun was in place. The minigun was a buzz saw of death-dealing destruction. Chambered in 7.62 mm NATO, the same powerful round as in the M-60 and M-14 rifles, it fired off at 1000 rounds per minute. The sheer volume of fire was capable of shredding any human target.

The powerful 7.62 mm NATO could punch through a brick wall with ease. At 1000 rpm, the minigun could slice a house in two.

He looked across to Belasko and Li, who were tucking their weapons into their harnesses, then affixing their fast-rope harnesses.

"I'll pop a flare when it looks like you've cleared enough," Bolan told the big man. "We'll need everything we can get on the ground."

Peters nodded. "Just don't forget about me."

"With the firepower you have, that'll be a hard thing to do," Li said.

Peters somehow managed a reassured grin. "I'll make damn sure no motherfuckers are gonna get close to you guys."

The big man patted the .45 Automag pistol holstered on his massive thigh. "Once this baby runs out, I'm coming down anyway, like it or not."

"We ready to get this party started?" Grimaldi called from the cockpit.

Bolan slapped the hull and gave the little pilot a thumbs-up. Dragon Slayer rose into the sky, the eerie whoosh of the stealth mode even more evident to Peters as he hung out the side door of the big helicopter. The wind blast was apparent, but the muffled thump of the helicopter was about a fifth of what it usually was when he had trained to be a door gunner in Canada.

It was eerie, like riding on the chariot of death.

He clenched the XM-134's pistol grip and leaned his weight on the nylon straps holding him up.

The big, silent chopper rocketed skyward. It would have thundered at the speed that it was moving, but again, there was only the rush and snap of wind across his face and the hazy blur of green of the world beneath him through the night vision goggles he wore on his door-gunner's helmet.

"We're thirty seconds from the drop-off, gang. We may be on whisper mode, but the moment I get over the lights of the camp, we're going to be noticed, just on rotor wash alone," Grimaldi's voice sizzled over the onboard communicators.

"Then let's give them a special preview," Peters spoke up. "Belasko?"

"Let it rip."

Peters swung around, grinning, his goggles showing the green-cast camp. It was a mile square, surrounded by a fifteen-foot-chain-link and concertina-wired fence. Every twenty yards a light shone, a blazing ball of green brilliance in the vision enhancement. He had his choice of targets, four squared buildings of one story apiece, and a two-story main office. There was a helicopter hangar, as well as a motor pool with jeeps. It was surprising how big a base that Chang could afford to keep in the open within fifty miles of a Thai city.

Bodies were moving around the teardrop-shaped helicopter that delivered his friend to his beating and Michelle Lam to her death. Alvin Warren was away from it now, and the frustrated big

Canadian flicked off the safety on the minigun and took aim at the helicopter.

"This one's for you, buddy."

The XM-134 suddenly shook to life in Peters's grip, the six barrels whirling wildly. Bullets ripped out so fast that there wasn't a chatter, but the sound of the air itself ripping to shreds as Peters held down the trigger for a full second, sweeping the helicopter's rotors and flank with seventeen high-velocity rounds. Bullets ripped and tore through the soft skin of the helicopter, snapping the ceramic of the rotor, and a moment later leaking fuel burst into flame, sending an explosive splash of torn metal and shrapnel spraying at the crew around the Little Bird.

SUA crewmen screamed where they didn't die instantly, and Peters snarled, swinging the minigun across the wounded in short tapping squirts. Bodies were torn to pieces as Dragon Slayer swung over the fireball that was once a helicopter. Peters was swiveling, aiming at a jeep that was rolling up, a security patrol bristling with rifles. Peters put the crosshairs of the XM-134 on the vehicle and hammered out a three-second slaughter-burst that chewed metal and flesh alike, slamming the vehicle to a stop as if it were smacked by a giant flyswatter.

Grimaldi at the controls had a .50-caliber GECAL tracking with his own helmet, the only weapon that was in a concealable turret. The three-barrel cannon swung toward other targets, smashing out its own payload at the one-story buildings, punching through brick and stone.

Peters spared a glance at the two figures sizzling down the rappelling ropes, and they dropped to the ground unslinging their weapons and sweeping for targets not driven to cover by the two heavy machine guns. "They're down!"

"But the bad guys aren't!" Grimaldi called back.

Peters swung back behind the minigun, milking the trigger and shredding targets wherever he saw them.

No, the bad guys weren't down yet, but death was coming for them.

THE EXECUTIONER HIT the ground and unclipped his harness. In his hands, his Colt Commando, retrieved from Dragon Slayer's arms locker, was fitted with a 30-round magazine, ready to rip against any opponent who would get in his way. A trio of Thai gunmen raced toward Bolan and Li, running from Grimaldi's and Peters's suppressive fire.

The Executioner milked the Commando's trigger, full-powered rifle bullets tearing across the distance between him and the enemy at 3000 feet per second. The Thai gangsters were punched backward by the hypersonic slugs, which pierced them as if they were made of tissue paper. Bolan leaped past the dead, his entire body having left behind its aches and pains, agony a distant memory.

Pain was suppressed.

Oxygen fed his muscles, displacing the buildup of acids that induced pain and fatigue.

Adrenaline sang inside his veins.

The Bolan blitz had just struck General Chang's home of homes.

He unclipped an M-36 fragmentation grenade, a little baseball of death, and flicked out the pin with his thumb, speedballing the bomb toward a doorway that was rippling and crackling with the muzzle-flashes of enemy rifles. Dropping down as bullets sizzled past him, thumping the air with their supersonic passages, he squinted against the flash and roar of the explosion. The fragger detonated, tossing a hundred feet of tightly corded wire out at supersonic speeds, the high-velocity metal making a lethal killzone for ten feet in all directions. The doorway cleared of gunfire, and Bolan rushed it, sweeping the entrance. The smoking muzzle of the Commando swept across the dead and dying, but Sergeant Mercy wasn't in residence in the soul of Mack Bolan at that moment.

He needed every shot he could get for the living.

Bolan stepped back, watching Li Quo fanning an area from a secured position behind the wrecked jeep that Peters had flattened with the minigun. Having good cover, as well as Dragon Slayer as a massive guardian angel, Bolan trusted the Thai to keep the camp tied up while he went about his business.

A burst of AK-47 fire caught the Executioner's attention, flickering from up the hallway, and Bolan clamped the tubular stock of his Commando against his hip and let the muzzle sweep toward the gunner, returning fire as he moved in a single side-step. The sweeping burst sent the San United Army thug tumbling with much of his face destroyed by high-velocity 5.56 mm copper-jacketed rockets.

Taking the hallway in three strides, he checked the doors, all open, scanning for signs of Warren, muzzle sweeping, checking for any more survivors in this building when he stumbled out the back door. A gunman hastily dropped his shovel, reaching for a propped-up rifle while his partner was shouting at him.

The scene was one Bolan had seen a dozen times before, but this was no less horrific.

Michelle Lam's corpse lay at the feet of a quartet of men caked in dirt from digging a shallow grave, weapons set aside for shovels, not quite sure what the hell was going on as war broke out all around them. Her one open eye stared sightlessly out of a moon-shaped face, draped on either side by her silken black hair, the destruction caused by her death shot mercifully covered by a sheen of her dark tresses.

Even with pain searing his soul, the Executioner took charge. He let the partly empty Commando drop on its sling, slapping hip leather for the mighty .44 Desert Eagle.

One thug cried out, showing off his emptied hands from where he was dropping his shovel, screaming something in Thai. It was useless. The first to move was the first to die. A single 240-grain slug hammered right between the digger's eyes and tore out the back of his skull in an explosion of gooey matter. His comrades began to scream, scrambling to get away from the tall killer in black, but none of them were faster than a .44 Magnum round. The Executioner planted each lackey with a bone and flesh-mangling missile that tore through them, slamming them lifelessly to the ground.

He looked down at the lifeless form of Michelle Lam, allowing emotion to course through his blood, a moment of regret.

"G-Force," he called, giving Grimaldi's nickname, "I found Michelle. Protect her."

"Sarge?" Grimaldi called back.

"I've got work to do" came the response.

The Executioner turned, feeding the Colt Commando a fresh magazine, heading out the door.

The killing machine wasn't going to stop until it burned out every ounce of pain raging like an inferno in Mack Bolan's heart of hearts.

28

Alvin Warren lifted his head to the roar and fury of war outside his cell and struggled to his wobbly hands and knees. The world spun, dizziness induced by concussion from his beating, the beating he had chivalrously taken to keep attention away from Michelle Lam.

Warren vomited on the floor of his cell, heaving up acid and water, making his crushed nostrils sting and lips burn. He leaned against the wall and crawled up helplessly, watching the huge helicopter flutter to and fro like a hummingbird or a bumblebee, spitting flames from its belly and from one of its doors. He clenched the bars, closing his eyes, wishing, calling for a bullet to come zipping at him, stray through the open window, or even shattering through the stone, exploding into his organs and ending his suffering.

Warren wasn't ashamed of the blood of men and women he'd shot down in his career. He had been fighting people who had been fighting back, or were planning to kill innocent bystanders in their sick crusades to make the world a better place for a twisted philosophy. But Lam's blood, staining his hands as surely as the caked blood that covered him from his ruined face, it burned like acid in his veins, squeezing at his heart. There was a little affection he'd started developing for the brave little Thai American social worker, but what truly hurt was that his efforts to keep her protected and in his shadow were in vain. She was a friend, a noncombatant who didn't deserve to be cut down like that.

The minigun in the door swiveled, and Warren braced himself. He looked straight down the merciless, unblinking eyes of the cannon's barrels, all glowing, making it look like an odd beast, a Siamese twin clinging to the side of the monster flying thing that hovered grimly, seeking flesh to rend.

"Do it!" Warren yelled, his raw throat cracking. He shook the bars. "Shoot me!"

The monster helicopter swung up and out of sight, and Warren cursed, pounding his fist on the bars once, aggravating the shattered tarsals of his hand and wrist. But he was beyond pain now.

Suddenly the wall exploded to his side, holes being punched through in an odd slow motion that Warren didn't realize was the effect of three barrels of a .50-caliber chain gun hammering through brick and mortar as if they were cheese, tossing debris left and right, sending the chunks tumbling to the ground.

A massive shadow appeared in the door, and Warren lunged at it, screaming wildly, but huge hands grabbed his shoulders, shaking him like a rag doll.

"Alvin! It's me!" the ebony giant spoke up.

Warren glanced up at his Canadian friend, then struggled to choke back tears.

"Kill me, man...just kill me," Warren whispered.

The battered CIA man felt a weapon shoved into his hands, and Kevin Peters squeezed his shoulder. "You are not gonna die. Not now. We need you to finish this out."

"I let her die," Warren said.

"You could barely crawl, let alone stand and fight to protect her," Peters told him. "We don't have time for this bullshit. Now take that weapon, lock and load, and start killing these mother-fuckers before I leave you behind."

Warren looked at the MP-5 in his hands, and braced the sloped hand guard against his forearm, slipping his head and good left hand through the sling. "I got one hand, you big dumb-ass."

Peters whirled, drawing his hand cannon, spotting a group of hostiles rushing up. He fired off three shots, sending two men spinning into oblivion with massive .45-caliber slugs hammering into them.

Peters grimaced and handed him a bandolier of magazines, shoving them back behind the cover of the wall. "We'll tape you up later. I'm sure you know one-handed reloads with that thing."

"I can improvise," Warren said, standing on shaky legs.

"Good. Now follow me," Peters ordered.

Warren took one step at a time back into the camp where he'd failed and let a dear, innocent life end. Warren and Peters rose in unison, their weapons ripping thunder into the blazing night.

It was time to start giving some bloody payback.

GENERAL CHANG CHI FU crawled into the jeep as quickly as he could, his driver already gunning the engine so that the toes of his boots scraped the hard-packed dirt beneath his feet while he was still clambering into the seat. Behind him, the flames and smoke of the wrecked motor pool looked like an open wound in the earth, revealing the maw of hell. Inside the flames, wailing souls shrieked in the agonies of immolation before gasoline and motor oil fed the roiling plasma to grant them mercy and strip the last of the flesh from cracking and exploding bones.

Chang lowered his head as gunfire streaked out from a couple of buildings, bullets chasing after the jeep and hammering into the armored plate he had tucked himself behind. The bucket of steel protected him from the whizzing rounds that were being poured out by a tall rampaging shadow that was surging through the darkness, sending fireballs of light issuing from his machine gun.

Belasko!

Chang swung up the AK-47 in the back of the jeep, leveling it and firing off half a magazine. Holding on with only one hand, and firing with the rifle braced in his other, he had no hope for an accurate shot, and the recoil hammered his arm brutally as rounds chopped high and wide.

Belasko went to the dirt, rolling, but the movements weren't in self-preservation. He wasn't dodging; he was still advancing, still pouring out gunfire as the driver gingerly navigated amid smoldering chunks of wreckage and smashed boulders that used to be parts of buildings, but had been blown to shreds by the massive helicopter. The wraith moved, crab-walking, obviously more used to shooting an automatic weapon with just one hand as he kept low and behind cover in between venturing out on his hands and feet like a three-legged spider with a turret gun.

Chang let loose with the rest of the magazine, and Belasko jerked, his weapon flying from his grip. But still, the executioner of so many of Chang's loyal soldiers was still rising to his feet, lunging and advancing toward the escaping general's jeep. Chang fumbled for a spare magazine lying on the rear floor of the vehicle when a burst of acceleration sent him jerking in his seat and the curved banana clip of the AK-47 skittering away.

With a curse, Chang dived for it, then felt himself thrown sideways out of the jeep as it lurched, the driver jerking and exploding in blossoms of blood. The driver died under a hail of bullets from above. The SUA general scooped up the magazine and scrambled away from the vehicle as it was peppered with a yet another blistering torrent of .50 caliber steel-cored rain. Obliteration exploded all around and behind him as his soldiers opened fire, throwing grenades, struggling to protect their base.

It wasn't enough. Each blazing weapon around him was snuffed out one by one, or sometimes a dozen at a time, by the shattering breath of the great dragon hovering above, and the dragon's human minions on the ground. How many of them were there? Were they all like Belasko?

Chang looked back and around, and saw only three other men on the ground. For a moment, the SUA general caught a glimpse of Han's familiar features, and suddenly realized that this had to be the only reason Belasko was so dogged. The little traitor, maybe even an undercover cop, was feeding the big bastard in black everything he needed to escape.

That big black wraith, he'd managed to find Chang's one weak spot, and turn him to his side with only a moment's effort! Chang glared. He wasn't human.

As if to prove the Thai gangster's fears, Belasko was back on his feet, right arm hanging limp at his side while he walked purposefully through the middle of the base, almost casually pumping rounds from a long-barreled machine pistol into soldiers who stumbled into his path.

Those eyes, those ice-cold eyes that the survivors of his forces reported, never left Chang, and the terrified conspirator ripped the empty magazine from his AK and hammered home a fresh 30-rounder.

Belasko didn't stop, letting the long-barreled gun drop from his hand, slide locked back, and reached across his waist, pulling a big, heavy-framed cannon from his holster. The draw was awkward, and he was off balance when two of Chang's men leaped at him, wrestling him down. Chang didn't take any chances, snapping up the AK-47 and holding down the trigger, letting the weapon spit steel and flame, sending flesh-shredding damnation into all three grounded men.

There was a scream of protest, and Chang whirled, racing away as gunfire spit after him. He'd finally put down the mysterious and deadly Mike Belasko, but had lost far too many men to do it. He ran and leaped atop a fallen light post that had smashed down the fence to make a bridge to escape. He had his side arm, and he had the few rounds left in his rifle——and he had the will to survive.

The woods might be protection against the gunship that was swooping and veering in the sky, hammering out messages of death to those who stood behind. Suddenly the great dragon spun as a fireball boiled out of an opened wound. Chang paused, then shook his head, continuing to move, knowing that the shell that had hit the killer helicopter only temporarily wounded it, and there were still avenging killers on the ground, hunting and slaughtering any resistance.

Chang put one foot in front of the other and began to run into the tangled woods and the encompassing night.

THE EXECUTIONER COUGHED and felt a knife of pain in his ribs. He felt where the steel-cored 7.62 mm slugs had been stopped by the combination of SUA soldiers and his own protective body armor. He pushed with his left arm, shoving one chewed-up body away from him, then slid out from under the other corpse, clawing for the Desert Eagle, which had been dropped in the melee.

He evaluated his injuries. His right arm had been made numb by falling to the ground to duck under a searing swath of lead spit out by Chang's rifle. His shoulder was smashed by his dive into a shattered piece of helicopter fuselage, making his arm hang numbly. It had been numbed enough so that it once again was subjected to a flesh wound, a cutting round that carved the flesh biceps deeply, letting warm blood seep down to prickled nerveless fingers.

Now, from the hammering that had killed the two men who had jumped him, he had received two broken ribs, and he was sure that if his stitches hadn't been torn on his leg, then he received a brand-new flesh wound down there.

Nothing that would stop him.

Just slow him down.

The Executioner struggled to his feet, Desert Eagle leading the way as he continued toward Chang, who had leaped the fence with the assistance of a fallen light pole that slammed down the chain link. Around him, caved-in buildings burned. Bodies were strewed about, some still twitching and screaming, but nobody was interested in waging war anymore, at least on the side of the SUA.

Still Peters and Warren opened fire on fleeing soldiers, slicing them down mercilessly with rounds to the back, killing for the sake of making sure the cancer of the San United Army wouldn't escape to regroup. Killing to make sure that the memory of Michelle Lam wouldn't be forsaken by allowing one of these heroin- and child-dealing bastards to walk one more step on this earth.

But there was still Chang, fleeing in the darkness, and Bolan took off at full speed, racing up the pole, feet nimble, mind cleared of distractions except for the trail of the escaping general. The mastermind of death and destruction, the provider of violation and despoilment was fleeing, and nothing short of the Executioner's own destruction would stop Chang.

Leaping off the end of the light pole, the Executioner landed in the jungle and started following the hastily crushed path made by Chang, a trail that couldn't have been larger if it had been made by a water buffalo. Long a hunter in Southeast Asian jungles, the Executioner moved surefootedly, not pushing himself at top speed, which would leave his lungs seeking oxygen and his bloodied leg collapsing beneath him. It was an easy, long-strided, ground-eating pace that took him into the darkness of the jungle.

That's when Dragon Slayer took the hit.

The Executioner paused, looking into the jungle after his prey.

Chang was escaping, fleeing on foot. He could be caught tonight, this nightmare crushed out once and for all.

But Jack Grimaldi was struggling to keep his aircraft from slamming into the ground and turning into his coffin.

The head viper, or his longest companion in the hellzones?

He thought back to Michelle Lam, remembering her shattered face, the way she was going to be shoved in the ground and packed down with dirt.

One more of Bolan's friendly dead, gone because the Executioner hadn't been there to protect her.

The life of a comrade in arms was more important than instant revenge. Chang's course was plotted; his fate was sealed.

Jack Grimaldi's fate was impending, and only one force could prevent his death.

Mack Bolan cursed and turned, running back to the fence, sparing his last grenade to blow a hole through and rush back to his friend's side.

General Chang Chi Fu would last until another day before meeting his judgment.

JACK GRIMALDI SQUEEZED back behind the seat as gunfire peppered the armored seat and smashed into the instruments of Dragon Slayer. He snaked his hand down into the well and grabbed for the Uzi submachine gun that he kept for occasions when he'd need some firepower inside of the helicopter, usually when it was disabled and downed by a cruel twist of fate in combat.

Outside, the remaining gunmen from the SUA had rallied

with the downing of Dragon Slayer, surrounding and pinning down Li, Peters and Warren as they tried fighting their way out against the last troops protecting the base. The rallying force was determined, and the little fire that the besieged soldiers could muster from their defensive positions was ineffective against a suddenly aggressive force.

It was to be expected. An advantage could be pushed only so far, Grimaldi thought.

A bullet pinged close to his ear, and the little pilot swung around, ripping off ten rounds into the cabin of the helicopter, crucifying a pair of gunners who had managed to board the wounded bird, slapping them to the ground.

The cockpit's armored glass suddenly starred, growing milky under the combined firepower of a dozen rifles avenging their brethren, and had Dragon Slayer not been built to shrug off small-arms fire, Grimaldi would have been dead.

As it was, another concentrated volley of steel-cored slugs could punch through the glass and splatter his remains across both seats.

The attackers lost their advantage. They had surprise, violence and audacity on their side, and they'd exploited it to the maximum, destroying the camp and slaughtering or driving off the San United Army force on hand. But with Bolan having been dropped, and then heading off after Chang, there was a pause in the merciless slaughter of Thai gangsters.

And in that space of a few breaths, someone had tagged Dragon Slayer with an RPG shell. Grimaldi was too low, doing too much, hanging around too long to avoid taking the blow that crippled the great war beast from the sky.

Everything went to hell after that.

Grimaldi tried to pull out of his harness when another salvo of 7.62 mm steel-cored slugs smashed the glass and drove the pilot to the deck. He crawled, cradling the Uzi, listening to the hammering of bullets like an insane drum solo on the hull of the helicopter.

"Sarge, if I ever needed you to bail me out..." Grimaldi growled.

He looked up and saw another group of four men racing around to the open hatch through which Kevin Peters had been

firing the minigun. They spotted him crawling, and Grimaldi
rolled sideways, firing his Uzi for a couple short bursts before
sliding completely behind the armored hull of the helicopter. He
knew that the four of them could rush him, or just simply throw
in a grenade and reduce him to a fine paste, ending his years of
actually fighting back for redemption.

A Thai gunman surged through the doorway, chopping down
his rifle and catching Grimaldi's Uzi across the frame, slamming
both weapons to the deck. The pilot let go, struggling to grab on
to the rifle barrel before it could be brought anywhere near him,
but Grimaldi realized that he was down and the standing attacker
had more leverage.

But he wasn't going down without a fight. He lashed up with
a savate kick from the floor, the tip of his boot connecting with
the SUA gunman's collarbone with an audible snap. The thug
grunted and kept twisting his rifle, trying to bury the muzzle in
Grimaldi's belly and open fire. Through the other hatch, blown
larger by the RPG shell's impact, another shadow appeared, and
Grimaldi cursed, knowing he'd been outflanked.

Death had entered the Dragon Slayer.

But Death was also packing a .44 Magnum Desert Eagle.

A single thundering report, loud enough to make Grimaldi's
teeth hurt in the confines of the cabin, sent the SUA killer tumbling bonelessly out the door. Mack Bolan quickly knelt by his
friend's side.

"One piece?"

"Except for Dragon Slayer, yeah," the plucky pilot replied.

"We can fix her later," Bolan answered. He swung and leveled the Desert Eagle out the door and cut loose with six booming shots, and Grimaldi knew he was cutting down the remaining
gunmen who were rushing the helicopter. Before the bodies outside finished tumbling to the ground, Bolan was returning his attention to the loadout cabinet on Dragon Slayer.

"I know you loaded light, but I hope you have one more cassette for the minigun," Bolan said.

"You know I always pack a spare. I'll load it while you give
us some cover fire," Grimaldi answered.

"Looks like Kevin left about three hundred rounds in the old
cassette," Bolan growled. "That should be enough."

Grimaldi scooped up the SUA gunman's rifle and took the side of the Executioner. His rifle wasn't much compared to Bolan's weapon, but the two partners laid down a field of devastation that shredded the ranks of the rallying SUA troops, the minigun's merciless six barrels chopping and pounding through unsuspecting flesh, Grimaldi's rifle hammering its backup staccato beat to tag down anyone who managed to dive out of the way of a sizzling crescent of high-velocity death at 1000 rounds per minute.

For eighteen seconds, the Executioner hosed down the hapless enemy, the flickering flames of the heavy gun spitting and smashing through their number until finally the mechanism stopped, wheeling around dead and empty.

Not that it mattered. Of the surviving SUA troopers who avoided the lethal death dance of the minigun and Grimaldi's captured rifle, nobody was interested in sticking around for the rest of the battle.

A few short chasing bursts to cut through those unlucky or stupid enough to get close to Li, Peters or Warren ended the last of the SUA's assets in the Nakhon Sawan.

As the five battered warriors assembled and began policing the dead and dying, sparing mercy rounds for everyone they could, they knew one last thing.

General Chang Chi Fu had escaped.

This war wasn't yet over.

29

It was dawn, and General Chang Chi Fu limped to a halt against a tree. Sunlight poured down upon him. He looked back through the forest and saw the boiling clouds rising from the darkness.

As he'd raced along during the night, leaving a trail a blind elephant could track, he'd detected no pursuit except for the first hundred or so yards. Then it disappeared before a final crescendo of autofire that marked the end of whatever war was going on back at the Nakhon Sawan base. As soon as the dawn came, he stripped off his uniform tunic and started toward the river, heading north toward Chang Mao province.

He'd pushed his luck at going after Mike Belasko personally. It was a mistake to go after the servant of an old enemy, on such a personal basis, especially when he had the money and the power to keep a relentless push against the man that would have ground him to fine hamburger before long.

It was the end of the day, his boots blistering his feet, his back raw from the sun, when he reached the river. It was a welcome sight, because he could travel along it, incognito for a while before he could arrange for proper clothes and communications to get in touch with the rest of his forces.

The San United Army was a massive entity, and even the three hundred dead left behind were only a fraction of the true power that Chang held. The prime minister would soon pay for his transgression of calling an American dog to hound him across the country. Even if Belasko had survived, he was injured and weakened from countless days of battle.

Chang had an army at his command, as well as the ear of every hired gun from Phuket to Chang Mao. Outgunned and outspent, there was no way this American vigilante could ever hope to do anything more than continue tilting at windmills until finally he died bleeding out in some thicket of jungle somewhere.

This quixotic quest to bring Chang down would fail, as it had before. And Chang was only growing stronger and stronger with each passing day. Even now he was in fine physical shape, and except for dunking his sore feet in the cool waters of the river, he needed nothing more to make things right in the world. Let Belasko come for him now; Chang would fight back and grind him into the mud like the worm he was.

Chang sat down on the muddy riverfront, pushing aside the tall blades of elephant grass, wincing as the razor-sharp grass nicked a piece of his forearm. Sliding farther through the bowing grass and prying off his boots, he scanned the muddy waters, looking for the telltale signs of a crocodile gliding through the murky blackness, moving with silent stealth to snap up unwary waders.

No shapes disturbed the surface of the water, and no needlefish darted in the tangled mass of cloying moss that started at the waterline and worked downward. The moss tickled his feet as he stepped into it, feeling the blisters on his feet cool with contact with the glorious mud.

A shadow started crawling the bend in the river, and Chang half rose, his hand going to a flap holster, when he noticed it was a teenage girl on a small, crude skiff. The girl pushed the boat along and sang a traditional old song, her voice melodic and bouncy.

"Girl!" Chang shouted.

She stopped, looking up in shock and surprise. In the shadows of sunset, Chang could tell she was beautiful. A sign, perhaps?

"Girl! I will pay you money if you give me a ride!"

The girl looked at the general, as if contemplating what to do, her dark eyes wary as she scanned the shore. Then, with aching slowness, the girl shoved hard on the pole and began steering the boat toward the shore, sliding up to Chang, who grabbed the bow and held on to it. The girl looked down at him, leaning on the pole she was using to propel the skiff.

"What is your name, girl?"

"I am called Rain," she answered.

"Rain. A beautiful name," Chang stated.

"Sir, you said you had money?"

Chang chuckled. Typical of peasants. Always looking for some way to earn some coin.

"Yes, I do. I just need to ride with you upriver. How far are you going?"

"I'm heading to the village of Bon Makai," Rain told him. "You are welcome to accompany me that far."

Chang consulted his mental map. Bon Makai was a small, negligible town, but at least there he'd be able to get some rudimentary transportation. The money in his pockets would be like gold from heaven, more than enough for him to buy everyone in the town, or to be treated as a king. He smiled.

"That would be perfect," Chang said.

Rain stepped on the opposite side of the boat, using her weight to oppose that of the stocky general as he slid aboard the skiff. It was a wobbly fit, but he finally slid into place, sitting across from the willow-limbed young girl as she put her weight into moving the boat.

"Who do you go to meet in Bon Makai?" Chang asked.

"My grandfather," Rain spoke up, slipping back to the stern and heaving against the pole, pushing away from the shore. "I needed to bring him medicines."

Chang leaned closer. "Medicines?"

"My grandfather, he is deaf and blind. He was injured by government soldiers many years ago. They thought he was with the SUA and threw a grenade into his home. My grandmother was killed," Rain said, sadness in her voice.

"That is horrible," Chang said. For a moment, he actually felt a pang of regret at the death of innocents who had nothing to do with his organization. He dismissed the feeling and scooted around, looking over his shoulder upriver as the skiff continued to glide along, propelled by the frail young girl who guided the boat.

She seemed delicate, but the effort she put into moving the boat showed a strength that to Chang was remarkable in one so young. He'd assumed so often that children were possessed of weakness, especially young girls, but Rain guided the boat with the strength and confidence of a full-grown man.

"Where are your father and mother?"

"They sold me," Rain said.

Chang perked at the sound of that.

"To whom?"

"I do not know. I managed to run away and stay with my grandfather."

"You've not seen them since then?"

"Why should I?" Rain asked. "They gave me up—thus, they have no claim on me. I am my own person now. And I have my grandfather."

Chang nodded. "That is...noble."

"It is living. There is nothing noble about surviving." Rain shrugged with that pronouncement.

Aside from the slosh of the pole through the water, and the sounds of the forest encroaching from each shore, there was an unnerving stillness in the air. The girl was practically a statue, standing with quiet stoniness that was unflinching, not even a grunt of effort as she jammed the pole into the riverbed and thrust the boat along. No more movement than necessary, simple, efficient.

"How much longer until we reach the village?" Chang asked, again looking back over his shoulder. The odd silence on the boat was starting to get to him, and he wanted off the skiff.

"See? The village is at up the next bend," Rain noted as they slid along in the water.

Chang sagged, relief flooding him. A good night's sleep, after perhaps a bottle of wine in his belly, would be everything he needed to forget the past week of terror and torment. He admitted it now—Belasko had been uncannily terrifying. He was a relentless shadow man who managed to elude his hunters, slaughter his soldiers and trace his most secret operations.

If it weren't for the fact that Chang had emptied an entire magazine from an AK-47 into Belasko, pinning him eternally to the ground, he wouldn't put it past the soldier to be waiting at this bend in the river, just before his first taste of relief, ready to gun him down in cold blood.

Rosenberg was still in America, and maybe he'd have his friends, his teammates who had assisted him those years ago, rise from the ashes like some phoenix and swoop down to once and for all obliterate Chang and the SUA from the face of the earth.

It wasn't going to be that easy.

Chang wasn't going to go easily.

He rose gingerly to his knees, getting a good sight of the village, and relief filled him to the brim.

Suddenly an iron-hard limb smashed into Chang's side, right along his belt. The pole struck hard, right on his holster, and with another savage jab, the soaking-wet guide pole was rammed like a spear into his side. Chang gasped, trying to pull his gun free, using one hand to hold off the pole, but it was too slippery, popping free from his grasp. He did manage to get the gun out of the half-torn flap holster, but a jarring impact with the slimy end of the pole made a sickening snap against his forearm. The pistol in his hand plopped into the murky waters of the river.

Choi Tranh glared at him, her lips drawn tight. "Can't have you being armed."

Chang started to roar in rage, ignoring the whistling sound of wood slicing air before he looked up and noticed the hurtling skiff pole swinging at his head. The general swung up his arm, feeling it break under the force of the second blow, but went limp and threw himself away from the skiff and whatever weapons that these two might pull on him. He crashed into the water, tangling in the very moss that earlier felt so good on his bare, sore feet.

Chang ripped free from the river bottom, pulling up mud and weeds, shedding water and tearing through the binding vegetation, crawling frantically to the shore. All the while he was expecting the stutter of a weapon to be the final sounds he ever heard, but he stopped, leaning back in the reeds.

Tranh looked at him with impassive intensity from the skiff, as if standing watch, waiting for some signal from on high.

Chang felt around and backed farther up the bank, cursing as elephant grass carved his arms, but never taking his eyes off the young attacker.

"You're not going to shoot me?" Chang spit in English.

Tranh shook her head. "No."

"Arrest me?"

"I'm not a cop."

"Turn me over to a cop?" Chang loosened his defensive stance. Clearly the girl wasn't carrying a gun.

Tranh shook her head. There was no joy in her face, no glee at causing the general any discomfort.

"You're not going to kill me?"

Tranh spoke up softly. "I am not your judge."

Chang swallowed. That was the message left on the corpse of the Frenchman.

"Why aren't you going to do anything?" Chang snapped.

"Because I will," a voice colder than the depths of hell announced, scraping across his spine.

Chang froze to the bottom of his black soul, every muscle freezing up, shocked realization coming over him. He clenched his eyes shut, trying to deny the reality of the sudden weight that crushingly intruded on his universe.

"You died."

"I died years ago," Bolan answered.

The general heard the sound of a safety being snapped off. He lowered his head.

"You wouldn't shoot me in the back of my head. You Americans have a sense of honor."

"Not to your kind," Mack Bolan answered.

Chang never felt the bullet that exploded through his skull like a freight train.

MACK BOLAN LOOKED at the corpse of Chang Chi Fu, floating facedown in the river. He wasn't certain there was much of a face left. And he didn't care.

His body ached, stitches torn loose, bruises discoloring on his skin, his ribs protesting with each intake of breath.

He glanced up to Tranh, who was watching Chang's corpse

being washed down the river, where needlefish and turtles would eat flesh.

Tranh had barely caught up with them before they left the military base that was a beacon for miles. She also knew exactly where Chang would be likely to run to. She suggested the plan. Tranh had helped finish off the man responsible for ruining her life.

Animal man had been stopped cold for now.

But the cost had been great.

Innocent bystanders and dedicated lawmen at a Washington party.

A good man's arm, and another's eye and ear.

Another with his face to be a crisscross of scars, just now being tended to by a former lover.

And Bolan's own deepest wound, the death of Michelle Lam. Her murderer was floating away, his brains blown out.

But the SUA was still a standing entity. Weakened, but there was still profit to be made in the trade of young lives and heroin.

The Executioner turned from the killing ground, aching wearily to his soul.

One enemy down for now, but the War Everlasting remained, as always.

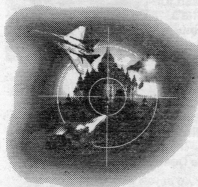

THE Destroyer®

UNNATURAL SELECTION

Sexy scientist Dr. Judith White, who first attempted to repopulate the earth with mutant, man-eating tiger people, is back with a new plan for world domination. She's putting her formula into a brand of bottled water that's become all the rage in Manhattan's boardrooms and cocktail parties. Remo and Chiun hit the Big Apple and find that it literally is a jungle—even the cops have gone carnivorous! And when one of CURE's own falls prey to Dr. White's diabolical scheme, his top secrets may give the insane doctor the extra bite she needs to eat The Destroyer for lunch!

Available in April 2003 at your favorite retail outlet.

TAKE 'EM FREE

2 action-packed novels plus a mystery bonus

NO RISK

NO OBLIGATION TO BUY

James Axler
Outlanders

TALON AND FANG

Kane finds himself thrown twenty-five years into a parallel future, a world where the mysterious Imperator has seemingly restored civilization to America. In this alternate reality, only Kane and Grant have survived, and the spilled blood has left them estranged. Yet Kane is certain that somewhere in time lies a different path to tomorrow's reality—and his obsession may give humanity their last chance to battle past and future as a sinister madman controls the secret heart of the world.

In the Outlands, the shocking truth is humanity's last hope.

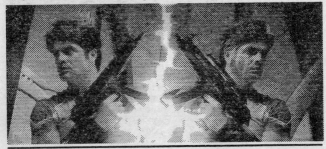

Or order your copy now by sending your name, address, zip or postal code, along with a check or money order (please do not send cash) for $6.50 for each book ordered ($7.99 in Canada), plus 75¢ postage and handling ($1.00 in Canada), payable to Gold Eagle Books, to:

In the U.S.	In Canada
Gold Eagle Books	Gold Eagle Books
3010 Walden Avenue	P.O. Box 636
P.O. Box 9077	Fort Erie, Ontario
Buffalo, NY 14269-9077	L2A 5X3

Please specify book title with your order.
Canadian residents add applicable federal and provincial taxes.

GOLD EAGLE

GOUT25

DEATH LANDS®

Skydark Spawn

**Available in
March 2003
at your favorite retail outlet.**

In the relatively untouched area of what was once Niagara
Falls, Ryan and his fellow wayfarers find the pastoral
farmland under the despotic control of a twisted baron and
his slave-breeding farm. Ryan, Mildred and Krysty are
captured by the baron's sec men and pawned into the cruel
frenzy of their leader's grotesque desires. JB, Jak and Doc
enlist the aid of outlanders to organize a counterstrike—but
rescue may come too late for them all.

W